PUMPKIN
M⚬⚬N

PAMELA E. CONRAD

HARCOURT BRACE & COMPANY

NEW YORK   SAN DIEGO   LONDON

PUMPKIN MOON

Requests for permission to make copies of any part of the work should be mailed to:
Permissions Department, Harcourt Brace & Company, 6277 Sea Harbor Drive,
Orlando, Florida 32887-6777.

"Sea Fever," by John Masefield. Reprinted by permission of The Society of Authors
as the literary representative of the Estate of John Masefield.

This is a work of fiction. All the names, characters, organizations, and events
portrayed in this book are either the products of the author's imagination or are
used fictitiously for verisimilitude. Any resemblance to any organization or to any
actual person, living or dead, is unintended.

Library of Congress Cataloging-in-Publication Data
Conrad, Pamela E.
Pumpkin moon/Pamela E. Conrad.—1st ed.
p.   cm.
ISBN 0-15-175301-6
I. Title.
PS3553.05185P8   1994
813'.54—dc20   93-23745

Designed by Lisa Peters
Printed in the United States of America
First edition
A B C D E

For all my friends who teach me
about charts, knots, and wind,
and for Barbara Fritz,
who shines a flashlight in dark waters.

At night when I wake up and hear the wind shrieking,

I almost fancy there is too much sail on the house,

and I had better go on the roof

and rig in the chimney.

—*Melville*

There is nothing like the sight of a broken child's body to help you across the river, from one side to the other. One minute you live in the illusion of your daughter's rebellious face, the remembered taste of her cheeks, the grime under her nails, and the next instant, under the autumn trees of blazing orange and yellow, you cross the river to reality: her head smashed like a pumpkin against the curb, tire tracks of hair and ribbon, and a high-top sneaker thrown up on a lawn.

You always hated when I made up things like this. And I could probably convince anyone but you that it was true. After all, I am a storyteller, a spinner of tales. I can still hear you telling me how my imagination was wild, that I was of a different ilk—a disturbed brand of thinker who spun warped illusions like mad spiders spin psychedelic webs.

You could tell me. I could tell you. But we have taken different roads, and for so long now we have said nothing. You left me here alone, and I went on writing my novels, plotting, revising, drawing characters into my life, you would say, like a magnet in a kitchen drawer attracts rusty pins.

But now in the drawer I have come across an old photograph of you. In it you are standing at the barbecue grill, in what you must have imagined to be some sort of unsmiling Napoleonic pose. You hold the long fork upright in one hand, and your other hand is pressed sideways across your T-shirt, across your heart. I study your shadowed eyes and try to read them. Did you know you would be leaving us, even then, as I snapped your picture? Now that you are gone, I press my fingers to your serious face, and wonder how you've changed.

Wasn't it you who once told me that the human body totally renews itself every seven years? So now it is seven years. Not one of the cells that were in your body in this photograph are still with you, nor is the woman who stands before you the wife you knew. And for some reason, a reason I am not certain of, I am yearning to tell you how I've changed. Maybe there is still in me a grain of habit, left over from a time when things were good between us and I told you everything, or perhaps I just need to clear the decks and be done with this. A way of setting you free. Or me. Whatever it is, I must tell you the whole of it—how in those darkest days a certain character came into my life, and how I attached myself to him, like a sailor snaps her lifelines to a boat when the seas begin to kick up. I want to tell you what happened, how this character took me the distance, and how, without meaning to, he left me dangling at the edge of the world, where I finally faced the sea monster of my darkest self.

2   PAMELA E. CONRAD

It began nearly three years after the smashed pumpkin, when the old fireplace in the living room started to belch little puffs of black smoke into the room. I could have let it go, stopped using the fireplace, as I had stopped using the rotting porch, the busted garage door, the sink in the back room, but the fireplace was my only comfort when I couldn't write, especially that spring when the mornings and evenings were so cold. Sometimes I would lie before the hearth and sleep, and in my dreams I'd hear the wood crackling and snapping and I'd think I'd fallen asleep near an open window and was being awakened by rain.

On dry, barren mornings I'd sit cross-legged and stare into the flames. Big chunks of stories would come to me as the wood would crack and tumble, and I'd be inspired by words, words like smudge, *that glowing bit of ash on the floor of the fireplace that kept me warm. Smudge. It would open a world flowing with words, and phrases, and metaphors. The whole universe would seem like a metaphor, an illusion of tinted Cello-tac over the great graph of reality, but I was beginning to have trouble finding the right words. The feeling was there, sort of an erection of the brain, but the words were coming harder and harder for me. It seemed I was growing content just thinking* smudge, *and nothing more.*

Who would blame me for getting the fireplace fixed? I had to. Everything in the living room was covered with a light dusting of soot. So I called a chimney sweep, and Max came.

You always thought I made friends too easily—people next to us at the movie, the waiter at the diner, the children in the park. I had tried to stop this once you were gone, suddenly embarrassed and awkward without you to frown at me. But with Max, I just couldn't help myself. And we didn't just strike up an intense conversation, the kind that used to drive you mad. I took him to bed.

And I'd do unforgivable things to him. Like if he came during the day, I'd tell him I couldn't stay. That I had to get my daughter at dancing school. I even left my clarinet out once and said it was hers.

Or late at night I'd sneak him up the creaking stairs to my room, shushing him, telling him my daughter, Casey, was sleeping in the room behind the pink door, and that we must be quiet. And then in my own bed, I would drive him close to screaming, make him want to call out, and then clamp my hand over his mouth, tell him not to wake her. He was young. He laughed and said it was like screwing a girl in a paneled basement while her parents were home. He made me laugh.

Oh, did he make me laugh. It was better than any medicine. Better than Cassis and white wine licked off warm skin. I'll bet you're shocked. I am too, now that I look back. But to misquote Whitman a bit—I am bigger, better than I thought. I did not know that I held such possibilities.

I thought I heard the doorbell ring that first morning. I was already sitting at my computer, struggling to come up with just one single novel idea for Charlie, my editor, and Jacobs, the publisher. Charlie was being so patient with me, so understanding since Casey's death, so trusting and sure that sooner or later I'd once again produce something wonderful for him. "I'll send you an outline real soon," I had told him six months before.

When I first started writing I had anticipated being a third-rate novelist, which isn't so bad. It's all I ever wanted—to make a living by writing, making things up all day, scenes, characters, confrontations, like playing God. So I wrote a novel about a woman who was relentless in acting out the same personal drama over and over again, with different people, in different settings. But instead of being third-rate, my first novel, *You Again,* drew some unexpected attention. High praise from literary circles. Scared me to death. My generic bachelor's degree and my provincial life embarrassed me, but I guess being an avid reader of good stuff and having an imagination that defies understanding, coupled with intense memories of some dense human interactions, all added up to a book that packed a wallop for some people.

Scary stuff. Especially with all the attention, and then these literary wizards at Jacobs's cocktail parties began to collar me. They seemed to know and understand things about *You Again* that I didn't know, and still didn't see even after they told me. They were smarter about my book than I was, and I was all the time trying to cover it. One time this slick magazine reviewer told me he thought my novel was something like "the quintessential example of Jung's concept of the animus." I had stared at him vacantly. "Animals?" I said. "There are no animals in *You Again*." I will never forget the look on his face; it flattened into a sort of stunned superiority as he mouthed, "An-i-mus. Jung. An-i-mus." I looked them up the minute I got home.

I was the emperor in new clothes. And any minute I expected a small, innocent voice in the crowd to call out, "But wait a minute! *You Again* was an accident. Brinkley doesn't have a brain in her head. Can't anyone see?"

Being literary, *You Again* didn't make me a lot of money, even after the initial surprising blast of reprintings. Sales began to decline, paperback rights had fallen through, no options on movies appeared (too literary, I was told), but it got me a hefty advance for my next book, right around the time I lost Casey. So there I was nearly three years later, without a word written, needing the chimney cleaned, and I had just enough money to last me another few months, as long as I didn't do anything or go anywhere. And I never asked anybody for a dime. Well, maybe just Charlie after I saw the sailboat. But that was something else.

So I was in the back room that morning staring at the black

screen and yellow letters of my computer when I thought I heard the doorbell ring. The house had been cold when I first got up, so I was wearing an old, red woolen shirt, and my mind was as empty as a forgotten fishhook. I knew I should just ignore the doorbell, but as usual I welcomed any diversion, any excuse to roll my chair away from the table. The doorbell rang again as I turned away from the screen, and again as my hand touched the front doorknob. I had forgotten all about the chimney sweep coming.

"Hail, citizen. Chim'man here." The door had opened onto a Dickens novel. A Mary Poppins movie. The chimney sweep stood on my doorstep, dressed in a black top hat and tails and, underneath, a Sting T-shirt. His face was beautiful the way some young men's faces are. And our eyes hesitated on each other.

It was then that I remembered the message on my phone machine saying the chimney sweep would be there at eight-thirty, and when I opened the door wide he swooped past me with his brushes and a large vacuum.

"Sorry I'm late," he said. He went right to the living room and began taking off his coat, his tails actually. "I had a few jobs before you this morning that I had to finish. A chimney cap. A damper installation." He looked up at me then as he dumped his things before the fireplace. Suddenly he was bashful. Born liars, we recognized each other. "Nah, that's not true," he said. "You're the first, and I'm just late. That's the way chimney sweeps are."

"No problem," I told him. "To tell you the truth, I forgot you were coming."

"Good. Good," he muttered, opening the glass doors to the fireplace and pulling open the steel mesh grating.

I noticed his hands right away—I always do—and his thighs as he squatted before the opening.

"It's a good chimney," I told him, but he put up his hand to stop me.

"Please, citizen. *I'll* be the judge of that." He moved the fireplace tools aside and put down a heavy cloth on the hearth. He ran his finger around the chimney's inside and then examined it as carefully as a doctor reading a thermometer. "It's a dirty one."

He made me smile. And although my computer hummed for me in the back room I sat on the sofa and watched. "It's been blowing soot into the living room," I told him. "Could it be stuffed up or something?"

Without answering he closed the glass doors, covered them with the heavy cloth, and stood back. He held very still, poised in his dusty top hat, giving me an instant to look him over— his long blue jean legs, his high young man's ass, his broad shoulders. Then he snapped his fingers once, loud. "There," he said. "It's clean."

I hate when men can make me laugh like that, lay me wide open like a loose drawer. He must have known he had me where he wanted me. But he couldn't have known how long it had been since I'd been there. I laughed and crossed my legs. Ran my fingers through my hair.

"Wanna come up with me?" he asked, motioning with his head, looping his thumb in his belt loop. I thought to my bedroom. "You look like the sort of modern woman who likes to go all the way with her chimney sweep."

I froze a little inside.

"Come on," he coaxed, picking up his brushes. "I'll bet you've never been up on your roof, now, have you? Have you?"

I flushed with relief.

"Well, come on," he said. "Haven't got all day."

We stepped out onto the front porch and the early spring day was bright and cold. I buttoned up the red woolen shirt and shivered while he went to his truck. The bite in April air always reminds me of when I was pregnant, when I walked around as the plump personification of hope and expectation. Expecting. The perfect word to describe pregnancy. My very body had harbored a new life, not like a seed, or an amoeba, I had thought, but an actual biography-prone life, a person who was going to have a job and a personality to give her grief, and opinions, a soul—an entire life pressed into the taut space between my two hipbones. I had had expectations. But that day, as I was led out onto my own front porch by a strange young man, I was thinner, smaller than I had been in years, and as empty of expectations as a dry gourd. I almost rattled.

His truck was in the driveway, white and dusty, with its front bumper slightly awry like a child's cleft lip. He lifted a ladder off the roof rack and hoisted it in the air. "Bring these brushes and poles, would you?" he asked, motioning to the pile on the grass. I picked them up and followed him around the back. He carried the ladder over his head, and his sneakers crunched their way down the graystone driveway. Forsythia twigs, like thin, delicately salted pretzels, scratched against his legs. He didn't even glance at the spectacularly huge yard, overgrown and neglected. He waded into the ivy and leaned the ladder up against the house.

"I'll go first," he said. He reached out for the brushes and poles and holding them in one hand, climbed the ladder in one clean, smooth ascent. He disappeared and then his head peeked over the edge.

I gripped the ladder and climbed steadily, feeling it bow a little under me. It was an old house, I'd always known that. But it was a big house, too, and it had never felt so huge before. I thought how I didn't even know this man, and I wondered where my fear had gone. His hand was there at the top, and it clasped mine and pulled me onto the roof.

"I forgot to ask," he said. "Do you come with a clean soul?"

"What?"

"Say, 'I come with a clean soul.'"

"Oh, come on."

"Please, say it. Or I'll worry for your safety."

"I come with a clean soul."

"Good. Follow me."

Without hesitation, he turned and walked up the steeply slanted roof as easily as he'd walked down the driveway. I walked up on all fours, not daring to look down, imagining myself sliding, sliding, sliding down into the rose of Sharon that always bloomed on my birthday. At the top was the chimney, a double chimney, actually, as wide as a park bench, and I followed his lead and straddled it. We sat facing each other.

I'd never seen the top of my house before. It was like an out-of-body experience, like rising up and looking down at my life. He looked at me. "You okay?"

"Fine."

He nodded, and forcing the round, black brush into the chimney opening, he began to screw one of the poles into it.

"So," he said. "Now you see what I do. What do you do?"

"I write."

"A writer."

"Yes. I sit at my machine all day and make up stories. Some people pump gas. Some people fold sheets. I make up lies."

"Sounds interesting. How'd this wonderful work find you?"

He forced the brush up and down, and then down further and screwed another stick onto the end of the first. The brush sank deeper into the chimney.

"I didn't like to talk when I was a kid, I guess. And I had a lot to say. So I wrote it down. And I lied a lot. I like to lie."

"Tell me a lie," he dared.

"Oh, I can't tell lies anymore. I have a daughter who catches me in them." My heart fluttered in my chest like a trapped bird. "I have to be straight as an arrow with her around. All my lies have to go down on paper. Certified lies."

He squinted at me. Weighing things. "Is that a lie?"

I shrugged.

Again another stick and the brush sank deeper still. "Are you married?"

"Divorced," I told him. "And that's the truth."

"Boyfriends?"

"Dozens," I lied.

"Okay," he said quietly. "I consider myself forewarned."

I didn't look at his eyes. I looked over the roof into the linden and sycamore trees that surround the house.

"Aren't you going to ask me how I got into *this* line of work?"

"I figured you probably inherited it from your cruel stepfather, who found you on the streets. You were a street urchin, and he taught you everything you know, and when he died— in the cardboard box you lived in with him and your sickly mother down by the railroad tracks—he left you all his tools and told you to carry on."

"Good. Good. But not accurate. You're way off. Actually I was a chief surgical resident at Columbia Presbyterian Hospital—"

I laughed.

"What?" he asked innocently, the corner of his mouth twitching with his nonsense.

I quieted. "Go on."

"Well, one memorable day, after ten hours on my feet in surgery—three brains, two livers, a swallowed church key, and a hair transplant—I looked out over the city and had a vision. I saw the landscape littered with dirty and potentially hazardous chimneys and knew what I had to do."

My laugh shocked me, it was so much like my mother's when my father would go after her.

"I like this lifestyle better," he told me, basking in my laughter. "I don't have to scrub up so much, and it leaves me time for other things.

"And I assure you," he laughed with me, "that despite appearances, I'm not in this for the glory!"

"What else have you done?" I asked.

"Oh, shipbuilding. I built wooden sailboats for a while in Annapolis." He was gently pushing the poles up and down, and the brush was so far down I could no longer hear it sweeping against the chimney lining. He stared out into the trees as he began to pull the brush back up, unscrewing the poles and handing them to me. "But the best job I ever had was crewing a sailing vessel one summer, the USS *Freedom Song,* a one-hundred-year-old double-masted schooner that's been going from Boston to New York every year since the bicentennial. I'd sit in the crow's nest," he told me, "and wave at motorists who sat waiting on the drawbridge of the Marine Parkway as we sailed by."

Unexpectedly the fine hairs stood up along my arms. "I love sailboats," I whispered. An image of my father's old boat floated and swelled to the surface of my thoughts. "Always have."

"You ever been sailing?"

And then, not knowing why, I said, "No." And he believed me.

The brush emerged from the chimney full of chunks of black creosote. "This is why your chimney's backing up," he said. "By the size of these pieces, I'd say this old stack hasn't been brushed in seven hundred years." He picked the chunks out with his fingers, sending them tumbling down the roof and over the edge. Some he dropped back into the chimney and I could hear them tumbling away.

"I have a sailboat," he said suddenly.

"You?"

"Sure, not wooden though, fiberglass. I have to sell it. The chimney business has been slow lately." He shrugged. "I don't know. It's getting rough."

"Oh, that's sad," I said.

He locked eyes with me. "Wanna buy it?" he asked.

"Oh, I couldn't."

"Why not? You look like an adventurous type. Independent." He took my hand and turned my palm up to study it. "Yes, see? Competent, seaworthy, and look, look at this—a jib, right here on your palm. See the jib?"

I took my palm back and looked at it. "What's a jib?" I pretended.

"The front sail, see?" His head touched mine as he took my hand back and ran his blackened finger over a long triangle that curved around my thumb's pad. A jib.

I eased my hand away, now streaked with chimney soot.

"What are you doing the rest of the day?" he asked.

"Writing. I'm supposed to be writing a new novel."

"Supposed?"

"Nothing's coming."

"Well, how about a sailboat book? You can write the *Woman's Guide to Cruising*."

"I'm sure it's been done. Besides, I write lies, remember? Novels."

"How about sailboat lies then? A story about a sailboat."

Sometimes ideas come this way. Beneath the sky, atop a chimney, unexpected, sudden, but fitting exactly right, as though it had been waiting in just that place to reveal itself to me. Something began to stir in me.

But I thought of Charlie. His good, sensible, editorial self would say, "Maybe you should stick with what you know, Ellie.

That's what has worked for you before." But he didn't know about my father's boat. Another thing Charlie didn't know was that I had felt as though I had put everything I had into *You Again.* I hadn't thought there was much else left of me. But maybe now. Maybe now I would find there *was* more. Troubling thoughts of that old childhood sailboat floated like jellyfish beneath the surface of my mind.

"What do you think?" he asked.

"I wonder if I could write a book about a woman who has a sailboat of her own?"

"Sure, why not?"

"Are there such women with their own boats?"

"Of course."

"I mean, they take care of them and can sail them alone and all? There are women who do that?"

He nodded. "You'd be great."

"You don't even know me."

"I know you. I know something very important about you, don't I?"

"What's that?"

"You're the kind of woman who will sit on her chimney in the morning with a perfect stranger instead of working on her new book."

"Ain't that the truth!" I laughed with him.

He licked his finger and held it to the wind. "A good westerly blow," he said. "Let's finish up here and we'll go for a sail."

"You're serious," I said.

"Chimney sweeps are never *serious.* We're *sincere.*"

Two squirrels suddenly startled us by scuttling wildly up the roof, tumbling past us, and disappearing over the edge. "Ah, squirrel love," he said, grinning at me.

He had the sharp, angular face of a gondolier. An angel. A dark-eyed silent-movie star. "What's your name?" I asked.

"Bond," he said. "James Bond."

"Really," I insisted.

"Max. Max Turkel."

"Ellie," I told him, shaking his hand over the blackness of my swept chimney. "Ellie Brinkley."

So, you see? I went with him. I know. You would say that I lacked judgment. That I barely knew him. You'd have all the reasons, all the safe reasons for not taking a chance with someone. But I knew all I had to know about Max. I knew he had invited me up on the roof to straddle my chimney with him, and that he had noticed things about me — noticed that I was competent and seaworthy, and that I could take chances. It had been so long since I'd been noticed.

I never mentioned this to you, but once, when you were still here, I went to the city and bought an exquisite china plate. It was imported from Holland, the softest possible blue and white melted together, and on its face was an image of a very still rabbit sitting near a fence in the snow, and pressed there on the edge of the plate, encircled with tightly sealed pinecones, was the year we met.

I brought the plate home and set it on the china cabinet that you passed every day, and I waited for you to notice it. For an entire year you passed by and never saw it. Never once noticed how beautiful it was. It called out to you. It called, "See how lovely I am, how soft, how good beneath my brittleness," and not once did you see it. Or if you did notice, you never mentioned it to me. And when you left, I wrapped the plate in tissue paper and put it way back in the drawer behind my grandmother's gravy boats and the soup ladles. Good riddance, my grandmother used to say. Good riddance.

I see your back, see you turning away in impatience. Wait. Stay with me a while longer. Here. You can even have your red woolen shirt back. It's perfect for cold spring mornings.

$\mathcal{M}$ax's truck hobbled over the ruts in the boatyard. It was a Tuesday, and like most boatyards on a weekday, there was no one around. Empty boats were tied with creaking lines to the short docks, white bumpers squeaked as they were nudged against the dock, and telltales fluttered on naked rigging in the breeze. Max pulled the truck to one side, its wheels deep in dried mud gullies, and we got out.

The scent of salt water filled my head and reminded me of something old—maybe of my father's packs of Chesterfields, and the sight of him tapping his ashes into the cuffs of his pants while he fished.

"You go ahead," Max said. "I'll find Captain and tell him I've got a buyer here."

"Max! I didn't say I'd buy her. I just said I'd look."

"P-shaw." Max spoke like a true comic strip. "Jump aboard. Third one on the left. The red one." He turned and I watched him walk toward the weathered boathouse. It was the pale, faded green wood of weathered boathouses, with the required outboard motor cradled by its doorway and an old dog asleep on a pile of torn sails.

I paced the length of the dock alone, the water glistening up in sharp bursts through the slats, like an old-time movie. I passed the boat he said was his without looking at it and walked all the way to the end, past another two boats—one a wooden motorboat, thick with varnish and flat paint, the other glossy with fiberglass buff. Behind me an automatic bilge pump blasted water in a stream, like an elephant peeing. I turned to watch it—a large sailboat, unaware, unashamed, automatic.

Slowly, almost like I was sneaking up on it, I returned to the red boat that was tied bow first to the dock. It was knotted carelessly from cleat to dock posts, but I could see even from the dock that its sail was bundled and covered the way my father would have done it. Water slapped at its hull without pattern or reason, and I was filled with an odd trembling joy. The boat was the red of poinsettias. The red of a cowboy's bandanna.

I grasped the jib stay, and with a long tottering stride I pulled myself from dock to sailboat, stepping over the secured anchor and onto the foredeck. I felt the boat sink slightly beneath my weight and then right itself as I made my way back to the cockpit. Clasping the shrouds lightly, I knew instantly they were a little too loose.

"Here," my father would say. "Feel this?" And with my back pressed up against him we would feel the shrouds together, delicately with our fingers. "See how loose?" And then kneeling, he would take a small tool from his pocket and tighten them one at a time, till they hummed like the strings of a bass fiddle.

The cockpit of this boat was strewn with blown leaves and bits of debris as if no one had been on it for a long time. Sitting along one side, facing the boathouse, I brushed the leaves into a pile and dropped them by handfuls over the side. All the while watching for Max. It wasn't till I looked away, looked out over the channel and forgot him for a moment, that I heard his footsteps on the planks of the dock. When I looked up, he was swinging his leg onto the bow, clasping the stay, and holding a six-pack of soda in the other hand. Max was not much taller than I, but he was broader, and solid. His weight tossed the boat more than mine had, and for an instant I remembered as a child thinking that my father's boat must have recognized him when he stepped on board, that it almost sighed beneath his familiar weight, and I thought that now of Max and his boat.

"Cap's outta beer," he explained, setting the orange sodas beside me and turning to unlock the cabin.

No brew on board, my father would say. He'd said it so many times it had become as familiar as *Ready about, Hard alee.* He'd said it often. *No brew on board.*

"That's fine with me," I told Max.

Max looked at me over his shoulder. "Pretty nice, huh? Is this paradise or what?"

I nodded and swelled inside. "Mmmm," is all I said.

I watched as Max prepared the boat to go out. He clambered about the deck, undoing, tightening, unlocking, unwinding. "Now you just sit tight, Miss Brinkley," he said.

"But how am I going to learn any—"

"This time out is purely for purposes of falling in love," he told me. "An afternoon out sailing and you'll be lost. I'll have you under my spell. You'll be so in love with this boat, you'll sell the bricks in your chimney to buy it." He paused and smiled at me from beneath his dark mustache. "Forget the bricks," he said. "You'll give me your firstborn child. That's how much you'll love it."

Imagine. He said that to me. Your firstborn child.

Then he stepped up to the boom and began to uncover the sails. The blue cover peeled away like an outer skin, and beneath it the white sail lay bunched and rolled. He patted and tugged and made the motions of checking everything out. He seemed to know what he was doing, yet there was an awkwardness about him and I couldn't tell if it was inexperience or excitement.

"Now come up here," he said. He patted the deck before the mast and I went up to him. "I want you to sit right here while we motor out, okay? Just sit back and enjoy." He turned his face up to the sun and stretched out his arms. "Just let the sun and the sea and the song of the gull seep into your soul." He suddenly bent over and brushed the spot where he had told me to sit. "Just be careful the puddles don't seep into your jeans."

I sat down where he told me. "You sure you don't want any help?"

"Not the tiniest bit," he answered. "Nothing. Absolutely nothing."

"What about the lines up here when we back out?"

He paused. "Well, yes, that you can do. But only that. Toss them off when I tell you."

I saluted him and he disappeared behind me. The metal mast was cool. I could feel it through my shirt, and while the gentle wind stroked my face and head, I thought of how ridiculous it would be for me to buy this boat. I heard compartment doors banging and clanging, crankings, and the anxious noise of someone yanking the cord on a gas motor. Again and again, the yank and nothing. It reminded me of the grass growing deep in the yard, when I would stand out there with beads of sweat sliding into my eyes, trying to start the lawnmower.

I turned to watch Max pull the cord, and as I did the motor caught, and as if he knew I was watching he gave a thumbs up sign in the air, and a puff of pale smoke floated over him. "Piece of toast," I heard him say to himself.

I smiled and crawled forward to the lines. "Tell me when," I called. I loosened their hold on the dock, but kept us bound there. I felt the motor drop into reverse and the lines tighten.

"All right, cast off," he said, and in that motion, that long instant of slack and good-bye, I released the lines from the dock posts and wound them into a neat coil as we eased away from land. I remembered this feeling from my father's boat. How I couldn't have called that dock back no matter how much I had wanted to, even if I had wanted to desperately. Sometimes there is that unalterable, irrevocable, lasting, permanent, irretrievable, never-going-backness of leaving shore.

Still on my knees, I watched as the barnacle-laced pilings passed on either side of me, and the land of the boatyard slipped away. Slowly the boat backed up, until it paused in the water like a dancer rising back on her toes before loping across the stage, and then it went forward. I almost saw myself as the figurehead on an old ship, a strong woman's face and mighty breasts driving ahead into stormy seas. Nothing so grand, with my soft, pale features and small, round breasts, I leaned back into the mast and watched as the boat turned itself out toward the bay. A peace I had forgotten washed over my body and I closed my eyes. I listened to the drone of the motor, the clear cut of the bow through the water, which really was no noise at all, but rather a silent sound, a hum along my limbs, and the sudden cry of a gull swooping by us.

"Pay attention now," Max called. "See how the land looks from the water? You need to know so you can find your way back. See the boatyard, how it looks from here?" I looked. "And the tanks back there? The cropping of trees, that white thing over there? Those are your landmarks."

I turned and looked, not to know or remember them, but just to appreciate them, knowing Max knew the way home. I wouldn't need to know them, didn't want to fill my mind with information I would never use. The boatyard looked like a painting. The two blue water tanks were like space creatures, and the white thing, the white thing, it wasn't important, a large rectangular white thing, and just before I closed my eyes and let the wind drape long wisps of my hair across my face I saw a green buoy pass us on the starboard side like the great insect eye of a submarine. I could tell the current was strong.

Max's voice interrupted my solitude. "Did you feel that?" he called.

I turned and stared at him blankly. I felt nothing. Then there it was. Kind of a vibration, a scratching.

"We're skimming the bottom," he told me, and then again a secret inner touch, like the tiny smooth heel of an unborn baby grazing the inside of me, the outline of me. I felt it and nodded.

"We'll have to get out deeper before we can let the centerboard down," he said. "Tide's going out."

I watched as the wind combed his wild, curly hair back off his face, like a mother would push a child's hair back to see him better. I saw the smooth, tanned brow, the eyebrows that, like Chinese letters, defined his squinting eyes, and then I watched his dark mustache deepen into a smile above his flashing teeth. In all the ways that I was soft and pale, a blend of silences and muted tones, he was solid and dark. I knew I was the kind of person one could easily lose at dusk, but Max's eyes held me in that moment, and the sun was bright.

"What's her name?" I asked, to change a subject that had not even taken form.

"Who?" His face looked sheepish.

"The boat."

"Oh, oh," he recovered. *"Nemaste."* He hooked his leg over the tiller suddenly, pressed the palms of his hands together, and bowed his head toward me. *"Nemaste."*

"Now *you* say it. Do it like this," he ordered, bowing his head.

"What does it mean?"

"Do it."

Twisting from the mast and lifting my hand, I pressed my palms together and said it. *"Nemaste.* Now what does it mean?"

"I was told it's Sanskrit for 'the God within me beholds the God within you.'" He took the tiller again.

He surprised me. Imagine a chimney sweep who seems magical, yet ordinary, who probably slurps beer with his buddies, sleeps late, and yet has a boat with a holy name. The *Nemaste.*

I tried to remember the name of my father's boat. It was there in the fringes of my brain, and yet, strain as I would, I couldn't find it. I pictured that old boat there on the long ago dock at Plum Tree Harbor, with its forest green hull, and the stiff, moldering sails, my father tossing buckets of water across the deck at the end of the day, but I couldn't see the stern. Couldn't in my mind step around the stern and read its name painted there. Maybe it didn't have a name. No. My father would say, "We're going to take—" What was it he had said?

"Look over there," Max called to me. His finger pointed at a distant stretch of water that the wind suddenly darkened and rippled as it touched the surface. "It's a puff," he called. "Here it comes." In seconds a stronger breeze passed over the boat, not affecting it at all without our sails up. "You have to keep an eye to the wind," he told me. "Always know where your wind is coming from. See?"

He pointed at the telltales up on the shrouds, little ribbons twitching in the breeze. "Those are your telltales. Nifty little high-tech devices that tell you where the wind is coming from."

I knew all about telltales. One spring my father had put the boat in the water for the first time, only to discover the telltales had rotted away during the winter. And he had taken the ribbons from the ends of my braids and had tied them to the shrouds. I remembered with strange twitchings of unexplainable shame that I was relieved he hadn't left them in my hair and watched *me* all day to see which way the wind was blowing.

Slowly we motored out into an open waterway. There weren't many other boats around, just an occasional fishing boat, or a small motorboat with a boy in it zipping by.

"Okay, matey," Max called. "I want to put the sails up now. But you just stay right where you are. Don't move a muscle, you hear?"

I didn't even look back at him. The motor slowed and softened, but kept humming raggedly. There was a cranking noise. I waited. I knew I was going to have to move, but I didn't want to appear too knowledgeable.

"Uh, matey," he finally called.

"Mmmm?"

"On second thought, I could use some help. Think you could step back here a minute?"

"Hold this," he said when I reached him and sat across from

him. He took my hands and put them on the tiller. "See this?" He moved the tiller from side to side to show me that when he pushed the tiller to starboard the boat eased to port, and when he pushed the tiller to port we eased the other way. "See? Easy, right? Now what I want you to do is watch the telltales there, and keep the boat heading right into the wind." When he let go of the tiller I realized his hands had been over mine. I was instantly at home. My hands had not forgotten; they could feel the rudder respond beneath the water.

"First I lower the boom," Max said. He stood on the bench and strained with the latch at the end of the boom. "You know when I was a kid, and my father left us and went to live in Monte Carlo—"

"I could have sworn he died in a cardboard box."

"That's what *you* said about my stepfather. My real father went to Monte Carlo."

I smiled up into the telltales.

"Anyway. Stop interrupting. So when he left us kids and my mother all alone, my mother sat us around the kitchen table one morning, and she said to us, 'Kids, I've got some bad news. Your father has lowered the boom. And we're never going to see him again. We're on our own.'

"Imagine that. Anyway, I don't know how old I was, maybe seven, and when she said 'lower the boom,' I thought she meant my father had hit her over the head. I don't know where I got that. Maybe cartoons. So I thought, *good.* I don't want anybody hitting my mother over the head, even my father, and I never had a moment's regret after that. And it wasn't till years later, after my mother'd remarried and I'd been sailing for a while, that I learned what lowering the boom really meant. It means prepare to sail, we're pushing off, I'm outta here! My father hadn't hit my mother at all. He was just outta there. That's all.

"Can you imagine a child misunderstanding something so completely?" He sat opposite me as if waiting for a response while the boom dangled between us.

"You know what Casey, my daughter, thought once?" I risked.

"What?"

"Well, when Casey was real young, maybe six or seven, and learning to read, I used to put little notes in her lunch box. No big deal, just things like 'We'll go grocery shopping when you get home' or 'Tonight is pizza night,' you know, that sort of thing. I'd been doing it for a long time, off and on, and one day she said to me, 'Ma? —' "

"That's what she calls you? Ma?"

"Mmm. So she says, 'Ma, how come—' "

"How old is she now?"

I cleared my throat. "Sixteen."

"And what does she call you now?"

What does she call me now. "Still Ma, I guess. Yes, she calls me Ma. Stop interrupting. So she says, 'Ma, how come you always sign your letters "I hate you, I hate you, I hate you"?' "

I couldn't see Max's pupils. His eyes were so dark and big, and the sky was bright and hard. He was watching me.

"So I said to her, 'What do you mean? I don't write "I hate you, I hate you, I hate you." ' And she said, 'Yes. See?' And she held out one of my notes. Before my name, or actually where I'd signed Ma, I had scribbled *XXX*."

"My God." Max sank back against the bench. He tipped his head way back, his face to the sky. "You must have felt awful."

Unexpectedly, a sob clenched my throat and I couldn't breathe. It had been so long since I had thought of those notes. And now they came crashing back to me, stirring up the old mud of guilt, and raising yet again the painful question of what had gone wrong. Could I have done anything different? Could I have been anything other than I was? And would it have mattered if I had written it out: I love you. I love you. I love you.

"Ooof." He punched his fist into his chest. "That kind of gets you right here, doesn't it?"

I nodded and turned my attention back to the telltales. We had swung nearly a quarter turn around. "Oh, dear," I mumbled. "What have I done?" He put his hand over mine and guided the tiller again until the telltales were streaming straight back. There was a new tenderness in his touch, and when I glanced at him it was through an unexpected swell of grateful tears. I looked away.

"Okay now?" he asked. "Just keep it there. Right like that."

He got up and leaped forward, untying and fumbling at the base of the mast. I knew he was attaching the halyard to the sail and I watched him, his concentration. How was it that he was so beautiful? How could a man be that beautiful? Not just his face, and his body, but the way he moved, the way he held himself. He was so beautiful that had I known him better then, had I been just a little bit brazen, I would've gone to him there at the mast, turned back his sleeve, and kissed the smooth skin along his forearm. He was that beautiful. And I was that grateful.

Then suddenly the sail lifted with all the grandeur of a curtain going up at an opera house. It lifted white and powerful into the sky. First the mainsail, broad and old, missing two battens, and then suddenly the jib, smaller and forward. I couldn't see Max any longer. I could just hear the lines pulling higher and higher. Facing into the wind, the sails luffed noisily. Then Max appeared from behind them like a puppet and jumped to the cockpit, taking the tiller from me. I was jealous.

I wanted to be the one to turn us away from the wind and feel the sails swell, but for now I surrendered the tiller to him and sank back to watch the sails.

The feeling was vast. Old. As familiar as the pattern of my father's beard on his heavily creased cheeks. I thought I remembered my father saying something about how a sailboat could be forgiving. Why had I forgotten all this? Why had I never thought I could have this in my life again? Suddenly it was as if I saw everything differently. A sailboat. Of course. It wasn't such a ridiculous idea at all.

Then as we sped along on linen wings, the boat tilted slightly and I went to sit alongside Max. Our legs touched each other in a familiar way, and feeling so trusting, I began to think out loud.

"This reminds me of a time," I said, "when a bird was trapped in our garage. Back at the house. You saw it. It's a big, old barn kind of building with a sloping roof, and it's got this window high in the peak at the back. I went back there late in the day to get something. The light was bright but fading, and when I got near the doors I heard a noise inside. I peered into the darkness. I was worried it was a couple of squirrels or something, but when my eyes got used to the light, I saw that it was this bird, a sparrow, and it was trying to get out of the garage through the back window that was shut tight. It would fly up, aim right for the trees on the opposite side of the window, and go for it. It'd throw itself at the glass with a clink and a thud and tumble down to the cement floor. Over and over. I tried to tell it—'Turn around! Here! Look here, at the doors, right behind you!' But my voice, my simple solution, terrified the sparrow. I tried getting closer and turning it toward the two wide-open doors, but it panicked and began throwing itself harder and harder against the window. Soon it wasn't even tumbling to the ground before it'd turn itself up and throw itself again at the window. I was making things worse, so I backed out of the garage and left it there."

Max looked at me. "What made you think of that?"

I shrugged. "I don't know. I guess I was just thinking how sometimes, an answer is so obvious, so close to you, and you don't even realize it."

I can still remember what it was like that day to watch Max when he was still new to me, his face turned into the wind and the mainsheet wound through his long fingers. He had listened to everything I said, took it all in without giving it meaning, without judging; he just listened. I had never been good at that. When I had seen that bird so long ago, you had still been here, and I had told you how I could see that you felt trapped with me and Casey, and that you couldn't see a way out, and that if you'd only turn around, maybe there would have been another way, a way that I could show you. And you had gotten angry.

But this day, as I cruised through the gentle waters of the Great South Bay with Max, I realized the story about the bird was about myself. Not the part where the bird is throwing itself against an invisible barrier, but the part just before the bird turns around and sees the doors wide open, like the gates of heaven.

I stood up then on the bench in the boat, a foot on each side, and spread my arms wide, to fly away. The same wind that pressed into the billowing sails gathered beneath my wings. I laughed and laughed and I felt this man, this Max, wrap his fingers around my ankle to steady me. I felt elated, thinking I was about to be released from the burden of throwing myself against incomprehensible barriers, and believing I was ready for whatever lay ahead.

I could not lie down in my own bed that night without feeling like I was on a boat, that my mattress tilted and swayed with the pulse of the sea. Such was my yearning for the *Nemaste*. I tried lying very still on my back, every muscle intentionally relaxed and smoothed, but my mind stayed wide awake. I thought of Max pulling down the sails in handfuls before we motored back, and later of him folding the sails neatly and binding them with stretched-out bungee cords before covering them with the blue cover. I turned over and buried my face in the down pillow, counting my breaths, and my mind hovered at the foot of the bed, waiting for me with pictures of the boatyard coming into view, the water tanks, the *Nemaste*'s slip. I felt over and over again the solid ground beneath my feet when I stepped off the boat, and memories of my childhood began seeping into my thoughts like an incoming tide flooding the moats of a sand castle.

There is my very first boat. I am little with thin arms and small hands that do not yet reach around a cup unless I use them both. I live in a tiny apartment in Ridgewood, Queens, upstairs from my grandparents. My own parents are very young—my father about twenty-three, and he has an outboard motor in a barrel in the back alley. He is a boy, and I am his little girl, peering into the barrel when the engine is still, its star blades glistening in the water, and then I am peering down from his arms, hands over my ears, as the noisy engine blasts away at the splashing water, and I am told, probably not exactly, but this is what I understand—this is a boat. I've seen enough illustrations in my picture books to know this is not a boat, but maybe, since my father should know—and he knows everything—maybe this is a sort of inside-out boat. I look for fish in the barrel.

My next boat is bigger, huge. And this time it is my grandmother who takes me to it. This boat will take us up the Hudson River to Indian Point where we will play bingo and go on a ride called the Caterpillar. I still see the piers, and feel clearly what it is like to be that little girl, behind my eyes, looking out at the dark posts of the pier. There is a slick film of oil on the surface of the water, and I can see rainbows there. I stand at the rail of the boat with Grandma and my mother who is carrying Peter, my brother. He has a bottle with a nipple on it that is so old and decrepit he can bury his finger in it all the way to the knuckle. He likes things easy, so this is his favorite nipple.

The boat pulls away from the pier, groaning, vibrating, heavy, and so big, bigger than anything I have ever seen, and the black water churns like nothing I could have made up in my worst nightmare. Grandma's fingers tighten along my shoulder blade as she probably imagines me slipping over the edge and disappearing from sight. I squirm from her grip and I'm scolded by her fear. She is the first person I will learn to adjust myself to, the first person I will be taught to take care of. "Grandma is nervous." "Grandma's nerves." I was told these things in whispers, and forced to be quiet, sit down, be still.

The boat leaves the harbor, and the water is no longer a black churning nightmare but a silvery gray rippled mirror of foam and mysterious creatures. I see jellyfish floating like the raw eggs my father poaches, and birds skimming close to the surface. The sun is shining, the air smells different, and the gentle movement soothes and calms my grandmother and mother. Soon I'm allowed to roam the boat. There's another little girl and we walk along outside corridors of sunshine and railings and glorious water, and inside corridors where there's a place where we can see the motor to the boat. Not a motor in a barrel, but a large room where we peek and see tremendous noisy workings, with chain-link gates and white pipes and hot, steamy heat.

Then up some stairs there is a dance floor, but I never see anyone dancing. Or do I? Am I chased away? There is a long bar with sparkling glasses and dozens of bottles.

I eat with Grandma at the tables indoors, where there are no windows, only open spaces to the outside. I learn where my mother and grandmother are set up, where my sweater is, my brother's disgusting bottle, and this is my base. This is where I return to sit on Grandma's chair and watch the water go by. We head up the Hudson River, but I don't see the Palisades.

Maybe I can't see that far. In my memories, my dreams, I am crossing the ocean.

The water at the Indian Point pier is clean—no rainbows. We spend the day, and when it is time to leave there is no water to wash my dirty hands, and Grandma persuades me to wash my hands in milk. I remember the smell of sour milk all the way home and how I must keep my hands far from my face.

The return trip at night is peaceful. I sleep, held and rocked by the water. And when we leave the boat in the darkness, with our parcels and sweaters, I feel the ground unyielding, uncompromising, unforgiving beneath my feet. I know this is what I like about water. It acknowledges me. It affirms me.

The clock bonged three times in the downstairs hall, and I propped myself up, almost sitting, thinking I would tire and sleep if I forced myself to sit up. Eyes still closed, the fishing trips came back to me, the ones with my parents and Peter.

My mother makes me wear a straw hat. Peter wears my father's baseball cap. My brother is older now; the bottle is gone. And I have my very own fish box. It's a basket and, after that first trip, will always smell of shiny snappers glittering like fleshy jewels.

We are a family of four in a small boat. My father isn't drinking. My mother is very quiet, dreamy. My parents say how good Peter is, how patient, how good. *I* think he is good, too. He sits without moving for hours with the fishing pole in his hands. They don't mention me sitting here patiently, but it's less astounding that I am patient because I am four years older than he is, and it's expected of me. But I am good. I am good, too. The sun touches the soft, pale hairs on my arms and my skinny legs and my sneakers. There is the softest breeze. We are in the middle of a lake. I can see the place where we got the boat, way off by a restaurant on the shore.

My father has turned off the engine and eased the anchor over the side. We drift and rock so gently to his movements. My mother tells us not to stand. Not to rock the boat. And my father, so happy when he's on a boat, not drinking, never drinking on a boat, sings, "Sit down, sit down, sit down, sit down, sit down, you're rocking the boat." All my life I will never hear anyone else sing these lines, but I will always think they must be from a popular Broadway play. I imagine Ethel Merman singing them. Peter and I sit still.

Fishing poles are prepared with bait and bobbins and handed to us. We are told to watch the bobbin floating in the water. Stare at it. Don't look away. And when it goes down, it means a fish is there, nibbling at our bait. Then, snap like this. The hook will hold.

Peter stares at his bobbin. He doesn't look away. His concentration is superhuman, or maybe superchild. I stare at my bobbin. I stare at Peter's bobbin. I look back at the restaurant. I think what if my father falls out? How will we get back?

I wait. My pole is wonderful. My very own. It's a small black pole, and my father has attached the guide rings for the fishing line himself. He had special thread that he wound around and around at night in our tiny apartment in Ridgewood. He wound it perfectly even, perfectly tight, like thread on my mother's wooden spools. The thread is black and yellow, and, wound around like that over and over, it looks like leopard skin to me. The reel is on the right side. I have a right-handed father. I appear to fish right-handed, but while the reel is under my right hand, my fishing soul is in my left hand, the hand that holds the pole, that feels the fat fish brush up against my line with their glimmery scales. My left hand feels their fins tap the hook, and it's my left hand that jerks the pole when the bobbin takes a dive.

I catch three snappers. My parents catch fluke. The snappers are small. The fluke are big. Life is very ordered. Everything is perfect. My father—dock worker and jack-of-all-trades, boilerman, bus driver, scab—shows Peter and me how the fluke swims on its side, white side down, so that any enemy fish underneath looking up will see his white side against the white sky, and any fish on top looking down will see his dark gray side against the ocean bottom. Enemies top and bottom. My father shows us how both the fluke's eyes are on top, a seeming mistake of organization in the world I am still expecting perfection of.

A perfect world. Before anything bad ever happened to us.

I slid deeper under the covers, and the cooled sheets jarred me, waking me even more. I wondered what it would be like to write about boats. Maybe I could talk to Charlie about it. What could he say? I couldn't remember him ever talking about anything nautical. Maybe boats were like cats, either you liked them or you didn't. But Charlie liked everything I ever wrote. I'd even shown him poems I had written when I was a teenager, and he liked those, too.

But always when I'd show him something I'd be nervous. I'd once heard a story about a little girl who came parading out of her bedroom during her parents' dinner party, pulling a shiny red wagon with a perfectly shaped little turd in it. That's a little what it had been like for me to show my work to anybody. Especially Charlie. What do you think, Charlie? You like it?

That sleepless night, I tried to remember the name of that editor from *Harper's Magazine* that I'd once met at Charlie's country place. He'd told me to send him anything. Anything at all, he was so impressed with *You Again.* Charlie wasn't too happy about that, but you don't have to tell your editor everything. I wasn't even sure I could tell him I was thinking of buying a boat when he knew how short I was on money. I wondered if he'd understand. If Charlie couldn't get me some more money, maybe I could get a short story together about a boat for *Harper's,* and maybe it would cover the cost of the boat. Or part of it.

But I wanted to write a novel. Something with weight and heft that could be printed on dull paper and lay flat between hard covers. A magazine, glossy and floppy, wouldn't count.

I paced the dusty wooden floors barefoot until the morning sun lifted over the neighbors' house and sent a swath of sharp, cold light across the dining room table. At nine thirty, when I knew he would finally be there, I dialed Charlie's number. I listened as the phone rang in his office, imagining the board over his desk, studded with tacked up book covers, memos, circled reviews, a Chinese take-out menu, and a map of Shelter Island. Behind him the huge window would be bright with city dirt. Charlie purses his lips together like this—

"Charlie? It's me. Ellie. Hi."

. . .

"Oh, okay. Trying to come up with something. You know. It's been hard. What can I tell ya?"

. . .

"You did? Well, I was probably out at the supermarket or something."

. . .

"Listen, Charlie, do you like boats?"

. . .

"Well, I've been thinking of writing something about boats, and I wanted to make sure you didn't hate boats or anything."

. . .

"I know. I know. Yes, I want to."

. . .

"I know a lot about boats. I grew up around them. My father had a boat when I was a kid."

. . .

"And it would be all right to do it in the first person, right? I know we talked about it, but I hated that one review."

. . .

"You're right. Out of my mind, right out. I'll never think of that jerk again. I'll read just the good reviews."

. . .

"I really did. I don't know. I guess it never came up. My father had a boat. I know all about that stuff."

. . .

"Okay. Well, I just wanted to make sure you didn't have an aversion to the sea. And umm, another thing. Do you think you could get me some more money on that advance? Three, maybe four thousand. You know, just to help me out a bit? I'll be needing to do a little research."

. . .

"Yeah, I could probably get together a chapter or two."

. . .

"Okay. Yes. And a synopsis. I know. I'll see what I can come up with."

. . .

"Thanks, Charlie. I'll be getting back to you."

. . .

"Yes. Okay. Bye."

The sun had barely moved. I walked into my office in the back room and sat down before the computer. I didn't even turn it on. I just sat there staring at it, and then in the dust on the screen I drew a small sailboat with its two sails up. Maybe it was too late in the day for me to start writing. I considered getting up before dawn the next day, like Sylvia Plath used to do while her fairy children slept in their little cots and their gaudy balloons tapped against the dusty floors. I used to have this theory about her that she wrote to lure men into her bed. I thought about that and startled myself by smiling. And under the boat I wrote his name in capital letters: MAX.

*L*ike a moon gathers filmy clouds to it, that's how I drew Max to me in the beginning. Easily. Effortlessly. I had told him I'd think about the boat, that I'd see if I could get up the money, and that I'd call him. But a week later, his head was silhouetted behind the heavy lace curtain on the back door, and his arm encircled his head as he leaned close to the window and peered in. He was wearing green work pants and a black-and-white plaid woolen shirt. His hands were stained with chimney soot around the lines of his nails and knuckles, and he was still smiling. "So, how've ya been?" he asked, slipping past me into the kitchen. "Thought any more about the boat?"

"Yes."

"Thought any more about me?"

"Some," I told him. Sparks flashed between us.

"I talked to my editor about writing something about a boat. He might be able to send me some money if I get him a chapter or two to look at."

"Did you tell your editor about me?"

"Why would I tell him about you?"

He shrugged and circled the table. "I don't know." He approached the stove and peeked in the coffeepot. "Not enough coffee here for the both of us."

I should have said I was working, but instead I said, "I'll make a fresh pot."

He surprised me. "No. Let's go out. I know this little place where they make the best coffee, in these neat little white paper cups that you can eat once the coffee is gone."

He grinned at me.

"And it's right near the boardwalk. We can watch the ocean. Drink our coffee. Eat our cups."

"I'll get my sweater."

Max was lean and young, and beautiful in a way I was sure women like me—women old enough to have teenage daughters—shouldn't have appreciated. His dark hair was too long, a mass of curls nearly to his shoulders, hair that spoke of the sixties, my flower years, but he was younger than I, maybe eight or ten years younger, and I was uncertain about what hair like that was supposed to mean today. Besides, his face had a beauty that was beyond fashion or trends. It was ageless, like the face of a Roman gladiator or a medieval French juggler. I couldn't place him in time, and when I finally sat next to him in his truck, it was easy to let myself be transported out of my life.

We drove down Long Beach Road with other workers and trucks and vans, everyone having jobs, journeys. Lights changed, traffic moved, gears shifted, and the cab of his truck took on a comical air, like a cartoon, or the inside of a crib belonging to a cherished child. There was a ceramic figure of a black-skinned boy fishing with a stick pole from the ashtray of his car. He tapped its knee lovingly, and told how it was on a trip to the Carolinas when he picked up Spanky here, who was hitching a ride. Max slipped in and out of reality, manipulating time and tide to suit himself, his truths as comforting and as childlike as his imaginings, and I found myself loving it. I'd met my match. More than that. I'd met someone whose lies were woven of a gentler weave. Someone whose lies taught me that mine were hard and less forgivable.

"Here we go," he said, pulling up in front of a roadside diner called Bertha's. We entered through a creaking screen door and an inner glass door. Inside, a couple of people at the counter looked up at us.

"Hey, Max. What's up?"

"Hey, how's it going? Bertha, give me two cups of regular coffee, to go, in your famous edible cups, and two toasted buttered muffins." He looked at me, and I nodded.

"Edible cups," she muttered and shook her head. We sat on the counter stools and waited for her to pour the coffee and toast the muffins. Bertha was hefty, slightly buttered-looking herself, but pleasant. "Where's Larry?" Max asked her.

"He's taking Virginia to the airport," she told him.

"Oh, I see," he said. As Bertha turned from us and snapped the covers on the coffee cups, Max leaned over and whispered in my ear, "Who's Virginia?" and I laughed.

It was like being with a child, unencumbered by reality's rules and boundaries, as if he could say to Bertha, "All right, now we're going to stop playing diner and play hospital. I'll be the surgeon, and you be the nurse."

Once Bertha had packed our coffees and muffins neatly in a brown paper bag, Max led the way out of the diner and headed up the block toward the boardwalk. From a distance the ocean glistened, and when we mounted the boardwalk steps the ocean spread out before us like a visual feast. The day was cool and slightly overcast, so there were few people on the boardwalk. Just some old folks bundled in sweaters and blankets, mesmerized by the waves.

"Come on," Max said, and he led the way down the other side of the boardwalk to the beach. My feet sank into the soft sand, and I watched them, feeling my thighs and calves tighten and struggle until we came to a newly painted lifeguard stand. Max climbed right up and I followed. We faced the ocean with the bag between us and became still. The sea pounded on the shore, clear and green, cold from a long winter.

I pointed to a small boat in the distance, a rowboat that seemed suspended in air above the horizon. It reminded me of an old Native American print: foggy, primitive.

"One morning . . ." Max began softly, his face calm and gentle as he drew out the coffees and peeled the plastic tops off them, ". . . when I was crewing on the *Freedom Song,* we were anchored off Mystic in the Sound. It was early, and off in the distance, just like that boat there, near the shore, we could see a small boat, a rowboat, heading toward us. It kept coming and coming, slow and steady, and soon we could see a man rowing and his two dogs sitting quietly with him. He came closer and closer, until at last he pulled alongside and handed up a basket full of eggs for our breakfast. He wouldn't stay to eat with us.

He just gave us the eggs and rowed off again, his dogs at his side and his oars dripping silver in the sunrise."

I looked at his face lit with the morning blaze of the ocean. I thought of kissing his cheek, tasting him, from the corner of his lips to where his cheek met his ear.

He sighed. "I'm living in the wrong era, you know."

"I know."

"I'm really suited to be the captain of a starship."

I laughed. I felt as if I were inhaling the scent of lilacs and had to hold my breath to keep the scent with me as long as I could. Or maybe it was more that I had just looked right into the sun, longer than was safe, and knew I would carry the image with me for too long.

We sat, the two of us, high above the beach, where no one could hear us. Maybe no one could see us. Time was suspended. Flattened.

"So tell me about this new book you're going to write," he said. "Does it have a sailboat in it?" He wasn't looking at me. He was sipping his hot coffee and looking out at the water.

I took a deep breath. "I think it might. I'm still just thinking about it. It might be about a man and his daughter. It's very sad. Troubling. The man has a sailboat in the story."

"Why is that sad? That doesn't sound sad at all. A man and his kid on their boat."

"The man is a drunk. And dangerous." A seagull saw our brown bag and circled close. It landed in the sand below and waited without moving. I could feel Max looking at me. I wondered if he was thinking about *my* cheek, about the taste of it.

"I don't like sad stories," he said. "Not unless they're love stories where at the end the lovers are together and everything ends happily. I like a good cry, but I like the ending to wipe my tears, you know?"

"Mmmm."

"Let's do a story together," he said suddenly, placing his cup between his legs and rubbing his palms together. "Let's do a story about a woman who owns a sailboat, and she has all these adventures."

"Romantic adventures?" I asked.

"Erotic, exciting adventures," he answered, "with all different men. Forget this sad stuff. This one's going to be a book of pleasure and adventure. It will sell like hotcakes. Sex and adventure."

"My editor would like you."

"How's that?"

"Editors like hotcakes, wouldn't you think? You should meet him. Maybe I *will* tell him about you. Maybe *he'd* like to buy your boat."

"No, no, no. Don't tell him anything about me. I'll be your secret muse. He doesn't ever have to know about me."

"Now how's she going to find all these men?" he went on.

"Bars?" I suggested.

"Nah."

"Marinas?"

"No, they have to be all different kinds of men, lawyers, detectives, professors, sailors,—"

"Chimney sweeps."

"God forbid," he said. "Chimney sweeps have such small dicks.

"I've got it!" he said over my laughter. "She can put a personal ad in the local paper." He wrote across the sky. " 'Lovely Long Island Lady seeks interesting, physically sound, reasonably sane man to go sailing, dining, and dancing.' How's that? And then she can meet each guy, and have a different kind of adventure with each one of them."

"Sounds great. Can I use that ad myself?"

"Of course not. I have another story for you. This one's for your editor who likes hotcakes. And then we'll start on your story, your real story, of a woman of great strength and stamina who sails away into the sunset."

"Lucky me. I'd rather romp with the personal-ad guys."

"When does Casey get home?"

"What?"

"Your daughter." He clasped my wrist to look at my watch. "She doesn't come home for lunch or anything, does she?"

"Uh, no. She's in school all day."

"So how about doing a chimney with me now?"

"It won't buy me a sailboat."

"True."

I sipped my coffee. "I should be working. I should be home. I promised Charlie I'd come up with something for him. And soon. So I can get the money for the boat."

"And then I'll teach you to sail."

"Yes. Then you can teach me."

"But you don't like my story idea? With all the adventure?"

"It's okay. It's got possibilities, I guess."

"Well, think about it. I know writers have to think about ideas for a long time before they start writing. Kind of like seeds germinating."

I put my empty cup back into the paper bag, but he took his and tossed it to the seagull. "Can't let a good edible cup go to waste." The seagull caught it midair and rose heavily over the beach. But we didn't make a move to leave. We just sat there.

I opened my mouth to say something, and thought better of it.

"What?" he asked. "What were you going to say?"

"Nothing. It was silly."

"No. Tell me. Nothing's silly. Tell me."

I looked at him head on. "Do I feel old to you?"

He didn't laugh. He shook his head immediately. "Not at all! No! Not at all!" And then suddenly, "How about me? Do I feel young to you?"

"Not at all."

We both smiled foolishly, too hard. "I like you," I told him. "You're very nice."

He shook himself. "Don't say that. I can't stand compliments. I can't stand getting them, and I'm really uncomfortable giving them." He rolled the brown bag between his hands and drops of coffee leaked out. "Not that I don't feel them, you understand. It's just that I want the compliments to be in the air. I want them just to be understood without me having to say anything. You know?"

"Yes." I nodded. "I understand."

He turned to me then, slid his arm along the back of the lifeguard seat, and paused. I thought maybe I was in a bubble, and if we touched, I would splash all over him. I leaned toward him to kiss his cheek, but he tilted his head, his lips met mine, I felt his mustache, and the kiss that I had meant to be two motions, toward and away, lingered in the toward, and his arms went around me. My hands were in his hair, in his long curls that were soft and good. I drew even closer there in the lifeguard chair, and our knees pressed together and slipped past each other. He chuckled deep in his throat. *At last,* I thought. *At last.*

He backed away, releasing me slowly, his hands smoothing my arms. "So, no roofs today for you?" he asked again.

"Not today."

"I'll call you, okay? How's that?"

I nodded and slipped down from our high perch. He followed and we headed back to the boardwalk, both of us with our hands in our pockets and heads down. I glanced at him out of the corner of my eye and he was looking at me. His face broke into a smile of relief when I smiled.

"What just happened back there?" he asked, motioning his thumb back to the lifeguard seat.

I shrugged and laughed, feeling bold at such a distance from him. "I don't know, but it was nice."

He shook his head in bewilderment. "I handled myself pretty well, don't you think?"

"You were terrific," I told him.

Sometimes I fancy my life to be like a May Sarton journal, but without the ocean out my window, and without the fame. Or the various cats and dogs. Like my imaginary Sarton I can stare at the bird feeder for hours. I can spend an entire afternoon wandering around the house, turning plants on the windowsills, spraying ferns, pinching dried leaves, polishing glass crystals that splatter rainbows on the walls, and admiring the slant of sunlight on a piece of polished wood. I don't feel as productive as she probably does, though. And I can't seem to justify it. I start to feel like a suburban housewife during an assassination week when the soaps are superseded by news reports, and she's no longer sure what her routine is.

Even though I'd had the discipline to refuse a chimney cleaning adventure that morning, the day was wasted. I couldn't sit in front of the computer even though I had left it turned on. I poured myself a cup of coffee, sat in my rocker in the middle of the living room, and thought about writing, writing about boats.

I thought of my father's sailboat. My younger brother, Peter, had never liked going out on it. He said being on a sailboat made him seasick, and we could see it made him green, and I would watch in wonder as his nervous hands would tremble over his eyes when the sails lifted. So my mother had insisted he stay home with her, and only my father and myself would take the sailboat out, sometimes with one of my father's friends, sometimes just the two of us. My father used to joke that I was his "only *son* who had taken to the sea." How proud that had made me then. But I was suddenly reminded of playing cards that night with my father in the cabin of the boat.

We play a sailor's game, cribbage, as the darkness curves beneath the boat and sways us. He has watched me lay out my hand—fifteen two, fifteen four, a pair for six—watched me lay it out, and he has laid his hand down faceup, and then, without skipping a beat, as casual as you please, he pulls a glass bottle of amber liquor out from beneath the bench. The only time. The last time.

The phone sliced through my memories like a guillotine and I picked it up.

"Ellie, it's Charlie."

"Charlie. Hi." The boat still swayed beneath me.

"I was thinking. Why don't you come for lunch and we can talk a bit. I want to hear about your boat ideas. Maybe I can help you along."

"Into the city?"

"The big one."

I was quiet. And still concentrating on my father's hand spread out on the table. He has three queens.

"Look at your calendar, Ellie. How's Friday?"

The calendar on the kitchen wall was from two years ago. And not even April, but November. "Friday's fine."

"One o'clock," he said. "My office," and he hung up.

The line went dead. But not my memory.

While he counts out his three of a kind for six, my father lifts the bottle to his mouth and smiles at me. Eyes the telltales in my hair. Tells me he is about to beat the pants off me with his three queens and his fifteen twos and runs and flushes, and his nibs.

When you and I were very young and had known each other for just a short time, I remember my eyes were still the darkest green-blue. My father used to say they were the color of the North Sea before a snowstorm. I would kneel on the bathroom sink at night and study my eyes, stare into them. And I can picture the color so clearly. So later on, when I knew you and you gave me that old jade ring—a pale oval of luminescent green—I liked it, but it never seemed especially mine. It was nice. It really was. Especially because it was from you, and in that it had its own meaning.

You'll be surprised to learn that after you'd been gone a few years, and Casey a few months, I had taken to wearing that ring all the time, and it was Max who noticed the color. I had touched my hand to my face while we were speaking and he gasped and told me my eyes were exactly the same color as my ring. How could that have been, I wondered? I stepped into the bathroom to see, and it was true. My eyes had faded to a green so pale, they were the color of the underbelly of a frog in early summer.

I told Max I had gotten the ring from a gypsy. That she had said I would have a life of ease and plenty, and that before I was forty my eyes would match it. He liked the story, and one night after we knew each other better he slipped it off my finger and put it on his own pinky. "If I were to wear this," he said, laughing, "it would be like you were always watching me."

I took it back from him.

Did you know all along that my eyes would turn so? You haven't seen my eyes in years. I wonder if you've forgotten the ring. And the color of my eyes.

The pizza box was warm on my upturned hands and along the insides of my arms. I walked soundlessly from the front door to the kitchen, my heavy socks padding along the carpeting and then on the linoleum. Max was sitting at the kitchen table and the windows were darkening with a spring night. The ceiling was so high the room almost echoed. He was smiling and waiting for me. We had this polite, cautious way with each other, because we hadn't made love yet. Neither of us was certain that we would, and the uncertainty had become our foreplay. Every motion, every glance, every word carried prismatic possibilities.

"Pizza," I said, placing the flat white box on the table. I opened it and steam lifted like a spirit between us.

"Mmmm, let's see," he mused, turning, and from his seat

he opened the refrigerator and began rummaging inside. "What can we put on it?" He pulled out cottage cheese, applesauce, and pickled herring. "There. That ought to do it."

I stared at him as he separated a slice of pizza from the circle and centered it on his plate. He dabbed a bit of applesauce on the end of the pizza slice.

I started to laugh. "What are you doing?"

"Don't worry," he said, adding the cottage cheese, and then slices of herring in a pattern. "Trust me. I know what I'm doing."

I watched in amazement, loving his silliness, his abandon. He lifted the full slice to his mouth and the end disappeared beneath his mustache. Silence. I waited.

"Sometimes I carry things too far," he said, simply.

I smirked and took a clean piece for myself. He dumped his piece back and took a fresh one.

"I *really* carried it too far once," he told me. "I was on a flight to Washington with a bunch of friends. We were going to a wedding, and the stewardess was real nasty ... I mean really nasty, no sense of humor at all. And well, the end of the story was I made lines of Cremora on my tray and snorted it.

"And she still wouldn't crack a smile, that old crab. Not only that, there were federal narcotics agents waiting for me when I got to Washington. Who would have thought it was a federal offense to snort Cremora in flight!"

"You're kidding!"

He crossed his heart.

"How about you?" he asked.

"How about me what?" Federal agents? The law? The merest hint of such things brought back unbidden images of flickering police cars pulling in front of the house, my bedroom ceiling pulsing with light.

"Have you ever taken anything too far?"

"Oh. No. I don't think so."

He leaned forward on his arms and looked at me closely. "No, I'll bet you haven't. You look like you don't even litter."

"You've got me all figured out, haven't you?"

He smiled at me.

"Fact is," I told him, "I robbed a bank in Georgia once. I was living on base housing with this army private whose wife had left him, and he got a letter from home saying his sister's baby had leukemia and they needed a lot of money for some special treatment. So he told me he was going to rob this little bank in town and I could join him or not, whatever I wanted to do, but he was going to do it, no matter what."

"What was the name of the town?"

"The name? Um—"

"Ha! Caught you! That was close. You almost had me."

"It takes me a minute to remember. That was a long time ago."

He was laughing.

"I can still remember what I wearing," I insisted. "It was a long green rubber raincoat."

"And a stocking over your head."

"That's right! With seams."

"Sequin-studded seams," he egged me on.

"And a straw hat."

"Of course a straw hat. You were in Georgia."

"So what were you doing in Washington?"

"Smuggling."

"Right. A shipment of Cremora."

"You got it."

Simultaneously we slapped a spontaneous high five over the table as if we just tied some game that was going on.

"Okay, let's get honest now," I said.

We grew silent for a few minutes, working on the pizza,

the crusts hot to the touch, the cheese stretching in long drips as we chomped and watched each other.

"Where's your Casey tonight?" he asked.

"Sleeping at a friend's."

He nodded. "Good pizza," he said.

"I *said,* let's get honest."

"It is!" he insisted. "I saw a bumper sticker today that said, 'Sex is like pizza. When it's good, it's very good. And when it's bad, it's still pretty good.' What was the best sex you ever had?" He said it just like that, as though he were asking me if I liked anchovies on my pizza, or mushrooms.

"The best sex?"

"Yes, the best sex. What comes to mind immediately?"

"Oh, it was with somebody much younger than you."

"Mmm?" He licked his fingers.

"Mmm what?"

"Mmm, why was it good?"

"What do you want? The details?"

"The facts, ma'am, just the facts."

There was a fine tension between us, like dim summer lightning on a horizon of cedar trees.

"It was at a party. Or I should say, it started at a party on New Year's Eve. I was with a girlfriend and we were dancing with these two young guys."

"How young?"

"Just twenty. Mine was. Hers was nineteen. Imagine, nineteen. She was such an easy tart."

"Obviously."

"Anyway, we danced all night, till after midnight, and then we came back here and built a fire."

"In *my* fireplace?"

"The very one you cleaned. I built a fire and we got quilts and spread them out on the floor. And talked."

Swallowing the memories again and again until the tension settled on my shoulders.

When it was over, and the Beast had been transformed into a fabulous Frenchman, the VCR hummed in its rewind. Max turned over onto his back and moaned. "Oh, I never want it to end like that! I always want him to die." He had one arm over his face and the other arm reached out toward me, and his fingers tapped on my toes inside their socks.

"Want some coffee?" I asked him.

He nodded and followed me into the kitchen. He leaned against the wall silently and watched my hands as I scooped out the coffee into the filter, followed me with his eyes while I filled a kettle with water and set a blue flame under it. We were very quiet. I could hear the clock ticking in the hallway.

"Did you notice," he asked, "how when he let her go back to her father, he didn't keep something important of hers to assure that she'd be back, but instead he gave her the most important thing of his, his magic key, trusting in her goodness and her love?"

"Yes. I noticed." I nodded and began to wash my hands. The cool water ran through my fingers, and suddenly Max clasped my wrists and held my hands together to cup the running water. He lowered his face into my hands and imitated the Beast's growly animal voice in French, lapping the water from my cupped hands the way the beast had done. "Oh, Belle, Belle," he said. I watched him, my heart aching, like it had once ached to watch Casey deep in a childhood fantasy, talking to someone only she was privileged to see. Without thinking I lowered my face into the curls of his head. *"Bête. Bête,"* I whispered. Then he stood, and without knowing what it would mean we put our arms around each other and stood without moving, just a constant pressure. We stayed like that a long time, until the kettle started to whistle and I drew away from him, my shoulder wet from the Beast's face, and his shirt wet from my hands.

He leaned back against the wall with his arms folded and watched as I poured boiling water over the grounds. In silence I got out two thick mugs and milk and two spoons. Then I poured the coffee. "Come," I said. "Let's sit inside."

"Go where I am going," he chanted softly. *"Va, va, va!"*

We sat on the sofa, each with our mug, turned toward each other. The room was so quiet, as if a black velvet comforter were settling down over everything. And the air was heavy like truth serum. I began to grow more and more anxious. And foolish. And doubtful. My hands trembled. When I glanced at Max I realized he was studying me. I closed my eyes. "I feel crazy," I whispered.

"Crazy?"

It was quiet a long time, the clock ticking.

"It's like we're animals, you know? We *are* a species of animal, with instincts and reflexes like other animals, and suddenly I feel as if I've just gone haywire, like some crazy bird that in the middle of winter, for no good reason, starts to gather up string for a nest. It's as if something is off inside me. Something's gone berserk."

"I don't understand."

"When I was really young, fourteen or fifteen, all my instincts and hormones were working, telling me to get ready for nests, and boys, and babies. It was all there right on the surface, aching, like a musky odor, and I attracted young boys like a cat in heat attracts toms. Nobody could tell me what was going on, nobody could explain it, but I just went along with it, because it felt natural. It felt good."

He didn't say anything, but his eyes didn't leave my face. My cheeks were growing hotter.

"That's a little how I feel now. Like that crazy bird. My instincts are flowing, I'm ready to go, yet I'm not fourteen. I guess I'm middle-aged, for Christ's sake. My body's not what it used to be, and my nesting days are long gone, and yet here I am gathering twigs for some ridiculous out-of-season nest."

I covered my cheeks with my hands and grew reckless. "I am so turned on! And what's the point? All these needs and feelings don't have a purpose anymore."

"That's not right," he said simply. "That's not a good way to think at all."

I felt foolish and sorry I'd said anything. "Sounds Catholic, I know." I tried to laugh at myself. "I just can't get comfortable inside."

Max leaned back against the sofa and grew thoughtful. "When I was a kid," he said, "I used to deliver newspapers to this nursing home in the neighborhood. I got to know the nurses and got to see what was going on in that place. And I remember one old guy, he must have been in his nineties. They called him 'Sugar.'" Max laughed. "What a character! They had to watch him constantly, because he'd get into bed with anything, and I mean anything! Old hundred-year-old ladies who didn't even know where they were, and there'd be Sugar, humping away."

"See?" I said. "That's what I mean. The instinct gone haywire. A useless, meaningless urge. That's how I feel."

"But what was wrong with that?" Max asked. "What else was old Sugar going to do? Stare at the TV all day and night? What harm was in it, if it made him feel good?"

"That doesn't sound right. Now I feel worse," I sighed, feeling misunderstood. I backed away inside myself.

"Forget Sugar, then," he said, a smile forming beneath his mustache. "You've been on my mind, too." Our eyes held in an arm wrestling grip. "But it wouldn't be any good," he added. "I'm a real lousy boyfriend. I wouldn't be any good for you."

"What do you mean?"

He seemed to be wrestling with his own thoughts, editing what he could tell me. His mouth even formed words, but no sound came, and his eyes seemed tortured.

"Tell me," I said. "I want to know."

"I'm no good at relationships. I don't like to have anybody counting on me for anything. You know? It doesn't work for me. I don't know why, but it just never works. I get these crushes, I fall in love, and it never lasts, it never gets ripe and good. And besides that I'm attracted to everybody! Everybody! Women, men. If I like somebody, I like them across the board. I can't just like them in compartments."

"You mean you're bisexual?"

He shrugged. "I don't know. There are men I love. If I like a man, I am drawn to him in every way. I've never had sex with a man, but I did kiss one once, for a while." He smiled. "This friend of mine, Teddy, but I couldn't do anything else." He smiled and watched me out of the corner of his eye. "You thought Sugar was bad!"

"I guess it doesn't sound so bad," I said softly. "Kind of like Walt Whitman or something, the way you put it."

"And I have no self-control," he cautioned. "I knew I was lost when I kissed you in the lifeguard seat the other day. One kiss and I'm a goner."

"But you didn't lose control at all," I reminded him. "You don't seem to be having any problem controlling yourself." I tucked my feet up under me.

"That's because you left right away. One kiss and I'm lost. But I'm not dependable, you know? All my relationships are bad. I always disappoint people." He rubbed his hand back and forth over his chin and one cheek. "Who knows how love happens. Maybe it just sneaks up on you, and changes you. I don't know. I've never seen it work. Never been in it when it worked for me."

"We'd be bad for each other, then," I said.

"Why?"

"Well, maybe it'd be okay if I thought I could separate love and sex, but I don't think I can. That's the way I am, and it's ridiculous. Being like that. It's like ... well, if a man were to get me into a motel I'd be building a picket fence around it in my mind."

We were quiet and I thought he was feeling sorry for me. Poor old, messed-up broad. But when I looked at him he was grinning.

"There's been something I've been dying to do," he said. Then he reached out and clasped my nose between his fingers and rubbed its tip. I laughed and pushed his hand away, tossing my head back, and our hands tangled. "No," he said, "there really *is* something I've been wanting to do." And he stood and moved so he could sit behind me, and he began to run his fingers through my hair. Down my back. Very gently he touched my hair, rubbed strands together, followed a wave from my head to the end, using two hands, gripping the full mass of my hair in his hands and then releasing it and smoothing it over my shoulders.

I turned to see his face, and his goofy, contented expression made me smile. I thought he must have looked like Sugar used to look.

"If you kiss me, I'll kill you," he said.

That's all it took.

*W*e kissed over and over. So long, and so over-and-over that my mind began to swim and I was thinking, What is this we're doing, pressing our faces together over and over, touching and searching with our lips? What a strange and wonderful thing.

"You have great lips," he whispered between kisses. "So soft."

"You're a great kisser," I told him.

"Yeah, that's what Teddy said, too."

I laughed, he smiled, and pressing our smiling teeth together he kissed me some more.

"We're not going to really *do* anything, right?" he asked.

"Of course not. We'll just do this." I held him tighter.

We kissed some more. Suddenly he was alert, his face turning from me. "What was that?" he asked.

"What?" I knew there was no one around. It was dark. It was late. No one ever came near the house, but he jumped from the sofa and peered out the front window.

"Oh, no. There are two guys out there."

"There are?"

"Yeah, and they're ... I don't believe it ... "

I was beside him peering out the window, too, my lips feeling swollen and tender. He put his arm around me. "They've got a posthole digger, and they're putting a picket fence around my truck."

"Oh, stop—" I laughed, but he had his arms around me and was leading me like a dancing rag doll back to the sofa, where he dropped me onto the soft cushions and laid on top of me.

"Let's do this, too," he whispered.

"But this is all," I whispered back.

He moved around and put his hand under my long denim skirt and began to stroke my thigh. "But how about this?" he asked. "It wouldn't seem right without a little bit of this."

"What did Teddy say? Did he let you do this?"

"Oh, no. I didn't even try. Teddy had such hairy legs. Yours are nice."

Max made me laugh. And laugh. My face ached from smiling and laughing, and to feel him there, pressed up against me, his hardness against my openness, I knew I would have him. I could not deny myself this. His stroking hand sent waves of turbulence over my skin, until he found his way through my clothes to my warmth and wetness and I opened to him.

After a while he removed his hand and I opened my eyes. Without taking his eyes from mine he brought his shiny, wet fingers to his mouth and delicately tasted them. "Oh, *Belle, Belle*," he growled.

He lowered his face into my throat, and I gathered myself up to kiss the top of his head. He lowered his face to my breasts and I watched him slowly rub his cheeks across them. Then placing his fingers over my breasts he lowered his face to my skirt, and taking it in his teeth he growled and shook his head. I began to laugh and couldn't stop. He dove beneath my skirt, growling and moaning, and still laughing I threw one leg over the back of the sofa, and let the other extend out far beyond us. He began to kiss me beneath my skirt as he had kissed my lips, slowly, deeply, probing, so soft, and I laughed like a madwoman, like I'd heard the funniest joke and couldn't stop. The laughter, the deepness, his hands along my shuddering hips and thighs, my skirt over his comical head, my laughter grew deeper and harder and I cried out over and over with a pure joy until I was limp and silent and found my hands around his head, my fingers in his curls.

He peeked over my skirt. "My. That was different. Do you always laugh like that?"

"Never. Come here."

He came up and laid on top of me again, and I couldn't hold him close enough, tight enough. He made it so easy for me to simply forget myself. He smiled and brushed my hair away from my face over and over as if he were exploring my hairline from ear to ear. "Pretty hair," he said.

I pulled his face down to mine and kissed him, tasted me on his lips. "Nice face," I whispered.

"Listen," he said, "we've gone this far, you wouldn't mind, would you, if I took my overalls off?"

I shook my head and smiled.

He stood up next to the sofa. He was wearing white one-piece overalls, shoulder to cuffs white and clean, like they were brand-new. He opened the snaps and revealed a lavender T-shirt. "You like this?" he asked, turning around to give me the complete view.

"Yes. It's very spiritual."

"Chim'man dresses up," he declared as he slid them off his shoulders and bent to let them drop over his legs. He danced and hopped around the room trying to get his sneakers through the legs of the overalls. I began laughing again, and he said, "Oh, no. Don't be laughing at me now. This is serious business. My manhood is at stake here." And hopping on one foot, his other leg tangled in the overalls, he hopped right out of the room at an odd slant and I heard him crash into the dining room table.

I was lost. When he emerged from the dining room he was completely naked. His clothes were gone. My beast. My beast.

He lay down on top of me again, and my laughter had softened to deep breaths as his fingers did their work, and without helping him he found his way into me. It was the last piece of the jigsaw puzzle. The last note of the symphony. He was in, and my bones turned to water as my legs wrapped around him and my arms held him to me. I had thought I would never have this again. Never even *want* this again, and here I was, wanting. He rocked easy in my arms, his breath in my ear. I remember smiling up into the darkness when he whispered, "Oh, baby, baby, baby," and then he was holding his breath, holding everything, suspended, aching, tighter, and we gripped each other until he collapsed around me like a hot-air balloon collapsing over a grassy field.

The room was still and dark, and all that was left was our quiet breathing, and then—

"Just give me a minute," he said. "I'll be ready again before you know it."

And we laughed.

Max and I fell asleep in that position that night, and in one soft slow moment, I felt him slide out of me like a thumb from a sleeping baby's mouth. I never felt him leave. Never felt him lift his weight from me. Didn't hear him struggle back into his white overalls, or tie the shoelaces on his sneakers. He was just gone, and when I began to wake up I was on the living room sofa, my skirt was smoothed down over my legs, and a scratchy afghan from the front parlor was tucked around me.

It was the clock radio that woke me, radio voices in the distance, and for an instant I forgot where I was. I thought I was in the center of my childhood. The bed of my girlhood was securely beneath me, narrow and soft, and there were voices coming from the kitchen. No, only one voice. The voice of the man on the weather band. It was as if I could hear the soundless snow settling on the roof outside my window. I could feel the cold making its way through the old plaster walls and into my bedroom, where the radiator never got more than barely warm. The voice was reporting the inches accumulated, the prediction for the day, the temperature, the barometer, the tides, the sea winds.

On winter mornings my mother would listen to find out about sending me to school, and I would hear the voice and imagine a man off somewhere in a down parka and earmuffs, talking into a microphone while a gale blew around him. He'd be in a barely heated hut by a railroad track, keeping tabs on things. And I'd stay in my bed under the warm comforters.

But in the summertime when I woke to hear the weather band drifting up the stairs, I knew my father was packing up food to go out sailing or fishing, and I'd get up quickly and pull on shorts and a T-shirt, wanting to go with him.

Had he left without me? I opened my eyes. My body was stretched the full length of the sofa. No. I was not a child. That was a life I had shed long ago. I was on a sofa in a big, old house where I lived alone. My clock radio had gone off up in my bedroom and someone was reporting on traffic heading into the Midtown Tunnel. It wasn't summer or winter. It was spring, and last night I had made love to a young man I hardly knew. I looked around the room and saw our coffee mugs on the floor, my underpants hung on a spoon in one, and then I saw there was something placed across my chest. Two work gloves. Two white chimney sweep work gloves lightly stained with ashes. I slipped my hands into them and smiled. I knew he wanted me to take them as a promise he'd left in my kingdom, a promise to come back. My beast.

I closed my eyes, snuggling back to sleepiness, and suddenly out of nowhere it came to me. *Little El.* That was the name of my father's boat. *Little El.* He'd named it after me. I used to run down the stairs and catch him turning off the radio and loading the car in the early morning light with tackle and poles, or a mended sail and a tin with sandwiches, chips, and soda.

"Where are you going?" I'd ask, knowing all the while.

"The *Little El*," he'd answer.

"Oh, can't I come, Daddy? Can't I come? Please?"

"You know if you wake your mother you can't, so pipe down," he'd say. "Leave her a note so she knows where you've gone. But be quiet about it."

And inside I'd write on the grocery pad: Gone with Dad to the *Little El*.

I rose slowly and walked naked through the house and up the stairs to turn off the radio. In my room I stood before the full-length mirror and stared into my eyes and then down at my body, my familiar body, and my bare feet that had widened like feet in some heavy stone sculpture. I squinted and tried to see myself as Max might have seen me. I wondered what he saw. Was he used to young, firm bodies? Had my soft body been enough for him? Was I the feast I had wanted to be?

I remembered how once in our early twenties when you and I were first living together, how one night we were getting dressed to go out. We were both standing before the closet getting things to wear. I was naked, and when you suddenly saw me there beside you, you gasped and clutched me to you, your hands all over me, and you had said how beautiful I was. I've never been that beautiful again, you know. I wish I'd known that that moment before the closet was my most beautiful moment. I would have gotten you to take a picture of me.

You know, I'll bet if I'd never joined up with you at all, ever, I probably would have gone to live in a small town somewhere, say in Minnesota, or Montana, and I would've worked in a diner on an interstate, and out there I would've been the most beautiful woman for miles. Men would stop their sixteen-wheelers and come in for a cup of coffee just to watch my hips across the counter, or my hands, and to smile at me and see my lips glisten without the need of any citified lipstick. Women would keep their distance, and as I grew older I'd have visitors who came, sometimes very late, to a house I rented at the edge of town, and my lights would burn late into the night, and my laughter would bounce out my open windows and across the grassy fields.

But this morning I was in the big, old house alone, the ruins of a life gone astray. And it was my day to go meet Charlie. Maybe I'd have been pretty in some places, but in the big city, amid spectacular metropolitan women of dazzling cosmetic skills and fashion savvy, I'd be decidedly unspectacular and go unnoticed.

I've always wished I could go into the city exactly as I am, with old jeans and sneakers still muddy from the garden, an old work shirt, no makeup, and my hair in a tumble. But my mother always made me feel the city demanded more of people, and it would chew me up and spit me out if I dared to enter its realm without putting on my war paint and my armor.

So I dressed quickly—my black skirt, a black cotton knit sweater, and a few colorful macramé string bracélets Casey had made for herself. I tied my hair up neatly, checked the train schedule, let my hair down and brushed it out, threw on a light jacket, and right before I left I fastened my hair up once more in front of the mirror in the vestibule, glad to be looking at myself for the last time.

I squinted my eyes and imagined myself in Buzzard's Breath, Montana. I would've hated working in a diner.

Charlie took me to Carletti's, an elegantly muffled Italian restaurant with thick carpeting, shiny brass trim, and mauve lighting. Sometimes it would occur to me to tell Charlie that I'd rather go to a coffee shop and pocket the difference, but I knew these lunches were as much for himself as for me.

"So how have you been, Charlie?" I asked as the waiter snapped open a linen napkin and draped it across my lap. I tried to act as though someone always put my napkin on my lap for me.

"Very well. Very, *very* well." He propped his glasses on the top of his head, which was scattered with long stray hairs over pale liver spots, and he looked at me. "As a matter of fact, I was out east at the country house this past weekend, raking up and pruning and trimming. It's going to be wonderful this summer with all the perennials I planted last year, and the stand of cedar trees I added."

"You like doing that kind of stuff, don't you?"

"I love it. Sometimes I wonder how I ever got into this business. I should have owned a flower farm, or a winery out on the North Fork. And just read *real* books, books between hard covers, in my spare time."

He picked up his menu and began to study it. "Do you remember the part of the garden, Ellie, in the back where it slopes down into the water?"

I thought of the steep slope and how the one time I had visited Charlie with Casey, she and I had accidentally slid down the slope side by side, our butts caked with mud, and our sneakers coming to a lucky halt at the edge of the water. If at that moment in the restaurant I had closed my eyes I would have seen with crystal clarity her laughing face with that little scar by her ear from when she'd had chicken pox. I kept my eyes open and only thought I heard her deep laughter, and a darkening happened for me as though a cloud had suddenly passed over the summer sun, or someone had dimmed the mauve lights. "I remember," I said softly.

He looked at my eyes. He remembered, too. But he was kind and looked away. "Well, I've had that all properly landscaped, so there's a rock garden there now, and wooden steps have been pressed into the center of the slope. It's not so difficult to get to the water now, to a little dock I had built. What will you have?" He rattled the menu.

Lunch was delicious—beyond food. Each dish was a tiny work of art arranged on our plates to perfection. We ate and talked about perennials and garden tools and catalogs, and when to plant tomatoes, and how to get a marriage of cardinals to look after them. He never mentioned Casey or anything that had happened, and it occurred to me that maybe he wasn't being kind at all, but just professional. Men didn't talk about personal things at business lunches as women did. A woman editor at a magazine that I had written for once took me to lunch, and by the time the coffee came I knew her deep, dark past and just where she stood in her life's journey. Men were different. Charlie was different. With me, anyway.

When the coffee came in small, steaming cups, he tipped his chair back and expanded. His jacket opened and I could see that his green lightweight sweater concealed a shirt that didn't button all the way to his belt. The waiter brought a heavenly cart full of dessert delights. We each pointed to something chocolatey that was piled with whipped cream and didn't speak again till we each had a dish before us.

"So, Ellie Brinkley," Charlie said, taking the first chocolate-riddled mouthful of cream. So, Ellie Brinkley.

I waited.

"Tell me about this new book idea you have. A sea story?"

"Well, not really a sea story." I patted the cream down with the back of my spoon. "A boat story, actually. A story about a man with a sailboat, and he has this daughter who goes sailing with him."

"What, like some sort of feminist *Old Man and the Sea?* He's going to take a girl out with him? Do they fish?"

I gave him a look that made him apologize. "I'm sorry. Go on. Go on."

I ate some whipped cream first and wondered why I had ordered it.

"Well, I thought maybe I could write about my daughter

now, too, Charlie. Not about her exactly, but you know. About a kid who gets killed in a car accident like she did." I glanced at him to see if he was believing me. "But I'd have her parents together, you know? Maybe they all go out on this boat every weekend, and somehow the kid will save the father before she dies."

Charlie was silent. His whipped cream was almost all gone. I felt nervous. I wasn't offering him much.

"And maybe, you know, maybe he could name the boat after her, and the boat takes on some sort of metaphorical heal- ing role in their lives. After she's gone. Or maybe she won't die at all. Maybe *he'll* die."

Charlie looked at me over the rim of his reading and eating glasses. I put down my spoon and waited, feeling like a child who's about to be lectured to.

"That's not much, Ellie. It's not even thought out yet."

"But it's the images that matter for me, Charlie. You know that's how I work. How can I explain it to you?" I closed my eyes and went on. "I can see this man standing on a weathered dock, smoking a Chesterfield without the filter. A squall is com- ing up and he taps the ashes of his cigarette into the cuff of his pants. He's not sure if he should go out in this weather. Then there's this kid with a big grin on her face. He doesn't want to disappoint her and she comes walking along the dock, carrying fishing poles and an ice chest. That's one image. Then I see this guy steering the boat on a bright autumn day. It's cool and very windy, and the sky is spectacular with white billowing clouds, piled high. The father turns the boat slightly into the wind, both sails swell, the boat heels way over, and there's the kid, grinning like crazy, sitting on the low side of the boat with her head thrown back and the ends of her braids trailing in the water."

Yes. Yes. Quickly I grabbed my pocketbook and pulled out

a pen and my railroad ticket. On the back I wrote: boat heeling. her hair in the water. grinning.

When I looked up, Charlie was smiling at me. A quiet, thoughtful smile, and for an instant I thought he looked like he felt sorry for me.

"What do you need, Ellie?" he asked softly.

"Need?" I looked at my whipped cream and full coffee cup.

"What do you need to write this?"

Oh. "I need money, Charlie." I breathed deep and put my hands flat on the table on each side of the plate. "The reason all this is finally coming to me is because of this boat I saw. It's an old sailboat, fiberglass, a real poor man's sailboat, nothing fancy, and memories just began swarming back. I think I can do it now, Charlie, it's just that I have to have the boat. And it's only four thousand dollars."

"Ellie!"

"It'll help me, Charlie. I know it will. I'll live on it a little again. Stay on it overnight, take it out. You know. Live it. I've gotta have it, Charlie. I'm afraid if I don't, I'll lose all these images. And I could sell the boat after I'm done with the novel. So maybe the money would be more like a loan."

"Heaton and Clark doesn't make loans."

We were silent.

"Ellie, you know the deal. You got money on signing and you'll get the rest when you hand in the finished manuscript. And it's all been on speculation, trusting that you have another novel in you somewhere."

I swallowed and my eyes were suddenly and unexpectedly full of tears. I let him see them. I took a deep breath and then, without taking my eyes away from him as they each spilled down my cheek, one at a time, I leaned toward him and whispered, "Charlie, I haven't been able to write a *limerick* since Casey ... died ... and ever since I sat on that boat things have been rushing in on me, images, scenes, dialogues. It's all there, Charlie, and then I start to lose it. If I could just have the boat—"

"What if *I* gave you a loan, Ellie? A personal loan from me?"

I folded my hands in my lap and stared at my thumbs.

"What am I saying?" He shrugged himself like a bear fighting off a mosquito. "Do you have any idea how much it costs to keep a boat? Where would you keep it? Marinas charge an arm and a leg! Town moorings are passed down in family estates! You'll have no place to keep it!"

I hadn't even thought of that. Max hadn't said anything about the marina. As a child I'd never heard my father say anything about the dock where he kept his boat. The room began to darken again. The waiter filled our crystal glasses with ice water and I looked at the pile of whipped cream before me.

"Unless . . ." Charlie was rubbing his eyes roughly over and over. "You could dock the boat at my place. Tell me, please tell me it's not over twenty-six feet."

"Twenty-two."

"Ellie! Twenty-two feet! Can't you find a little dinghy to puff around in to stir up your memories?"

"It's got a cabin, Charlie. A V berth, and a centerboard to crank up. An outboard motor. And lights for at night, for sitting in the cabin, playing cards. It's so much like the one I grew up in. Did you ever sit in a car, a car model that you drove all the time years ago, and your whole body remembers exactly where the pedals are and the radio knobs and the windshield wipers? And then you start to remember all the songs that were popular then? That's what this boat is like for me, Charlie."

The waiter was by our table. "Is everything all right?" he asked, looking at our untouched coffee and my pile of chocolate-laced whipped cream.

I nodded and Charlie asked for the check. "All right," Charlie said to me, putting his glasses back on. He leaned forward and glared across the table, his eyes magnified and moist. I started to feel giddy with hope. "All right," he repeated. "I myself will loan you the money for this boat. And you will dock the boat out at my weekend house."

"Okay," I said.

"On one condition, Ellie. No, two. This will be for one year. You can use my dock for one year, this season only. That's plenty of time to get the bones of a novel going. Then if you have something to show me, I will try to get the rest of your advance and then you can do whatever you want with the boat. If you have nothing to show me after a year, you sell the boat and pay the loan off." He scribbled on the bill the waiter had placed beside him.

The dessert was beginning to look good again. I looked at the waiter and grinned. When he smiled back, I pointed to the pile of whipped cream before me. "Do you think you could put this in a bag for me to take home?" He laughed and didn't believe me.

I left my napkin rolled in a nervous knot beside my plate and followed Charlie out into a spring day. The lunch hour hum was slowing down and we stood outside the restaurant facing each other. "I'll mail you the check from home tonight, all right?"

"Thanks, Charlie."

He held out his hand to shake mine, but I hugged him instead and turned away before I could see his expression, whether it was pity or awkwardness. I could've taken the subway back to Penn Station that day, but it was glorious out, the wind from the northeast at about ten to twelve knots, so I tacked all the way uptown.

When I got home from the city that day, the first thing I did was put in a call to the chimney cleaning service. I was flying with hopefulness and smiled when I heard his voice.

"Greetings, citizen. Chim'man here. I can't speak to you right now, so if you'll leave your name, phone number, and a brief message, I'll call you back as soon as I get in."

Beep.

"Hey, Max, it's me. Ellie." I hadn't even taken my jacket off yet, and as I spoke I slipped it off, draped it over a dining room chair, and pulled the clip out of my hair. "Where are you? What are you doing? I've been in the city all day, so I'm just gonna whip up a quick salad tonight if you want to stop by. Around seven. If you can't make it don't worry. Just give me a call." I wanted to say more, something seductive and funny, but I just said, "Bye, Max."

The air around me seemed filled with the ticking sound of the old regulator clock, as if all day in the silence of the house, the ticks had collected and grown deeper and denser, and by that night, the phone as still and silent as a dead crab, I stood waist deep in the collected ticking of the day. It began to occur to me that Max could just disappear. The thought swept in on me like a tidal wave: people change, you can't count on anything. The marrow in my bones told me.

Even you, I had grown not to count on you. You, changing from the lit side of the moon to the dark side of the moon, from clarity to an unknown, a cold stranger. I once thought I had never known anyone capable of greater kindness than you. And always when I think of your kindness I think of that warm summer night when you came home late to find an opossum lying in the middle of the road out front. I was waiting up for you, and from our bedroom window saw your tall form turn the corner and head toward the house, disappearing into the leafy shadow of our linden tree and the neighbor's thick forsythia shrubs. I got back under the covers, hid my book under the bed, and waited for the sound of your key in the door, your footstep on the stair. But you didn't come, and soon I peered out again and saw you out front in the middle of the street, bending over and studying a still form in the road.

"Honey?" I called softly through the screen. "What is it?"

When you straightened, the streetlight caught the ridge of your nose, the line of your bottom lip as you looked up to me. "Come down here a minute, Ellie."

A car turned down the road toward you, and in the headlights I watched you wave and motion the car to swing around you.

I threw on a pair of shorts under my short nightshirt, ran barefoot down the stairs, out the door, and down the cool wooden steps. As I drew near I heard what you said to the limp pile of fur at your feet. "Hang on there, ol' fella. Take it easy now. You'll be all right."

I could see the opossum in the circle of the streetlight. Another car drove up, and again you waved him aside with both arms. I remember the face of the driver as he went past, staring down at the animal and then up at our faces. The opossum was in a crouch as if he were about to sneeze and had frozen that way. Half his face was scraped, and as the three of us stood poised there in the middle of the road, a dark puddle was forming around him.

"He's been hit," you told me. "We've got to get him out of the road."

"Don't touch him," I warned. "You might hurt him more. He might bite you. Raccoons have rabies. Can opossums?"

"How can we lift him?"

The opossum's naked pink tail extended out behind him. Suddenly he whimpered and I jumped back. "Jeez!"

"Go get the snow shovel and my garden gloves," you said. "At least we'll get him to the side of the road, so he doesn't get hit again."

"I don't have any shoes on," I said. "And it's dark."

"Then stand here and make sure no cars go over him again. Direct them past."

"Honey . . ." But you were gone, crunching down the driveway in the darkness, leaving me alone with the opossum. I could hear it breathing, short shallow breaths like a baby that is full and falls asleep still clinging to the breast. Headlights came toward me and stupidly I waved them past, standing there barefoot, in my nightshirt. The car passed, taking with it the pocket of laughter and the sound of an old Beach Boys tune. The opossum got up on all fours

and fell down again. "Easy now," I told him, crouching to see his face. "Take it easy." He got up again, took three or four shaky steps, and I jumped back and threw my arms around myself. Now instead of being right on the yellow line that ran down the center of the road, he was smack in the middle of one lane. If it had been up to me I would have just gone to bed and let life, or death, take its course. I'd have called village sanitation in the morning and looked away.

But another car's lights shone in the distance. Jesus, what was this tonight, the Cross Island Expressway? When it was close I waved it aside as you had done. "'S that your dog?" someone inside yelled. I shook my head and smiled, trying to look casual and unconcerned, and as the car roared away someone inside yelled, "Road pizza!"

Soon you came back with the shovel and the gardening gloves. "He moved?" you asked.

"All by himself," I said. "Maybe you can just shoo him over some more."

"Ma? What're ya doin' out there?" We looked up to see Casey standing in the open doorway. She was little then, and so warm and delicious on summer nights, her hair smelling like cheese. I walked up the path to the house and gathered her into my arms.

"It's just an opossum, sweetie, that's all. He was hit by a car crossing the road and Daddy's trying to get him up on the grass so he won't get hit again."

"The possum didn't look both ways," she said.

"That's right."

"Let me see."

"I don't think . . ."

"Ellie, come here and help me," you called.

Casey scrambled from my arms and ran down the walkway to the edge of the road. She stood there watching, her small, tanned toes curled over the curb. "Is he dead, Daddy, that old possum?"

"No, Case, he's just hurt real bad."

"What is that, Daddy? Is that blood in the road?"

You handed me the gloves then. "See if you can shoo him onto the shovel, Ellie, and I'll lift him over to the grass." You held the shovel in front of the opossum, and then without me having to do a thing it obligingly stepped onto the snow shovel like an old woman stepping into an elevator. In the light I saw your arms bulge and strain to lift the heavy animal at an awkward angle, and you walked it back to the grass and set it down.

"Can we keep him, Daddy? Can we bring him inside?"

Casey and I watched as you eased the shovel out from under the wounded animal and it rolled onto his side and stayed like that. "No, we're going to leave him right here for tonight and we'll decide what to do in the morning." I took the shovel from you and watched Casey scramble up into your arms.

"Maybe his friends will come for him," she said softly.

And remember? You answered, "Oh, wouldn't that be nice, if his friends came for him and got him home safe where they could patch him up . . ."

"And give him chamomile tea." Casey loved Peter Rabbit.

I knew you so well then, knew ahead of time that you'd sit at the bedroom window all night, and then just before dawn get up and bury the still, soft form behind the garage and tell Casey that his friends must have come. I followed you up into the house that night, the hall light making silhouettes of you and Casey, her small, tousled head leaning toward yours as she looked in your breast pocket.

Click. I saved you like that in a sweet mental photograph, with the summer night draped around you like French lace, and a dying animal on the curb who would later be carried off by gentle friends. The sound of your steps on the wooden stairs consoled me. And Casey. I thought you were the kindest man I had ever known.

But, click. Later, the other picture: your face an inch from *mine, the veins bulging on your forehead, the words roaring from somewhere deep inside you. Without touching me, without laying a hand on me, you pinned me against the kitchen wall like a knife thrower pins the lady against a backdrop, with knives tearing tiny ruffles of her costume here and there. And all I could think to say was, "But you love me," to which you sneered, like a face in an old Elvis movie, and you smelled of booze, that old cologne of my childhood, and at that instant—just like our regulator clock can suddenly stop without any noticeable slowing down and leave me a cappella—at that very instant it was over. I stopped loving you.*

People change.

Max didn't return my call the next day or the day after. I'd dial the chimney sweep number and hang up when I heard the recording begin. I paced. I wound the old clock that hung in the dining room. I wiped counters. I made a hundred excuses for him: Work had picked up and he was busy cleaning chimneys. Impossible. He was irresponsible and spontaneous. Maybe something had happened to him. He'd had an accident with the truck. I could see it turning over and over as it leaped the center rail on the expressway, his fingers spread wide, vividly against the windshield. Maybe he was dead. More likely he'd been kidnapped by pirates.

Two days later Charlie's check came in the mail. Four thousand dollars and an extra five hundred. The note said, "Boats always need extra things, right? Like ropes and flags?"

It was then that I went to the boat on my own, drove out to the marina in the spring rain all by myself. It was late afternoon and my windshield wipers flapped back and forth over a constant drizzle. It felt like they were scraping on my brain. I retraced Max's route back through the neighborhoods where canals lined the yards, to the muddy parking lot where I could see the wooden dock and its long line of softly bobbing boats. I zipped my yellow slicker to my chin and flipped up the light hood as I started down the dock now slick with rain. I felt frightened, not knowing what I would find, and not knowing why that frightened me. The slip was empty. The *Nemaste* was gone. She'd taken her lines and left no wake, no trail. The deep green water in her slip swelled and ebbed with a distant storm.

I looked over at the marina building, but it was closed up and locked. The dog was gone and a crate of empty soda cans stood beside the door. Where could Max have taken her in the rain? Or was she sold to someone else, gone off to a different slip in another life? I crossed my arms in front of me, my hands buried up to the elbow in the opposite cuffs. And if he had sold the boat, had he no need for me anymore?

I decided to will Max back. I sat down on the wet dock, my feet dangling into the slip where the *Nemaste* would return, and I willed him back. I had been doing this all my life. It was as natural to me as floating is to a duck, or spinning to a spider. I think in another life I may have been an Eastern monk living on a hilltop, spinning my prayer wheel and chanting my days away. Or maybe I'd just been a frog, croaking out the same sad tune over and over. Whatever. It came easy.

I had originally learned this *willing* trick when I was still living at home with my parents in that old tract house by the side of the railroad tracks where we had eventually moved when we left Ridgewood. I remember being embarrassed when they had company over for family barbecues. Now I know it must have been my father that I was ashamed of, and the four or five Rheingold beer cans that circled his paper plate, plus the can on the grill, the can by the lawn mower, and the can on the windowsill where my mother would hand out trays of hamburger rolls and pitchers of iced tea. But in those days I still thought I was embarrassed by the trains that kept running past, stopping all conversation with their clacking rumbles, while we silently ate our ears of corn or cranked the ice-cream maker, ignoring the round, blank faces of curious commuters who sped past.

I knew that once the company left after the barbecue, I would no longer be ashamed of the trains. I even loved the hill that led up to the rails and the wild mint that grew up its stony sides, so much so that today if I sniff some fresh mint in a market, tears of stinging memory fill my eyes and I can barely breathe.

I was the only one in the family whose bedroom faced out on the tracks, and it was there at my window I learned to spin my willful webs. Sitting on my bed in the darkness before the open window, sometimes without any clothes to cover me, I'd will a train to come to me. At night there were fewer and I'd will them to come by sitting very still and seeing them in my mind. I'd empty myself and listen for them. Sometimes I'd recite things quietly, quirky incantations that always worked: "Frankie and Johnny were sweethearts. Lordy, how they could love. Swore to be true to each other. True as the stars above. He was her man. But she done him wrong." I always tried to remember as much as I could. I used to will my father to come to me this way, too. I think, sometimes, it worked. But it's the times it didn't work that come back to me again and again like paper cups thrown into the wind.

A strong biting wind was blowing off the water toward the marina, and the tide was rising, lifting the water closer and closer to my dangling sneakers as I sat by the *Nemaste*'s slip. But I felt and saw none of it. I was a million miles, a million years away. "Frankie and Johnnie were sweethearts." I am standing in the back of an old Ford, the backseat as big as a dentist's waiting room, and the noisy heater's blowing hot air only on the front seat. "Oh, Lordy, how they could love." I'm standing behind my father while he drives and my chin is tucked into the hollow of his shoulder and I am listening to his rumbling, rambling recitations of an old ballad. "Swore to be true to each other." We've just come from a warm, cozy tavern where I got to balance atop a high stool that didn't spin around like the one in the candy store, and I got to eat peanuts and drink a small soda while he drank a fast, tiny drink and a frosty beer. "True as the stars above." He is happy, very, very happy, so happy all his vowels are full and round like chocolate-covered cherries bursting in his mouth, "Now don't tell your mother that we stopped off," and so happy he reaches back and touches my head every so often, telling me I'm his special one, his sweet patootie, his classy dame. "He was her man." So happy that when he drops me off at my clarinet lesson and tells me he'll be back in an hour for me, I believe him. "But he done her wrong."

The doors to the music school are locked, the windows are dark, and the Ford has driven away, back in the direction it came from. No one from the school is around, not the teacher nor any of the other students, and on the quiet business street where there's a pharmacy and a photographer's studio and a lingerie shop, people are beginning to close up and leave, bundled up in their long woolen coats and bright scarves. I sit down on the curb, my clarinet case across my knees, and I begin to wait. To wait and will my father back. "Frankieand-Johnnieweresweethearts.Lordy,howtheycouldlove.Sworetobetrue-toeachother." The streetlights begin to flicker above me. The few cars at the curb have pulled away. "Trueasthestarsabove. Hewasherman.Buthedoneherwrong." Once everyone is gone, but while there is still light, I open my clarinet case, snap the familiar pieces together, and taking my gloves off, I do my lesson. When it's too dark to read the music I just play long melancholy notes and listen to them echo down the empty street. I try another magical conjuring: "He floats through the air with the greatest of ease, the daring young man on the flying trapeze, his movements are graceful, all the girls he does please, but he's stolen my poor heart away." It's just me, waiting for Daddy. Willing Daddy back. True as the stars above. Until my fingers are too cold and I put my clarinet away.

Finally I begin to cry. I know now I will never get home. I miss my dog. I miss the lamp beside my bed and the brightly lit train that flies past my window at night. I'm sure I'll never see any of this again. I sit there crying quietly for what seems like hours in the darkness, and then I vacantly watch a bus begin to wind its way toward me up the long avenue. Through a light, icy snow that's beginning to swirl I see its headlights, the lit banner sign across the top, and the glowing windows. It comes closer and closer until it stops right across the street from where I'm sitting, and once it hisses, moans, and accelerates, it's gone. Standing there on the curb are my mother and my brother. Peter has a scarf wrapped around his neck and face so only his eyes show and he's holding my mother's hand. I spring to my cold, stiff feet and we face each other. I am so happy to see them I begin to laugh, but my mother, if she is at all relieved to see me, puts her relief aside and comes storming across the street at me. I'm afraid she's going to hit me, but instead she begins jerking at my coat, pulling it tighter around my throat. She pulls my hat out of my pocket and then she hits me with it. "Why don't you have this on? Are you crazy? Out here in the cold night without your hat?"

"I've got my gloves on!" I say holding up my hands to show her.

Again she slaps the hat off the top of my head, again and again. "How many times do I have to tell you? Can't you do anything right?" She is gritting her teeth, hating me, and all I can think is not to tell her that Daddy and I "stopped off." She couldn't beat it out of me. I will never tell her, I think, shielding my face and head with my arm. Peter starts to whimper. It makes her stop, and she just stands there. She stands there with her gloves in fists, her face in a fist.

"Mommy," I plead, but she says nothing.

"Get your things," she finally says, pointing to my clarinet and music books, and she heads off down the street in the same direction my father had taken hours before. I scoop up everything and run after her. Peter has to run to keep up and he's crying.

"Are we walking?" I ask. We can't walk. We're so far. It's a far drive to clarinet school. That's why my father drives me.

She spins around, nearly knocking Peter to his knees. "Do you see a goddamned bus? Do you? Do you see any more buses at this hour of the night?" She turns again, nearly jerking Peter's arm out of its socket and I catch up with them, and shifting my clarinet and books in one arm I take Peter's other hand and squeeze it. Our eyes meet. Our eyes meet. Swore to be true to each other. True as the stars above.

"You're stupid!" he shouts at me and I let go of his hand. I drop behind them. And follow them from bus stop to bus stop, my mother always looking over her shoulder for those lights and glowing windows. And she never says another word. And I swear, Daddy, swear I'll never tell her we "stopped off."

The tide had reached the bottoms of my sneakers and the cold had seeped into my slicker and down to my very bones. A fog had slipped in, like the memory of an old poem, and covered everything. I knew the *Nemaste* would never find its way back tonight. "The man he was graceful. All the girls he did please." I knew nothing would work now, and I looked over the edge at my reflection in the water, my wiggly frog head peering up at me from the darkness. "He has stolen my poor heart away."

The little red light was glowing on the answering machine. Without taking off my rain slicker, I stood there in the dark house and pressed rewind. My slicker dripped soft rain onto the wood floor, and the machine kept rewinding. There were either a hundred messages, or one long one, or else my machine was broken.

I pressed playback.

Beep.

"Hail, citizen. Chim'man here." I smiled despite myself. "This is a meteorite alert. Just want you to be informed. You know about it, right? Tonight. This very night, in this our beloved northern hemisphere, there will be the most spectacular meteorite shower known to man, modern man, anyway, and not expected to be seen again for eons. Three or four years anyway, and who knows if we'll all still be here by then, right? So don't be a square. Be there."

Beep.

"It's me again, the chim person. Listen, it's raining. But who cares, right? I'm calling from Amityville. I've got the boat out here and I'm going to see if I can take her out past the city lights for this. Wish you could come. Where are you when I need you, citizen? I'll bring you back a meteorite."

Beep.

"Guess who. Listen, you might be able to see this from your roof. Don't you have a roof off the side of your house that you could get out to from a window? You know, over the porch? Yeah, the porch roof. Well, listen, at 9:43, squeeze your little old body through that window and perch out there. It'll be in the northeast. From 9:43 to early morning. Bring a sleeping bag. And something to protect your head, if a meteorite falls. Or maybe a catcher's mitt, hadn't thought of that . . . You could—"

Beep.

"And don't forget. Make a wish on the first meteorite you see falling through space. I swear it's good magic. It always works. Works for me anyway. Well, that's it for now. Ten-four, out the door. Over and under, life's asunder."

Beep.

I looked at my watch. Five after nine. I didn't take my slicker off, but climbed the stairs in the darkness to Casey's room. I opened the door and walked across to the window. I didn't put the light on and I didn't look at what was there. In three years I had tried only once to pack away her things. Boxes stood opened, half full, some drawers still as she had left them.

And the room smelled stale, an undefined scent I imagined to be a mixture of stale cigarettes, Cheerios, and the lingering pungent hormones of a young girl. I held my breath and unlocked her window. I was surprised to find the storm window wide open—still wide open—as though she had just escaped onto the roof this morning. This is what she used to do, I told myself as I extended a leg out the window. This is Casey's escape route, the way she eased herself out of the safety of this house and out onto the roofs of daring and danger. I slipped through the window, feeling the adolescent knot inside me tighten and stretch. It was raining, but I stood up on my daughter's roof and looked up into the sky.

I calculated northeast, imagining myself lying facedown like an old trembling compass, head to north, left to west, right to east, the south at my feet. Being left-handed I'd always had a fondness for west, and now turning northeast there was no kindness in the drizzle that covered my face. There was not a star to be seen and the sky was covered with a pale gray light, neither dark nor bright, like the inside of a feather pillow. And nowhere around me was there a horizon. If I'd had my sextant there'd have been nothing to take a fix on; the horizon was a riot of trees and houses. How could I ever know where I was, if there was no horizon in my life? Max would have understood that.

"No life of dead reckoning for me!" I said out loud into the rain on the roof. And then with thoughts of stars and meteorites and Max still drifting through my mind, I went inside to find my old poetry books.

It was much later when I finally got into bed. I pulled the phone onto the covers beside me and spread the books out on the quilt. I had marked pages and passages, and now with the rain pounding on my windows, I imagined Max on the deck of the *Nemaste,* staring up into the night, his soot-lined hands each tucked under an armpit, and his face, his mustache, his crinkled eyes watching for a shooting star in a wet fog. I dialed the chimney sweep number.

"Greetings, Citizen. Chim'man here. I can't speak to you right now, so if you'll leave your name, phone number, and a brief message, I'll call you back as soon as I get in."

Beep.

I started hesitantly, opening the first book on my lap. "Max. It's raining out. You must be disappointed, so I thought I would send you some star poems." I took a deep breath and smoothed my hand over the page. I was trembling.

" 'When he shall die,
    Take him and cut him out in little stars,
    And he will make the face of heaven so fine
    That all the world will be in love with night,
    And pay no worship to the garish sun.' "

I paused a minute. "That was Romeo and Juliet."

And then, the next book opened to the mark—" 'My tavern was the Big Bear. My stars in the sky rustled softly.' Rimbaud. Do you know him?"

I laughed nervously. "Oh, no, is this as silly as it feels? How about this one: 'We are all in the gutter, but some of us are looking at the stars.' Can you guess? Oscar Wilde."

"Okay. One more and that's it for you." I cleared my throat, breathed deeply and tried to still the panic and the thought of the unretractability of a phone message. I opened a small book of sea poems, a book with my maiden name, my father's name, still on the bookplate. " 'I must go down to the sea again, to the lonely sea and the sky, And all I ask is a tall ship, and a star to steer her by.' John Masefield. So where's my tall ship, Max? Please call me."

I placed the phone gently in its cradle and hugged my knees against me. I knew I was being ridiculous, but an excitement was pushing up against my chest, an excitement I knew well enough not to trust, but a feeling that nonetheless comforted me. I was doing it. I was willing Max back.

I turned out the light and tugged the blanket up over me. Books tumbled to the floor and the phone clattered and quieted. Reading the poetry had stirred my brain, the way hearing French words spoken on the street could suddenly start me thinking, *"La même chose, la même chose."* The poems churned up some dark and troubling waters. In the darkness of my bedroom a poem drifted back, like an image of a seagull afloat on the water, appearing and dropping in the unbroken swells.

" 'Colder and louder blew the wind, A gale from the Northeast, The snow fell hissing in the brine, And the billows frothed like yeast.' "

There on the dock in the late afternoon, my father is tossing the sleeping bags and fishing gear onto the boat. He is booming out another of his rhyming stories for me. If the hidden whiskey bottle thumps against the tackle box or clunks against the water jug, I do not hear it. I haven't a clue about what is to come. All I am concerned about is that no one witness his recitation, but I see a head peek out from the cabin of the boat in the next slip and then disappear. I wish he would wait until we're alone, until we are out on the water away from strangers.

" 'It was the schooner Hesperus, that sailed the wintry sea, And the skipper had taken his little daughter, To bear him company.' " Leaping onto the boat, I wait on my knees to untie the lines at the bow that hold us to the shore. Somewhere behind me he goes on and on while he prepares the sails. My cheeks burn hot, hot, and I don't dare look at the boat next to us.

I bear him company.

The night after the phone message of poems, I half heard someone drive up the driveway and continue along the house to the back. I waited, not really certain it was what I'd thought. I waited for the doorbell or a knock. It could have slipped by, a mistaken sound, but something made me get up and peer out the kitchen window. Way back, under the pine tree, Max's truck gleamed, catching the reflection of his headlights against the garage, and it wasn't till that very instant when I saw it there that I felt an unexpected anger well up in me. Why so long? What did he want from me now? I would just buy the damn boat and be rid of him.

When he didn't come up to the house, I went to the back door and opened it.

"Max?" I called.

No answer. I grabbed a sweater off the hook and I went down the steps, letting the screen door bang behind me. I crunched up the gravel driveway to the truck. His window was rolled down on the passenger side and I looked in. Max was sitting there looking straight ahead, his hands clasped on top of the steering wheel. Slowly he turned and faced me, and somewhere beneath his mustache I thought he might have been trying to smile.

I didn't mean to say it. I never do. It came out before I could think, an impulse, like reaching out and gripping a life preserver, a detonated life preserver. "Where have you been?" I said.

He didn't answer.

"I hate that you didn't call right away."

His mustache flattened out and his eyes became distant. "I

told you I'm no good at this showing-up stuff. Relationships. Girlfriends. I don't do it well." He shrugged.

Now I stared off into space. It was true; he had warned me. I looked back at him. "How was your meteorite shower?"

"Not a single little pop," he answered. "Just rain and fog and more rain. It was all going on up there. But the clouds kept it all covered. What a rotten thing to do, don't you think? So selfish."

"Yeah, real rotten," I answered about something else, and I turned back to the house. I heard his door open and his footsteps. I sat on the back stoop and waited for him, buttoning every button on my sweater. He sat close beside me, our thighs and arms touching.

"My friend has this big dog," he started. "And that dog is always so glad when he sees me, you know? It makes me feel great. And he really lets me know it, too. You want to know how this dog does it? Can I show you?"

I looked at him skeptically.

"I swear. It'll make you feel great. And I *am* so glad to see you."

I tried not to smile, and nodded.

Max put his arm around my shoulders and drew me close. Before I knew it he had given me one big lick up the side of my face and backed off and waited for me to react. He wasn't there two minutes and he already had me where he wanted me.

"Oh, I hate you," I said, laughing and wiping my cheek. "How can you do this to me? You make love to me, you're all over me, and then you disappear. You're gone. You don't even call."

"I called."

"Mmm. None too soon. I was beginning to hate you by then."

His arm dropped from around my shoulder. "See? That's what I can't stand about all this. I don't want you to feel that way. I feel terrible to upset anybody. I want to be like Tinker Bell!"

"Tinker Bell?"

"Yeah, everybody's always so glad to see Tinker Bell, but no one really notices if Tinker Bell isn't there."

"That would be convenient, wouldn't it? Jesus. You've gone beyond the Peter Pan syndrome, all the way to Tinker Bell. To fantasyland. There's no help for you, Max."

He grinned wickedly and drew close. "Did I ever tell you," he whispered, "about the time I did peyote in high school with my friend and we painted ourselves up with war paint?"

"Max. You're changing the subject."

"You seduced me," he said.

"*I seduced you?*"

"That's right. I know me. I knew just what would happen—that we'd be sitting here a week later, you mad, me sorry, trying to work things out. I've done this dozens of times already."

He turned on the step, easing himself away from me, and then he laid down and put his head in my lap. "I just want you to be happy to see me. That's all."

"I am happy to see you," I said reluctantly, despite myself. I stroked his hair, let my fingers brush through the big, dark curls. I let my lips settle on his cheek right in front of his ear. He was warm. He closed his eyes.

"What am I gonna do, Ellie? I'm too old for this."

I thought of Sugar and smiled.

"And you ain't seen nothin'," he added. "See, there's this girlfriend ..." His eyes opened and he watched my face as he told me. "I've been Tinker Belling in and out of her life for two years. She's a wonderful girl. She's a teacher, and her car is always full of bulletin board stuff—giant cardboard bumble-bees, flowers made out of crepe paper, remember them? And snowmen that leave soap flakes all over her coat. And she's good to me. Her family even likes me, and I'll be watching TV with her and eating some cake she made herself. She even grinds her own coffee. Anyway I'll be sitting there and all of a sudden I'll think, *If I don't leave right now, right this minute, I may never get out of here again. I'll spend the rest of my life sitting on this sofa with this same woman next to me for all eternity.* It comes over me like an oil spill, and she sees it in my face. She knows me. Then I just get up and leave."

Oddly this comforted me. It felt like a little victory to have him there with me. Right this minute he wasn't backing away from me. He was in my circle. I nodded with understanding, and like settling into a saddle that knows my shape and weight I knew then what a familiar thing I could be to him—the woman who could understand him, be on his team, keep his secrets, be his classy dame. I stroked his hair and watched his profile. He turned his face into my thighs and pressed against me. I expanded, puffed up, like an anemone on a secret reef. And like something strange and secret in the depths of a calm ocean, I barely moved. My hand on his head. His face against my lap. A peaceful breeze hummed through the large pine tree and two small night birds chased each other in large sweeps past us.

Suddenly he sat up, and with a light pressure eased my head down into his lap, reversing positions. "Now," he said, "tell me about you." And his hands were in my hair, smoothing it away from my face.

I looked at the back garden sidewards, felt his legs against the side of my face, and smelled the sooty ripeness of him. I smiled. "I've got the money for the boat."

"No kidding! Oh, I'm so glad. I want you to have her. Only you. I took her out yesterday in that rain. The wind was really ripping for a while and I reefed her sails and she just held steady and patient. She has a good soul, the *Nemaste*. She'll be good for you. And you're perfect for her."

He gathered my hair up in two hands and twisted it into a bundle. "What else?" he asked. "Tell me something else about you."

"I love to have my hair stroked. My head rubbed."

"I knew that. Tell me something I don't know. Like, what about you, Ellie? Have you ever sat across the table from somebody for all eternity?"

Then like minnows in a bucket, images of you and Casey flashing through my thoughts. I saw you sitting at the kitchen table, the cigarette smoke drifting up into the overhead light, and Casey beside me. I remembered the two of you flipping a matchbook back and forth to each other, somehow making touchdowns and points after, laughing, bending to retrieve the matches from the floor after an energetic score.

"Yes, I have sat across a table from someone for all eternity." I almost whispered.

"Oil spill?" he asked.

"Oil spill," I agreed.

Now he was spreading my hair down the side of his leg, fanning it like feathers, touching my head so tenderly. "So what do you want?" he asked. "What do you want right now?"

"I want you to hold me." He folded himself over me and his arms encircled me, his hands on my neck, along my arm. His breath on my cheek.

"And what else?"

"I want you to make love to me."

"That's all?"

"But I want you to do it very, very quietly. Casey's asleep."

"I will do it very, very slowly and so quietly that in the morning this Casey will say to you, 'Ma, I thought I heard something so quiet last night. It sounded like a ship sailing over the house through the trees.'" Max's breath was mixing with mine and I turned my face up to him. "'But so tremendously huge, Ma,' she'll tell you, 'so huge that I thought it sounded more like a big pumpkin moon lifting itself right out of the sea.'"

$\mathcal{W}$ e crept up the stairs quietly. I
held my finger to my lips and pointed at Casey's closed door as
we passed it. Like two shadows we continued on to my room
and silently I closed the door. The street lamp across the road
sent the gentlest light through the thin lace curtains, and I
crossed the room to close an open window. It was chilly.

We were then on opposite sides of the high brass bed. Without speaking, we stood facing each other and began undressing.
Max bent and took his sneakers off, and then sent his socks
sailing across the room to the rocking chair. Without bending I

slipped my own shoes off and sent my socks sailing after his. I knew he was smiling. Then I unbuttoned my sweater, and he followed me like a mirror, even though he had no sweater on but a zipped jacket. My sweater and his jacket went flying across the room together. I began to unbutton my blouse and he stood very still watching me. We were both leaning into the bed across from each other, out of each other's reach, the mattress thigh-high, and barely seeing each other in the faint light. I slipped my blouse slowly down my arms and let it fall onto the bed. Cold air touched me. Silently I unhooked my bra and let it drift down my arms as well. In the frail darkness I could tell Max was watching me. I looked down at my own breasts, round and soft in the dimmest of light, and looking back up at him I touched my own curved thumbs to my nipples. The room was cold and they were hard. Max's arms and T-shirt rose over his head and his shirt flew across the room. More gently, not wanting to move so quickly, I gathered my shirt and bra and tossed them also. We were both naked from the waist up. The brightest thing in the room must have been his teeth. Grinning at me. A clear, white grin. Oh, what could have been so hard, he made so easy for me.

He opened his belt. I unsnapped my jeans. Together and slowly like musicians sounding a note to tune their strings, we lowered our zippers. Stepped out of our pants and tossed them across the room. Knee for knee, we mounted the bed. Our arms at our sides. I trembled with cold and an old craving that felt so new. We knelt opposite each other then with our knees touching, our soft breathing the only sound. I didn't move as he lifted his hands and touched only the very tips of my breasts, my nipples, their darker moons, and as if he had walked through an arbor and caught on a spider web, I felt the accompanying tug in my crotch. I arched my back, leaning into it. Then, placing his hands on each side of my thighs, he touched his lips to my breasts. His nose. His cheeks. His ears. His hair. He painted swirls of himself on my chest and breasts until I couldn't help myself anymore. I gathered him to me with glad and eager arms. For the second time.

Max made love to me with all the vigor and enthusiasm of a small boy opening tons of Christmas presents. A friend of mine once told me how her three-year-old son had come into the bathroom one night just when she was stepping out of the shower. Before she could cover herself he had caught sight of her wet and glistening bush and had exclaimed, "Oh, Mommy, that's so pretty!" This is what Max was like. He could have been a virgin turned loose on a warm and erotic terrain. There was no touch, no sensation that couldn't stand being repeated over and over until I would beg him to stop, to start again, to come closer. And for all he was, I was more. I was my best with Max, my skin stretched smooth and tight so that everywhere he touched me I hummed like well-tuned shrouds.

Afterwards, lying there sleepily in each other's arms, I was thinking how sex with Max was different from anything I could ever remember when he asked, "Did it get boring for you? With this guy you sat across the kitchen table from for all eternity? Making love to the same man every time? The same face day after day?"

I got a flash of turning my face away from boozy breath and then, like a whore, being entered without being kissed. "Why do you ask?"

Max was spooned behind me, his chin fitting perfectly in the hollow of my shoulder. "Because it scares me, I guess. It's always so good at this stage, and then you know, it gets old. Doesn't it? Or is it just me?"

"So," I offered, sighing back into his embrace, "we'll just do it till it doesn't feel right anymore and then we won't do it anymore."

He sat up suddenly, nearly dumping me out of the bed. "You mean it? You really, really mean it?"

I laughed. "Sure. As a matter of fact, let's not wait until it gets boring. Let's quit before we have to, like Mickey Mantle did."

"You've fucked *Mickey Mantle?*" He suddenly looked at my body, my thighs as if he expected to find Louisville Slugger branded there.

I pulled the sheet over me. "All right," I said, "let's decide right now, on this date, May whatever, that you and I, Max Turkel and Ellie Brinkley, will make love only five times with each other, and that after five times we will stop, even if it's still good, because on the sixth time it probably won't be so hot anymore."

"That's great!"

I looked at him. It wasn't that great.

"Now let's see," he mused. "This is the second time, right?"

"Right."

"Even though I came twice?" he asked.

"I came *seven* times."

"But our feet never touched the floor."

"That sounds like a good cutoff," I said. "As long as our feet never touch the floor it's a single time."

"But what if one of us has to go to the bathroom?"

"Well, then, how about it's a single time until we get dressed?"

"That's better," he said. "But what if we eventually get into kinky clothes? You know."

"We probably wouldn't get into kinky clothes until the eleventh or twelfth time," I speculated.

"That's true." He nodded. "Then we only have three more times to go."

"Three more."

He sank back down behind me, collected me in his arms, and held me tightly against him. "Then we will never be lesser or greater than we are right now." He placed his hand against my face and turned me to look at him. I tumbled naked beside him until we were face to face. "You know, Ellie, in that great amusement park of the universe, on that game where you hit the weight with a giant hammer?"

I nodded.

"We just rang the bell."

"Oh, Max."

We made love again that night, never touching the floor, never needing to get dressed, and finally he slid off the bed in the darkness and went for his clothes.

"Max."

"Mmm?"

"What about the boat?"

"It's yours."

"I need to get it out East where I can dock it for free, at my editor's country house."

"I'll sail it out there for you." He grunted, struggling with his clothes.

"You would?"

"Sure. You'll come. Won't you? It'll be great."

"Okay. And maybe we can do number three on the boat," I suggested.

"Well, it'll be a two-day trip, so that might be an opportune time. You may be right."

I smiled up into the darkness.

"Ellie?" he said.

"Mmm?"

"Could you put the light on a minute? I can't find my watch."

I reached across the bed and turned the lamp on. The clock said 4:45 A.M. I looked over at him and burst out laughing. He was standing at the foot of the bed in a combination of both our clothes, everything crooked and bulging, my bra over my sweater, my bikini pants over his jeans.

I began to howl hysterically and watched in disbelief as he flew across the room at me. "Shhh! Shhh!" he begged. "You'll wake your kid!" When I couldn't stop, he straddled me and pressed the pillow gently over my face to muffle my cries. Somewhere in the struggle, I became exhausted. I could no longer tell if I was laughing or crying, but when my breathing leveled out and I was still, he lifted the pillow away from me and stroked the hair off my face. I didn't open my eyes. I listened to him turn off the light and heard him leave my clothes on the foot of the bed. I couldn't hear his feet on the stairs. Or the door close behind him. But in my sleep I heard the truck start up, and when I opened my eyes into the darkness, I heard the gravel crunch in the driveway.

"Shhh," I whispered. "You'll wake Casey."

Casey, the little ghost who haunts the hallways of my dark days. Alone, when I am tired and sad, and I let myself think of her, the whole story seeps into my defenseless thoughts. It's funny, but sometimes I think that if you and I had had a little daughter spirited away when she was a very young child, she would have been an angel in my life, an angel to mark my path. But because she was older and ripped herself out of my life, the way a paw is ripped from a bloody trap, there is no going back to it in a gentle way. There are no angels. No angels for me. Her death could not have happened at a more terrible time. And yet, looking back, I can see

it could have happened only then. It had been building and smolder-
ing and coming for a long time, with its odd little moments of half-
hearted healings.

Do you remember the Christmas before she died? How when
you came to pick her up on the weekend, I had all those tiny white
lights tacked around the front stoop? The tiny little pinpoints of
brightness that were nearly blinding there were so many of them? I
never told you how that came about, did I? And you never asked.
But when did I ever need you to ask? When have I ever sat still
and waited?

It was about two weeks before Christmas and I found myself in
a garden store, in the greenhouse section, needing to buy tinsel and
a new tree stand. I was in no hurry, I was alone, and I startled
myself by beginning to cry. Sobs escaped me like pollen exploding
into the humidity. No one was around, so I stopped a moment and
leaned up against a rack of philodendron. It used to happen to me
like this sometimes. Not often, but enough. Even though our divorce
was no longer a word that set my teeth on edge, and you'd been
gone for over two years, a simple thing like walking through a
garden store like we had done a hundred times could still shake me.
Do you remember that marriage counselor we went to see and how
we sat apart in his office making lists of what we liked best about
each other, what we liked to do with each other? I never would
have thought to put this on the list—walking through pungent,
fertile aisles together, barely able to breathe, touching leaves, singling
out funny-looking cactus. I never would have thought of this in a
million years, but there I was sobbing beside a little bubbling foun-
tain buried deep in the palms and ferns, missing you terribly, and
thinking that this might have been my most favorite thing of all to
do with you.

I bolted through the aisles then, holding my breath to keep
the green air out of the great storerooms of my melodramatic

soul, and I let myself through the glass doors into the back of the garden center, where the Christmas decorations were. I've heard it said that people should never shop in a grocery store when they're hungry. The same holds true here: they should never shop in a Christmas store when they're sad. I set about to buy good cheer. How odd that word sounds to me now, so old-fashioned, like gladden, hark, and gaslights. But I thought I could find it. I bought an armful of red-berried holly, a mistletoe, clusters of glass balls, and I don't know what I was thinking, other than they were on sale, and I had enough money in my wallet, but I bought five boxes of strings of outdoor lights, tiny pinpoint white lights, each containing one hundred tiny bulbs, each smaller than a ladybug, five hundred in all, five hundred painful burning lights and three packs of thumbtacks. I don't know what I was thinking.

At home I arranged the holly on the kitchen table, hoping Casey might like it, maybe she'd say something, and we'd have gentle words for a change. Maybe she'd buy into my fantasy, and look around the house and feel safe. I'd always believed if I could just create the right atmosphere in the house, things would change. I had read articles about the colors of rooms, how a red room could be stimulating, a blue room calming, so to surprise her once I painted her room a cool blue, to soothe her, to erase her scowl, but she hated it, and her hatred triggered an untapped frustration and a rage so deep in me that in her cool, calming blue room I had flung her radio across the room and against the freshly painted wall. Its shape is impressed on the plaster still, and she mocked me by letting it be the only spot she didn't cover with a poster of nightmarish-looking rock stars, men like motorcycle murderers in Halloween drag. But this was Christmas—surely a little holly, a red ribbon twining up the staircase would give me a magazine life, make it all simple.

104 PAMELA E. CONRAD

But she came home from junior high silent, her thickly black-rimmed eyes not even looking at me, or the holly. I added to it by not even saying hello as she disappeared up the stairs to her room, leaving a trail of stale cigarette smell, and another indistinguishable odor that I remember only from my brother when he was a sweaty teenager. Maybe it was gym. Or beer.

"I'll be back at six," she mumbled a few minutes later as she passed me going the other way.

"Casey," I said.

"What?"

Someone once told me that all adolescents are psychotic. There were times when I didn't even recognize her. Her expression was one of a terrorist holding a gun on me. I used to try to remember her baby face, that strenuous smile that would grip her whole body and make me automatically respond to her. Her short fingers that I would hold to my mouth and taste. She, of course, remembered none of this. She knew me only as the barrier to all that she thought she wanted.

"I'd like you to ask permission to go out instead of just informing me." I don't know why I'd said that. It was like pushing the first card over, standing back as the others begin to topple, topple, topple, and I'd stand amazed at myself, not even trying to step in somewhere before the last card is flipped, the door slammed.

"May I go out, Mother dear?" she whined at me, her voice hard, and I could see how dirty her hands were. I could see the bandanna wound around her knee. Her face formed a perfect sneer, like something right off one of her posters, and I wondered if she practiced that in front of her mirror.

Well, I'd been a teenager once too. I'd learned facial expressions on my parents as she'd been learning on me. Thoughts of my own mother flickered in my mind, and when I answered her, when I spoke to her through hard, hateful lips, it was my mother's voice that I heard. "Get lost," I whispered. She slammed the door after her. In that instant I had hated her, the instant I saw her so clearly before me, so distant from anything I had ever thought was possible with us, but the minute she was out of my sight, as always I began to sink, promising myself I'd do better next time. But thinking about her could be like carrying splintery logs from the garage to the house. I could never do it all in one trip. I always keep putting them down, even though it's so much harder to pick them up again.

Trembling, I touched the holly on the table, adjusting the stems deeper into the vase, and a sharp edge of a leaf jabbed me and made me bleed a holly berry on the side of my finger. It was three-thirty, and still light outside. I longed for the numbness of performing a task, and without thinking, without joy, I put on my long coat and gloves and gathered up the boxes of lights and the cards of thumbtacks.

Winter lived gently on our front porch, partially protected by the overhang roof and side screens and muffled by the late afternoon sun in the west that held only the empty promise of warmth. For some reason the porch has always reminded me of the depths of a padded baby carriage where there is only the smell of milk and the sound of folded flannel. I laid the tacks and the lights on the porch swing and opened one box. The lights were strung on a cord, and the cord was wound around a piece of plastic. My breath hovered in the air about me as I unwound the cord and laid it out on the floor. One hundred tiny lights. I plugged the end into the outdoor outlet and I could see they were all lit, very pale, dim lights. Maybe they wouldn't show. Maybe I should have gotten different colors, the kind that look like candy. Everything I did, every choice I made had the tinge, the unmistakable hint of regret. But my need to not return to the garden store was greater than my regret.

Turning the lights off, I began at the door, tacking them up one side, across the top, and down the other. I continued the string across the side of the porch to the steps. There were seven wide steps. Slowly and methodically, I plugged strand after strand into the next and secured them by pushing the tacks into the soft wood of the porch steps, trailing the strands back and forth. A winter sparrow swooped close to the porch, close enough to catch my eye and then disappear into the dormant rhododendron bushes. I had taken off my gloves to push the tacks, and my fingers ached with the cold. When I was done, I crumpled up the empty boxes and plugged in the lights. I tossed the boxes in the garbage can at the side of the house and stepped onto the front lawn to admire the porch. I could barely see the lights. Each one looked like a spiritless prick of weak electricity. I crossed the street and looked from there. It was even worse. The sky was lavender with winter dusk, a harsh brightness that totally obscured my lights.

Maybe in the darkness they would show more brightly. And then I went in the house. I jammed my gloves into the pockets of my coat and hung my coat in the closet. Then I went to the kitchen to make dinner.

I didn't think of the lights again until the doorbell rang. I left a pot steaming on the stove, some beans bubbling in their casserole, and went to answer it. I pulled the curtain aside and grew angry when I saw Casey's back standing at the door. She knew not to use the front door. I'd told her countless times to come around to the back door, where she could let herself in and not have to pull me away from whatever I was doing. I unlocked the door. "How many times have I told you—"

Casey turned to look at me, and her eyes were shining like a million lights. Behind her a million lights were shining like some brilliant enchantment. In the darkness, the front porch had been transformed into a blazing winter wonderland.

"Wow!" she said when I opened the door. Just "wow," and

then she turned and swirled, her arms held out in the air, her head thrown back. Comically she began to shuffle a faked tap dance across the porch floor. I stepped out into the cold.

"I feel so important!" she cried. "Like I'm a star on Broadway!"

I watched her shining face in the brightness, loving her face in that moment, thinking someday someone would love her for her face alone, and for her laughter. And believing, or wanting to believe that this was all just a phase she was sure to outgrow. I remember the moon that night hanging like a pale fingernail over the house across the street where the sun had gone down just a short time ago.

And now, so much later, I was lying in bed in the pale hours of a cool spring morning, my vagina still damp with the seed of a man I had never visited a greenhouse with, a man who had never seen my porch at Christmas, but he had been very careful to be quiet. Very quiet, so that he wouldn't wake a child he thought was in the next room, a sad, troubled girl whom I had never been able to love enough, but who had tap danced for me anyway one night so long ago.

$\mathcal{I}$ once heard something that made me so sad. I was down in the basement taking laundry out of the dryer. There were the usual sounds of the dryer door closing, buttons clicking on the lid, and I remember how warm the towels were that morning, as though a large dog had been sleeping on them. Then I heard the unmistakably clear sound of a cricket throwing his voice from some indistinct place. I searched and eventually found him in the deep metal sink next to the washing machine, sitting right on top of the drain. His chirping echoed down the pipe and filled the laundry room with cricket music. It reminded me of the bravado of juvenile delinquents—teenage kids standing in a tunnel with their black leather jackets and their glowing cigarette butts, singing some popular tune and reveling in their echo, as though it was the best thing they'd done all day. Like the cricket. So loud, so futile.

Tell me, when was the last time you heard that expression—juvenile delinquents? Nobody says that anymore, kind of like colored, or ladies. *Not that we don't have juvenile delinquents; certainly Casey would have fit the bill. Only black leather and cigarettes were quickly to become child's play to her. I used to have this theory about who the first juvenile delinquents must have been. Had I ever told you?*

Probably not. You weren't around for much during those difficult times, and besides, I'll bet you never even heard the story of "The Twelve Dancing Princesses" yourself, have you? Maybe you did. But I have this prejudice that tells me that only people who've been sneaky children, smuggling flashlights under cotton comforters to read Grimms' fairy tales, would know about them. But who knows? There are probably lots of things I don't know about you. Things I never understood. Lots of things.

There was once a king who had twelve lovely daughters, and every morning he would go to their room to wake them, and always at the foot of their beds would be their shoes, worn through. Even though he had just given them new shoes the day before, there they would be, tattered and in shambles, where their delicate toes had danced holes in them. Such a mystery.

I thought of that king this one particular morning when I came down to the kitchen early. I was up before Casey, ready to stick a quick salami sandwich and a can of juice in a brown bag for her, when I noticed her sneakers by the back door. They were caked with mud, and their broken shoelaces were wet. It had begun to rain during the night. Long after I was in bed. I remembered getting up to tighten the latch on my rattling rain-streaked window and the clock had said quarter past three.

I stared at her sneakers and that's the first thing I thought of—this fat king, in his long ermine-trimmed robe, with a golden crown upon his head, a staff, a clunky ruby ring on his pinky. He would have frozen just like I did, the twenty-four little slippers worn through and smoking. He would have scratched his head. He would have said, "What the hell is going on here?"

I turned at the sound of Casey shuffling into the kitchen. She looked as though she had slept in her clothes. Her hair was flat on one side and there were still grains of sleep sand in her eyes.

"What the hell is going on here?" I asked.

She stared at me blankly. "Give me a clue," she said.

I walked over to the sneakers and picked up one by the soggy shoelace. "Clue number one. A wet, muddy sneaker."

"So?"

"Did you go out last night? In the middle of the night?"

The twelve dancing princesses awake from their dreams and stretch, languidly waving and smiling sheepishly at their father. "Hi, Daddy."

"Did you go out last night?" he asks. "After your mother and I went to bed?"

"Oh, no, Daddy. We were all right here, sound asleep." They fluff their pillows and collapse back drowsily, their silken nightgowns wafting down over their tired, deceitful little dance-till-you-drop bodies.

Casey shrugged.

"Where did you go?" I asked her.

The king, obese with wealth and opulence, not used to

lifting the slightest thing, bends his bulk and lifts a tattered slipper into the air. "But your shoes . . ."

She ignored me, but I could see the tension curling across her shoulders as she turned and reached into the pantry for a box of Cheerios.

"Casey, I'm talking to you."

"Talkin' to you," she mocked. She opened the cereal box, and tilting it, held it over her head and began pouring. Some went in her mouth, some tumbled over her hair, her shoulders, onto the floor. It had the desired effect of shocking and silencing me. She sat at the table, dumping the box on its side. Little O's poured over the table and at my feet. I suddenly had the thought that she was drunk. But there was no smell. She was something else. Something unfamiliar and unrecognizable.

The king must have been stunned as well by the obvious lies and deceit. "I will put a guard at your door tonight," he tells the lovely princesses. "And you will stay where you belong, in bed, in the castle, under my power."

They probably giggle and say, "Of course, Daddy. But you don't need a guard. We don't go anywhere. Nowhere at all."

"I can't do this anymore, Case."

She pinched her nostrils together and winced. "So don't."

"I told you I'd go to family court. If you gave me one more reason, I'd go and have you put someplace where they can take better care of you than I can. Where you can get help. You're only thirteen. You can't go out in the middle of the night at all hours. Doing whatever it is you're doing."

She looked at me and I thought her face had softened. Maybe I had reached her. Maybe there was a little chink in her wall. "Oh, Casey," I said, collapsing in the chair opposite her and extending my hand along the oak table toward her, little O's sticking to my arm.

But she immediately bolted out of her seat. Her face was a

stranger's. "Fuck you!" she yelled. "Just fuck you. You got it? Anything else you want to know?"

I heard the king close the door behind him as he leaves his daughters' room and I heard the silence of the princesses who are so sure that no guard, no prince, can stop their night passages. I tried to imagine how the king would feel when at last there is a soldier who outwits them and saves them from their own devilishness.

I guess Casey never thought I'd really go through with it. And I guess I never thought that there would be no soldier waiting for Casey, no soldier waiting to figure out her enchantments and save her from herself. Family court was its own ruthless kingdom. With even less protective power than my own. And with its own sort of evil spell.

I opened the back door and swept out the kitchen floor. I was being quiet and keeping busy while Max studied the nautical charts. He sat hunched over the kitchen table, a cup of hot coffee beside him and the old ceiling lamp carving a circle of light around it all. Folded and tucked under his cup was the check for the boat. It was finally, officially, mine.

"I can't decide," he was saying. "Should we sail around the southern fork, around Montauk? That will take a little longer, I think. Or should we cut through Shinnecock Canal, through the locks, which might be a little trickier?"

Charlie had said, "Why don't you trailer it out? It will be quicker. A few hours. If you sail, it will take days."

"Only two days," I had told him. "And it could be material for my book."

Now I sat down next to Max. I pulled my chair close to his and leaned my chin on his shoulder. It was decided that our next lovemaking, number three, would be on our cruise to Shelter Island, so we had become like affectionate sister and brother.

Like two puppies. Except when leaving each other. Then he would nip my lip, or I would run my hand down his thigh when I'd bring his jacket.

"I vote for tricky," I said, gazing at the charts with him. Max's charts were bound in books, like road maps. The pale tan for land and green and white for water, with its sprinkling of numbers to indicate depths and shoals, reminded me of the charts my father used to use, big, cumbersome charts that were rolled and tossed into the forward berth when not in use. On those occasions that he did use them, reading them intensely while he blew his cheeks up like balloons, his lips pressed against the back of his fist, I used to wonder what he would have done without me, how he would have ever kept his charts from coiling with a snap if it weren't for me, his ship's girl, pressing the curling chart open with my two hands and some-times lying my whole body across the top of the chart itself to keep it from rolling up.

Max traced a line with his finger. "We start here, sail along the Great South Bay, to here, sail in the ocean for a while, then head north, cut through the canal, which can be really treacher-ous, depending on the current that day, and then we're home free in the Peconic Bay. Paradise. You could sail it yourself from there."

"And the other way?"

"Well, if we didn't cut through the canal, we'd continue along here, out to Montauk Point, which has its own set of problems. The Race. And it would take another day, probably."

"The Race?"

"Strong currents. Depending on the tide. We could catch it right."

Why don't we aim for the canal?" I suggested. "And then if it's too rough there that day, we'll continue on."

"And what if the Point is too rough?" he asked.

"We'll turn into a teacup and fly away."

I still had my head on his shoulder and he reached across himself and cupped my head with his hand. He rubbed my head and ear and I felt loved. "And where would we fly?"

"To the apple tree."

"And then?"

"Then I would make you some applesauce."

His hand over my ear silenced everything. All I could hear was a dim heartbeat somewhere, his or mine.

"Is that how you begin to write a story?" I head him say. He turned to face me. "You just go off like that?"

"Well, there's that part, and then there's the part where you finally have to plan it. Shape it. In your mind you draw a big circle and you tell yourself it starts here and it ends here." I drew a circle in the air, beginning and ending at the same point.

"I wish I could write a story. I would tell a story about my stepfather. About when he had Alzheimer's. He's dead now."

I took his hand between my two, like a sandwich, his skin darker and rougher. "It's not hard. You could do it."

"How do you make a circle? Tell me a story."

I turned his palm down and brought the tips of his fingers to my forehead.

"Start with a woman," he suggested. "She's in love. She's found the love of her life. Now make a circle."

I closed my eyes and let his fingers settle to my eyebrows. "There was this young woman," I began, "okay, a young woman who has found the love of her life. A young man that she thought the world of."

"That's the beginning of the circle?" Max asked.

"Not yet. The young man loved her, too, but he liked to be smarter than she was, and she knew it, so one day she made a mistake for him. The sun was setting, and it was just the kind of day that turns the sun a dull orange as it's going down. The sun was so dull you could look right into it. They were walking along together and not giving it much thought, when she said to him, 'Oh, look at that beautiful moon.' "

"It was the sun," Max said.

"That's right. And the young man laughed at her. Beginning of the circle." I opened my eyes and held his hand in my lap. "So the story goes on, and you can tell it a number of different ways, but always there's that memory of the mistake she made, and it's their little joke, about how dumb she is, you know—this dumb broad who can't tell the sun from the moon kind of stuff. And they go on, and they buy a house and have a little girl. And everything seems to be okay, but you know, it gets to be one of those sitting-across-the-table-for-all-eternity sort of situations, and one day he starts to pack. 'Where are you going?' she says to him. 'Away,' he tells her. 'Away from me?' 'Yes.' 'Away from our child?' 'Yes.'

"She begins to spin. Her whole world is slipping away from her, and she needs him so much. She spins down the stairs, through the house, scooping up their little girl, and together they spin out of the house and far away."

"She doesn't want the kid to see him packing," Max said.

"Mmmm. So they go to the duck pond to feed the ducks until he's all packed and gone."

"And what about the circle?"

"This is where it comes in. You see, they're sitting there at the duck pond, sitting on this nice little park bench under the trees, and across the pond in the west—"

"Is the sun going down," Max whispers.

"Right. And it's the kind of sun that is dull orange and you can look right into it. And the little girl points and says—" I turned up my both palms to him and waited.

"Oh, Mommy, look at the beautiful moon."

"You got it."

Max's eyes glistened, then closed. He bowed his head and pulled me toward him till our foreheads touched. I was feeling nothing, graced by the distance of a storyteller. "Now you," I said. "Now you make a circle. It's easy."

He straightened and leaned back in his seat. Slowly he tucked his hands in his armpits and looked past me, over my head, into the next room. "A circle," he said softly. "There's my stepfather who is forgetting everything," he started. "He forgets where his bedroom is. He forgets how to button his shirt sometimes. He has to ask people to help him." Max looked down at me, I guessed to see if he was doing it right. He paused.

"That's good, but give it some distance. You can't see someone if you're dancing with them. Let them dance with someone else so you can watch. And unless it's significant to the story, let it be a father, and not a stepfather. Simplify. Start it: there's this guy whose father was forgetting everything."

"That's hard," Max said. He closed his eyes, and went on. "Okay, so there was this father and his son." He paused. "I'm trying to see the circle."

I waited quietly.

"And when the son was young they used to watch the horse races on TV together. At Belmont. And they would bet each other. A dollar, a couple of bucks, whatever it was, and the father always won. He really knew his horses. Used to get the racing sheets, drove my mother nuts."

"Drove the boy's mother nuts," I corrected.

"Right. So anyway, the kid was forever handing over money to his father. And his old man had no mercy. He wasn't easy on the kid. He'd pocket those couple of bucks his kid had mowed lawns for as easy as he'd take a check from his own boss. No mercy."

Max smiled and looked at me. "I see the circle," he whispered.

I leaned back and waited, reaching out to sip Max's coffee.

"Well, it went on like this for years, until the kid was grown and out of the house. Then one day—this kid was a man now—he stopped in to see his parents and his father was sitting in front of the TV. By this time his old man had Alzheimer's and everyone was kind of used to saying things over and over and showing him familiar things as if he'd never seen them before. So his old man was watching TV and the son sees he's watching the races at Belmont. Now what the father doesn't know is that what he's watching is a video of the race that already happened. His son heard the results of the race on the way over and sees his big chance. He pulls his wallet out and slaps a ten down on the coffee table in front of his father. 'Bet you ten, Pops. Ten on Splendid Rapture.'

"This old guy may be losing some bolts but he hasn't lost his confidence. He reaches into his back pocket, pulls out an old, flat leather wallet, and matches the ten. 'True Deal,' the old guy says, 'by two lengths.' See? So the son goes along with it. 'Okay, True Deal and Splendid Rapture.' You know how it comes out. Splendid Rapture wins and the old man is flustered. His son pockets the money, grinning. And then there are two more races. And it's the same thing each time. At post time, his father doubles the bet, doubles it again, and each time the son pockets the money. Gets back all the money he ever lost to his father, all those years of mowing lawns and delivering newspapers. What goes around comes around."

"And that's the circle?" I asked him.

"No. Not yet. You see, a true circle here would be for the son to lose again. So what happens is the old guy is so impressed by his son's horse luck that he insists they go to the track together the next weekend, and he wants to bet all his money, on whatever his son says. Luckily the old lady only lets him bring a couple of hundred, but even that wipes the son out. You see, the son places the bets, hoping he's got a winner—of course he never does—but whenever any horse at all wins, the son cheers and yells and jumps up and down as if he's won. Now the old guy—from the time the horses start till they finish—he's forgotten who they bet on, so he's believing he's winning every time."

Max leaned way back in his seat, tilting it, pressing the heels of his hands into his eyes. "Geez," he laughed, "did that cost me. That was a lot of chimneys!"

"Full circle," I added.

"Full circle. A good story, don't you think?"

"I love it," I told him. "I can imagine them at the racetrack with the son losing and having to cover himself."

He smiled. He was far away. "I was glad to do that for him. He died a couple of months later. Left me a little money and I bought some flowers for the funeral home, a big horseshoe-shaped thing, you know, like they put around winning horses' necks. My mother hated it."

He looked back at me and we smiled. "So should I copyright this story or what? Think it has movie potential?"

I laughed as he leaned forward and squeezed my kneecaps to make me jump. There was a sharp pain that ran the ragged edge of pleasure and I struggled to slip away, but he held me. "You won't tell anyone my story, will you? Will you steal it from me?"

Still laughing and struggling, I strained to release myself from him, swearing and promising I'd never write it, that I had already forgotten it. We wrestled there on the kitchen chairs, tickling, twisting, forcing, and hooting.

But look at this. Just look at this. Eventually I did write it down. And I'm even telling you.

I learned all I have ever needed to know about promises from my father. I learned about whiskers, and about boats and beer from him. And I learned about a soul anguish from him the way you learn about an apple that you never bite. You will always know only the slick, dark exterior, but never what is inside. You never bite through the crisp skin to the juicy pulp. And even though you may never uncover or bite into the tightly sealed brownness of the tiny apple pits, you are sometimes sure you can taste the drops of their poison in the back of your throat.

———

My father prides himself on the barbecued chicken he concocts every summer of my childhood. No one is allowed in the kitchen when he makes the sauce, and gathering from my mother's puckered face I think that he must put beer in it, or maybe even whiskey. But the chicken is delicious; even my mother has to admit it.

I cannot count the number of Sunday afternoons we sit in the backyard in the shadow of the railroad tracks, watching while the smoke rises from the grill, and my father, his belly escaping from beneath his shirt and above his belt, tilts his head way back and drains a beer can. "Get me another brew, son," he says to Peter, and Peter runs inside and returns with a can and the opener, which my father takes from him. I know if Peter goes quickly and comes back running the can of beer might spray over my father's hands. Or if Peter goes slowly and walks deliberately, his little feet sure and heavy as they cross the lawn, the beer will open with a precise hiss and nothing will be lost.

This one time I am in the kitchen when Peter comes trotting up the steps. He doesn't speak to me but goes right to the refrigerator and opens it. Cans of Rheingold line the shelves, and oh, how I long to be a Rheingold girl, one of those beauties whose faces line the glass at the deli counter down the block. I always vote for the blond, the one who most closely matches my own sun-streaked and sandy hair.

"Peter," I whisper, suddenly inspired.

"What." He turns with a cold beer in his hand.

"Wanna see something? Wanna surprise Daddy?"

"What."

I take the cold beer from him and shake it. I shake it and shake it as hard as I can. Until my neck aches.

"There." I hand it back to him.

"So?"

"So, go ahead. You'll see."

Peter gets this expression on his face that says I am the most inconsequential person he's ever encountered in the entire five years of his life and heads out the door. I follow him into the late afternoon sun. My parents have pulled the barbecue table back into the shade of the house, and I sit beside my mother, who sips her iced tea and stares into space. The bench rocks in the uneven grass and dirt when I sit down and she turns in annoyance to look at me. "Sit still."

I watched as Peter hands the beer to my father. The can glistens in the sun, dripping wet and icy cold. The chicken sizzles on the grill, sending up a cloud of fragrant promise. As the can switches hands, I can see Peter's hand is wet. He wipes it on his shorts as my father tousles his hair. "Thank you, son." I suddenly look at my father's face. There is something in his voice, a cloying gentleness that warns me something is going on. He is pulling Peter into his corner with his voice, pulling Peter away from my mother. Yet when Peter sits down beside my mother, and rocks the bench as I had, she reaches out and encircles him with her arm, drawing him back against her. My father picks up the can opener. His loose-jowled face tightens and I see him glance at my mother and my brother.

His brawny, thick hands put the beer can on the table and hold the opener to it. I hold my breath. I will think later how I could have stopped him right here. I could have yelled "Wait!" and swiped the can out from under his nose. I could have gotten another can. But I don't. I hold very still. I can't take my eyes off the can.

The opener loops itself around the edge of the can, then gently its point presses into the lid. I can see the metal give an instant before the can explodes all over the table. The basket of potato chips, the clean dishes, the macaroni salad. Everything covered in stinking beer. Even me. Even me. I look down at my flat chest and hold my T-shirt away from my skin. Then I look up at him.

Beer drips from his nose. From his hair. He flicks his wet hands before him. My mother says, "Jesus."

Then he turns on Peter. He draws his arm across himself and flings it. "You little bastard." I think he has hit my mother, but she doesn't move and Peter tumbles off the bench. "You little shit!" I glance at the neighbor's screened windows.

Peter starts to whimper. And I begin to vibrate all over. I hold my hands over my ears to stop my head from trembling. And to block the sound of Peter's voice.

"I didn't do it!" Peter cries. "I didn't do it! Ellie did it! Ellie shook it!" He is crouched in the grass with his arms over his head. His fingers look like dead starfish that my father would pin on a board and varnish.

I don't move. Frozen beside my mother, the two of us don't move. I keep my hands over my ears. My father's eyes dig into my own eyes with a rage that is no stranger to me. A rage that appears with a certain predictability that escapes me, a pattern that has something to do with the number of beers, or a bottle of whiskey that is never capped. Or the expression on my mother's face.

"Is that true?" he asks, suddenly calm. There is an undertow here, a drawing out of strength and might. I walk into it.

"Yes, Daddy."

"Why would you do that?" he asks, winding his heavy fingers around Peter's wrist and drawing the boy to him. Peter softens, goes toward our father. "Now why would you do that, Elizabeth? Do you want Peter in trouble? Huh?" The storm is building. Suddenly he has Peter hanging by a wrist in midair. Holding Peter up in the air with one hand, dangling like a large blue fish, he smacks him hard across the behind with his other hand. "Is that what you want, Elizabeth? Tell me. You want Peter in trouble? You like this?" Again the broad flat of his hand flies through the air and catches Peter across his legs. "How about this? You like this?" His legs, his behind, his chest, his one skinny swinging arm. Bright peonies seem to bloom on my brother's skin.

Until finally it stops. I squeeze my eyes shut, and when I open them Peter is scrambling away toward the house and my father is turning the chicken. My mother is sopping up the beer, patting a paper napkin over our dishes, on top of the chips, even on the macaroni salad.

"Get me a brew, Elizabeth," my father says calmly. And I do. I go inside and slide it carefully off the shelf of the refrigerator, all the while hearing the muffled squeals coming from my brother's room. And I carry that can, that beer can, that Rheingold beer can out into our backyard. I carry it before me with two hands as if it's some sort of holy chalice filled with nitroglycerin.

Max and I had finally set a day to meet at the boat, for a check to see if anything had to be done and what had to be gotten for our trip out East. I arrived a half hour before the agreed-upon time so that I could be alone on the boat for a while. It was a hot day, the first day of summer heat, and I had worn a bathing suit under my T-shirt and shorts.

The sky was bright, though dark around the edges, and there was the lightest of breezes brushing over the marina. The telltales fluttered sleepily, and the marina's flag, heavy and limp, barely moved. The water from the bay lapped quietly against the red side of my boat, and I was filled with an inexplicable joy. My boat. My own boat. Fearing there might be someone looking out at me from a nearby galley or out the marina building window, I busied myself with opening the hatch, trying to hide my grin. I unlocked the bolt with the key Max had given me and then I lifted out the three sections of the hatch door one at a time. Brittle and weathered on the outside, I noticed they were varnished and still shiny on the inside.

I gathered the sections under my arm, stepped down two steps into the cozy galley, and lowered myself onto the cushioned bench along the side. It was so quiet, so still, so small, a tiny parcel of finite space in the center of an endless pulsating universe. I could barely breathe for the elation I was feeling. I ran my fingers along the teak storage shelves, along the knobs of the shortwave radio. We had never had a radio in the boat when I was young. I would have to learn this. Picking up the small hand-held mike, I held it to my mouth and whispered, "Mayday, Mayday."

Then I pushed the red cushions aside to check in the storage areas. There were a couple of life preservers still in their plastic covers, a box of old, rusty fishing tackle, an old sweater, propane bottles, and bundles of heavy, damp line. There were two sailbags, one marked "Gennie," a long-handled broom, and an old yellow rubber raincoat. Under one cushion was a table. I tossed the cushion into the forward berth and struggled to set the table up, latch it against the wall, and pull the single support leg down. It was difficult and awkward, and in the heat, sweat broke out across my lip and forehead, but once it was in place I sat at it, my arms resting on its dusty surface, my legs underneath. I could imagine Max and me playing cards here at night, the darkness curving and swaying beneath us. Here, at last, on my own boat, I wouldn't hold back the memories; they would come and I would write them down. I'd let Max be a part of it, and I would play it out with him, whatever it was. I would lean into my karma. Embrace it this time.

"Ahoy, matey! Or is that a pirate aboard? Yo ho ho and a

bottle of rum. Sailing, sailing over the bounding main." The boat rocked as Max climbed aboard and made his way back to the cockpit. I went to him.

"It's the matey," I answered.

"Well, look at this," he marveled. "Already she's got the table up, making it all homey and comfy. Have you decided where our children will sleep?"

"In a hammock off the boom," I answered in the same silly tone.

He threw one arm around me and tilted me back over the tiller. "Ah, and will ya marry me, dearie?"

"Not if I'll need special clothes."

He released me and I realized he was clasping a large brown bag in his other hand. "That's good," he muttered. "I'll have to remember that. Good answer." He bent over his bag and took out two sandwiches, two beers, and two Cokes. "I hope you like liverwurst with lettuce and horseradish and Swiss with a touch of mayo." He studied my face.

"My favorite."

"If not, I also got roast beef and cheddar with mustard and sliced tomatoes."

"Either," I said.

Bending over the bag he held out a beer to me. "Beer?"

I shook my head. "No, thanks."

He looked at me, handed me a soda, and popped a soda for himself. He put the two beers back in the bag, and reaching into the galley tossed them forward. I heard them land on the cushion. I sat down on the bench opposite him and watched him over the can of soda as I sipped it.

"On the way over here," he was saying, "I remembered something." We were facing each other, knees pointing at each other like arrows. "It's a vague memory," he said, "and I'm not quite sure how to explain it, but I remember now who you are."

He opened the sandwiches, and dividing them so we would each have half of both kinds, he handed me two pieces.

I put my can beside me. "So? Who am I?" It made me nervous. Had he seen that awful Sunday afternoon interview show, where the man in the tweed Barneys jacket had asked me how I saw myself in the greater scheme of things? Side by side with other American authors? Did Max see when I had answered, "I would wish to be a daughter to Melville," and the interviewer had made the audience laugh by lifting his open hands to me in shock? *Indeed,* his face had said.

I blushed now, remembering.

"Yes, I remember," Max said. "You are my assignment."

"How's that?"

"Well, that's the part I'm not remembering. I can't remember if I'm supposed to teach *you* something, or if you're supposed to teach *me* something. But you are definitely my assignment."

We sat looking at each other. "Well?" he said.

"Well, what?"

"Well, what do you think of that?"

I shrugged. "I don't know. Will there be a written test? Or a term paper?"

He leapt from his seat and sat roughly beside me, rocking the boat, and grabbing me in a wrestler's lock. "You're feisty today, aren't you?"

"And you're silly today." Despite his arms around me, I managed to bite the liverwurst sandwich. Mustard squirted out along my cheek, and without hesitating he bit my cheek and licked the mustard away.

"Ooh, salty girl on rye," he said.

When the sandwiches were mostly gone, and the garbage tossed in the cabin beside the unopened beer cans, we made ready to go out—a sailing lesson and an opportunity to make sure we were in shape for our longer voyage. The wind was beginning to kick up and the dark edges of the sky were growing thicker.

"Think it's going to rain?" I asked him. I was nervous about storms.

He looked up from adjusting the roaring outboard motor and squinted into the sky. "Rain, shmain," he said, "What's a little water to old tars like us." But suddenly there was my father's booming voice, as though tossed out upon a long ago wake—*Come hither! come hither! my little daughter, And do not tremble so; For I can weather the roughest gale, That ever wind did blow.*

And then me: "He wrapped her warm in his seaman's coat, Against the stinging blast; He cut a rope from a broken spar, And bound her to the mast."

I had said it out loud. Max froze. "What was *that?*"

"What?

"What you said—cut a rope from a broken spar . . ."

Shame nailed me to the bench. A child's shame of a shameless father. "Wreck of the Hesperus," I mumbled. Max didn't turn back to the motor, and it roared on. He just stood there waiting. "It's about a sailor," I told him, "a sailor who takes his daughter out into a storm, and they both die."

"How does it go?"

I tried to make light of it. Make fun of it. "The snow fell hissing in the brine," I chided, "And the billows frothed like yeast."

When Max didn't laugh, I grew bolder, more ridiculous. I began to act it out, clutching my hands beneath my chin and rolling my eyes. " 'O father! I hear the church-bells ring, Oh say, what may it be?' 'Tis a fog-bell on a rock-bound coast!' And he steered for the open sea."

I tossed my head back and threw open my arms, diving past regret. " 'O, father! I see a gleaming light, Oh say, what may it be?' But the father answered never a word, A frozen corpse was he."

Max had folded his arms across his chest and was grinning.

"It gets better," I warned him. And suddenly the shame was my own, the shame of making fun of my father, but I couldn't stop myself, and the bad taste of betrayal began to fill my mouth. "At daybreak, then, on the bleak sea-beach, A fisherman stood aghast, To see the form of a maiden fair, Lashed close to a drifting mast."

My voice cracked with the last line, and I was suddenly afraid that Max would think I was crazy. He was studying me.

"That upsets you?" he asked.

"It's an awful poem," I said. "I don't know why I remember it. I heard it when I was a kid."

He shook his head. "Well, there'll be no frothing billows today," he promised. "Why don't you cut us loose?"

Embarrassed and subdued, I made my way forward and unwound the lines from the cleats. I stared into the dark water at the widening distance between the dock and our bow. The lines coiled around my arms, elbow to hand as my first captain had taught me, and I sat back against the steel mast. I tried to calm the trembling in my rib cage, I took deep breaths.

Max wove the *Nemaste* out past mooring markers that tossed like bobbins from my childhood fishing poles, only no snappers came to nibble, no sharks, no got-aways, no father to bait my hook again. I was wound in a shroud of sadness there on the bow of my boat, and leaning against the mast, where Max couldn't see me, I wound my arms around my legs, and biting my knee I cried.

But Max called. "Look there!"

I looked off to where he pointed and saw a handsome cabin cruiser moored among other boats like itself. Only it stood out because it was covered with huge seagulls as big as turkeys. The boat was strung with cord and plastic flags, obviously a seaman's sort of scarecrow, but it was evident that nothing had frightened these gulls. They sat motionless facing into the breeze, ignoring all the other boats and shitting endlessly.

We started to laugh: Max, probably because it was not the *Nemaste* these gulls had decided upon that summer, and me because I suddenly thought of my childhood, Peter and my parents, and I wondered if things would have been different for me if I'd wound myself in cord and plastic flags.

As Max steered on out into the bay and into the new summer heat, we could see whitecaps beginning to dot the inlet and the seagulls following fisherman who were heading home early. Max proceeded cautiously, slowing the engine. When I turned back to look at his face, to read his expression, he was standing at the tiller, squinting ahead, looking up at the sky, and watching the boats pass us going the other way. He had taken his shirt off and stood bare and tan.

"What do you think?" I called over the roar of the outboard.

He shrugged. "I don't know. It doesn't look that bad. I don't know why everyone's heading back in."

"Maybe they know something we don't know," I suggested. It occurred to me to lash myself to the mast. A part of me wanted to go home, but I ignored it.

We motored further and further out into the center of the bay, while the dark clouds loomed higher and higher, developing layers and depths that didn't seem possible, as if there were cities in the sky. We were alone, our mast and the furled white sails somehow crisper and more finely focused than any other detail around us. A hot wind whipped at the *Nemaste,* and when thunder rumbled in some distant height above us, I crawled back to Max along the gunwale, holding on nervously. If my father had been at the tiller I would not have been afraid. There'd been no storm, no squall, or tornado, even, that he couldn't have tamed, couldn't have ridden through with assurance and calm. I sat on the bench alongside Max.

He looked back at me. "Don't worry," he said, reaching out to touch my head as though he could see the little child that sat before him.

"All the boats are coming in," I said tentatively.

"They're coming in off the ocean. It won't get bad here in the bay. We'll be okay." He sat beside me as the lightning flashed across the water, reflections everywhere. I pressed myself against him, wishing for the bulk and softness of my capable father, but Max was lean and hard. "Get that old slicker on so your clothes don't get wet," he said, motioning with his chin to the cabin.

"Don't *you* want it?" I asked.

He shook his head and began taking his jeans off. Down to bathing trunks, he tossed his jeans into the cabin. A little shift happened in me, from fearful to fearless, from endangered to indestructible. Following his lead and ignoring the yellow slicker I could have had, I took off my T-shirt and my shorts and tossed them into the cabin along with his clothes. The air seemed warm, then cool, and goose bumps rose along my thighs and arms. There we were, motoring in circles, nearly naked beneath a stormy water sky.

He slipped the motor into neutral and we floated. "No sailing today," he finally admitted.

"Mmmm." I trembled.

Max's arm went around me, his hand encircled my waist, and his fingers eased into the waist of my bathing suit. He was smiling. "Ever do it on a boat, in a storm?" he asked.

I leaned against him but said, "I don't want to do it on a boat in a storm." If I was going to die, I'd just want to die. But he laughed, and pulling my head against his shoulder he kissed the top of my head four or five times, his fingers in my hair. "Maybe we should head back then," he said. "Try this again later in the week."

I nodded. The sky exploded above us. Thunder cracked and lightning tore across the sky and hit the shore. Max reached back and eased the motor into forward and we turned toward home. We sat cupped into each other on the bench, Max in front, his hand on the tiller, and me behind, my arms around him and my cheek pressed against his shoulder. The rain was easy at first, wetting us thoroughly, and when we pressed against each other I could taste the sweet drops on his skin. Then it pelted hard.

"Holy shit!" Max shouted. He stood up and I stood with him, pressing myself against his back, the wet lines coiling beneath our bare feet. The rain got harder and harder, faster and louder, until it stung like a million pins, and then like hundreds of pebbles. Hail bounced around the floor of the cockpit like popcorn over a fire. I tried to watch ahead over Max's shoulder to the marina, but the hail hurt my face, forcing my head down and my eyes closed.

"Go into the cabin," he yelled over his shoulder, but I just started to scream and laugh at the same time. I wondered later how he had done it, steered us into the slip alone, with me huddled uselessly on the bench. I was doubled over, my chest against my thighs, my arms wound over my head, laughing hysterically when he was getting us in and tying us up.

"Hey, Queequeg," he called.

I glanced up and he was in the cabin. We were tied to the dock and the motor was off. I dashed through the hailstones into the cabin and collapsed beside him, exhausted. We tumbled over with my arms and legs all around him. "How did you do that? How did you even keep your eyes open?"

"I can weather the roughest gale that ever wind did blow," he said. And then he popped open the beer can and grinned.

$\mathcal{I}$'d never seen my father drink on the boat. And this maybe is why I have loved boats so much. It was the rule on board, not a promise. I wouldn't have trusted a promise. He'd promise my mother that he wouldn't drink at a family dinner or at a christening, and he'd always make the promise, and then when coffee was being served, or when people would start to leave, sometimes I'd hear him whisper to my mother, "I'll be right back, Tina. I need cigarettes." And he would back away from her sheepishly, or else he'd turn his back defiantly, and I'd know that was it. The next time we would see him it would be as though he'd gone out and collected a hurricane in the space between his eyes.

For the longest time he never drank on the boat. But I must tell you this now. And as I begin to tell you, it is not words that come to me first, but rather a slow hum deep in my throat, in my ribs even, beneath my breasts. It is the hum of a tired woman rocking an infant to sleep, or perhaps the hum of a young man pouring himself a drink aboard a boat that gently rocks. I don't know. But there's a humming and a rocking, and as I tell you this I want us to be in a dark and secret place. I would pull a blanket over our heads, like I used to do with Peter, and we would face each other in this darkness. The smell of our childbreaths and our cotton socks and leather school shoes would be with us, and I would begin to tell you, but instead of words this resonant hum would build inside me, and it would be all I'd need. And you would know.

My father drank that day on the boat. For the first time ever, in that place where I felt the safest in the whole world, he drank. Maybe I had known he would that afternoon when the clouds were a rumbling tumble above us and I had gathered the docking lines into my hands, cutting my chances as we left the dock. He drank, and I'd never be the same again. I would come back to shore changed. Altered by regret, scarred, and here, beneath this blanket, I would show you. I would lift my skirt, roll down my sock beneath my ankle, and in the darkness show you the nicks and gouges. Where it happened on me. And as I would show you, you would hear me humming. A tuneless series of notes that string after each other in clusters and crooked lines like senseless barnacles on the bottom of a poorly kept sailboat.

Here and here, see? Mmm, mmm, mmn, mmmmmm...

Max would sometimes ask me questions about Casey. And when I couldn't change the subject or brush him off, I would tell him how it was when she was little, the good things, the things that I could still remember almost as though they had happened to someone else in some other life, or I had seen it on a sitcom.

One night he stopped by very late and we sat out on the front stoop with the porch lights off. The huge maples and sycamores at the front curb towered over us, swishing in a summer air, and the breeze was ripe with honeysuckle and roses. We were lying on the steps, like waterfalls, our feet crossed on the bottom step, our heads resting on the top step. Max's arms were crossed over his chest, while my fingers ran along the wood of the steps touching the rough holes where Christmas lights had once been tacked. We balanced there on the cusp of the summer solstice, me aching and nostalgic for other seasons.

"She was born the end of October," I told him, "and there'll never be anything in the whole world for me like the air in October and the way it feels inside my face. Reminds me of woolen coats, and fancy knitted carriage covers, and big orange pumpkins on people's porches. I see a pumpkin today and I can almost smell Casey's baby breath. And taste and feel her tiny toes on my lips."

I smiled, then chuckled to myself. "I remember one Halloween she was studiously coloring pictures of big pumpkins, and I was telling her about the pumpkin we had bought right before she was born. She ignored me for a while and then she said, 'Mommy, get your shadow out of here.' She was never a sentimental kid, and I was blocking her light."

"Why don't you want me to meet her?" Max finally asked that night.

"And who would I say you were?"

"How about the chimney sweep? Tell her I came to clean the chimney and we hit it off."

I snorted.

"Or tell her I'm selling you a boat. Haven't you told her about the boat yet? We can take her out in it. Take her for a sail. I'll teach her to do stuff, and before you know it the two of you will be doing it on your own."

"I haven't told her about the boat. She's difficult."

"What do you mean?"

I shrugged. "She goes to a special school." I sat up, suddenly nauseous. "Listen, I don't want to talk about it. She doesn't like it when I date. And she doesn't like men around here."

He glanced back at the house, as if pondering her possible appearance at the door. "She would like me," he stated flatly, beginning to knead my shoulders. "Kids always like Chim'man."

"We'll see, Max," I said softly, feeling his fingers ease my restlessness. "Maybe someday."

I didn't think I'd ever gather up the courage or energy I knew I would need, to tell him the whole story. Besides, where would I have begun? The first time she ran? The rolling papers falling out of her pockets? The first arrest perhaps? I guess if I really had to chart it, to mark a beginning and then a waypoint where everything finally fell apart, I guess I could start with the first time she stole, that time she stole money from her friend Jessie's mother. Maybe if I'd been different, maybe if I'd known some other way to react, another way to be a mother, maybe then things might have been different. But I was an empty well, and when Casey lowered her bucket and pulled it up, it was as dry as dust.

Casey was about nine then, and you were watching TV, spread out long and relaxed on the floor. I can still feel myself standing over you — "That was Jessie's mother on the phone."

"Just a minute," you answer, holding up your hand and quieting

me while the set bursts into cheers and leaps. Two men in helmets and shoulder pads hug each other, jumping up and down. In one helmet white teeth flash, a smile trapped in a hard moon. You jot some figures on your numbers pad and then finally look up at me. "Phew! They're wiping them out. A complete upset."

"That was Jessie's mother on the phone."

"Mmm? So?"

"After Casey left yesterday afternoon, she discovered a five-dollar bill missing from her dresser. She said Casey had been in her room. She thought we should know."

You are so easy, relaxed. You sip your beer. I want to kill you, but instead I say, "I could kill her."

"Oh, I don't know. Kids do stuff like that. Did you talk to Casey? Maybe she didn't do it."

" 'Kids do stuff like that'! I never did that. I never stole money. Did you? Did you ever steal money from your friends' mothers when you were nine? I'm so embarrassed. How could she do this?"

Your eyes touch lightly on my face, the pad, the TV, as the commercial finishes up. Your attention slices in half like a hard apple and I don't want it any more. I turn and you do nothing when I run up the stairs to kill our daughter. The door to Casey's room is closed, and when I push it open I find her at her desk with a decapitated Barbie doll. There's a paper funnel down the neck hole, and she's pouring baby powder into it.

"What the hell are you doing?"

She flinches. "Nothing."

"Nothing? Lie one. Mrs. Ferri just called." I grab the powder from her hand and Barbie topples headless onto the desk.

"Yeah." Casey's face grows soft, transforming into what I know is supposed to pass for an honest expression. "So?"

"She's missing some money."

"I didn't take it." Casey stands up to meet whatever is coming.

"A little touchy, aren't we?" I hold my palm out to her. "Let's have it."

"Have what?"

"The money. You know exactly what."

"I didn't take it. Honest."

I stare at her. I am transformed. I am a jailer, a torturer, filled with shame. Without feeling I watch as my empty palm claps across my daughter's cheek. I am my mother. "You're lying."

But Casey stands her ground, eyes meeting mine. "No, Ma, I didn't take it." Her eyes are like two black tunnels to the pit of her head, and I can see right in. I can see the lie.

"Give me the money, Casey."

"I don't have it."

A football cheer rises from downstairs like smoke, and again the slap, this time her ear, harder than I mean to.

Casey wails. "You never believe me. I tell the truth and you don't believe me."

"Casey. I am leaving this room before I kill you, and I'll be back in five minutes. You will have that money in your hand or you will be in a world of trouble."

"I don't have it! I don't have it!"

I leave Casey's door open and slam the bathroom door behind me to sit on the edge of the tub. I am shaking, my legs, up the back of my neck. "I didn't beat her," I reassure myself. "I only hit her twice." I press my burning palms into my eyes. I would cry, but crying is for sadness. There is nothing for rage. A beer commercial plays in the background. I turn on the hot water and lean my cheek against the cold sink. Casey's crying has stopped, and now I hear mutterings and slammings. All my strength keeps me at the sink and away from her. Steam begins to seep into my hair, but like fog on an old steel bridge, it does nothing. Then there is a gentle scraping, a sliding, a bucket lowering into the well. Quietly, a badly wrinkled *five-dollar bill slips beneath the crack under the door. I win, we lose. The bucket goes back up empty.*

It's hard for me to recall the exact details of her first arrest; there were so many visits to family court, and soon they all blended together. It never changed. Family court in the fall was like family court in the summer. Rain or shine. The same sullen guards at the doors. The same wooden chairs, the fearsome judges hidden behind closed doors. There was a terrible sameness, like a sore throat is always the same.

I would go alone. Ten or twelve times, whatever it was. I would pass through the metal detectors with lowered eyes, have my pocketbook searched, and then I'd be directed upstairs to the waiting room outside the judges' hearing rooms. It was a large room with two sections of hard chairs facing each other, like a standoff. Mostly it was women with their children, many of them poor and black, coming to demand child support. Most of the white women were gaudily dressed in dark silk suits and flashy jewelry. These were the lawyers.

And then there were the men who skulked in the hallways, smoking, beckoned there by summonses and edicts, like bad boys called to task. I remember how these men would look at me. The eye contact, the body gestures. If we'd been just a little more savage, these men with their backs up against the wall, fighting for children and paychecks and pride, would have strutted naked before me, in display. Homo sapiens like peacocks. Threatened. Tails spread. Hands would squeeze their own balls. "I'm a man," they each would've said.

I guess I do remember the first court appearance; it is the only one you came to. You are there, a half hour late, as is your custom, but still earlier than Casey, who has not yet been delivered by the people who have her in custody. The cloud of Scotch around you shocks me. God knows why. It is as familiar to me as the odor of my own skin, yet when I am away from it for any length of time, alone and clear of it, it always jolts me with a vague sort of terror.

We greet each other. No, Casey hasn't arrived yet.

I tell you what the guard said, that the couple of kids coming over from the detention center could be two or three hours late.

"Jesus," you say. "I can't stay that long. I've got work to do."

I try for a split second to find your puffy eyes through your tinted eyeglasses and then I look around the room. You're the only one here today who's missing work. Everyone else is here for kicks. *I don't actually say this. I remember thinking it, adding to the volumes of things I had never actually said to you.*

Casey arrives two hours later with a social worker, a woman I've spoken to only over the phone. They arrive like two related strangers — they could be mother and daughter — and I think that I am the only one in the room who knows about the lines that bind me to this angry girl. I am the only one who can see the thick lines disappearing beneath the dark and turbulent waters. And only I can feel its anchor's sharpness dug in the deep sands of my heart.

She nods to me from the doorway while the social worker signs her in, and then the social worker introduces herself to me. She calls Casey "Cassandra," and Casey strews her rumpled bags on the floor at my feet. I think of them being searched. Then the two of you, father and daughter, retreat like comrades to sit across the room. I remember how you give Casey a cigarette. It's the first time I actually see her smoke. Her tiny toes dancing along my chin, her sweet milky breath, her full lips turn to you and your lit match.

I wonder if anyone would have arrested me that day had I pulled a silver gun from my bag and shot you. Yes, I would have preferred you dead then, but that thought, like the sharp end of a splinter gone too deep, burned with a pain too horrifying to hold. So I didn't look at you.

Another hour and they call out "Brinkley, Elizabeth and Cassandra," and we are all ushered into the hallway outside the judge's hearing room. You and the social worker come, too, even though your names have not been shouted into the smoke-filled room.

I am brittle and tight, preparing to say and to admit that I can no longer live with my own child, I can no longer care for her, I have exhausted all strength and reason. I clasp my hands together in front of me and hold my breath against the stench of Scotch that fills the airless hallway. The doors open and we are ushered into a bright, clean room. The judge shuffles papers as we approach. I go forward with Casey—who has grown stormy and sullen—and the social worker, while you drop into the back row of seats. The judge asks who you are, staying in the back the way you do, and the social worker mumbles that you are the father, but you are not involved in the court action. The judge and I meet eyes and I imagine he looks at me with pity.

The statements are rattled off. Minor was found tossing burning papers out window of home onto roof. Fire department summoned. School found drug paraphernalia in her locker. Continuously out overnight unsupervised. Nine accounts of running away.

The judge peers over his glasses at her. "How old are you, Cassandra?"

"Sixteen."

"She's thirteen, your honor," the social worker says.

He stares at my daughter. "This is quite a track record you're stacking up against yourself, young lady," he says, shaking the papers before him.

Casey shrugs. "So what," I hear her mumble. I cannot believe my ears.

"Your mother claims you're unmanageable," he states.

"And you're pretty fucking ugly," she comes back.

The judge hesitates, staring at her. He looks at me. I am not *breathing yet tears stream down my cheeks, my neck.* Take her, *I silently beg him.* Take her.

He bangs the gavel. "Remanded to Our Lady of the Shepherds. Bring her back to me in six months." He begins stamping papers and handing them to clerks. It's over. We are dismissed.

"Big fucking deal," Casey says, and the social worker, stone-faced, leads her out past me and past you. I feel like I am walking through deep water. Against a current. In lead shoes. You wait for me and step out behind me as I pass. "I guess you're happy now," you say quietly. I look at you and think: full circle. There's a full circle here somewhere, and if I could only think clearly for a moment I would see it. But I keep on walking, not looking back, not looking ahead, vaguely wondering where this full circle began.

Later when I am in the shower with my forehead pressed against the green tiles, the hot, steaming water rinses over me. The house is empty. She is gone. Casey is gone from my life, leaving a familiar emptiness. And suddenly I feel like a dangling plastic fish on a baby's mobile that has gone haywire. All balance is gone, and no matter how hard I scrub and no matter how long I stand there with water streaming over me, I cannot rinse away the sorrow, or the lingering stench of Scotch.

$\mathcal{M}$ax decided that my job—a few days before our sea journey was to begin—would be to take my car out to Charlie's country house and leave it there so that once the *Nemaste* was safely anchored at his dock, we could drive home. I was to take the train back alone, and his reasoning was that after two or three days sailing we'd both be exhausted and appreciate the luxury of a car ride home. That didn't make too much sense to me, knowing that since it was my car, I'd be the one who, exhausted, would probably do the long drive home. But seeing as how it would probably be Max who'd be doing most of the serious sailing, and I could have done none of this without him, I didn't object. I drove out.

It was a Saturday and I had just shaken a nasty headache, the kind that lasts for a couple of days and then leaves, changing my perspective on everything. A knife slides out of my left eye, rendering me painfree, euphoric. The very road I traveled on seemed slicked with grace.

I drove out over the Long Island plains, along the six-lane parkways, not just admiring, but beholding the long stretches of trees and grass and wild flowers, and then I headed up through Noyack, along a twisting, curving Grand Prix sort of road where after nearly two hours of the gentlest of driving, I found a deli and stopped for a Styrofoam cup of coffee and a bran muffin. I couldn't help but remember the time I had come out with Casey. With a child along I had stopped at a 7-Eleven and we had bought slurpies, gigantic, sweet, icy drinks, so thick they needed special wide straws, so cold I had gotten a pain deep in my ribs. Now, driving on, I balanced the hot coffee between my legs and picked at the bran muffin that lay broken and crumbling in the empty seat beside me.

There was no wait for the ferry, and like a smooth machine the emotionless men collected fares, pulled the guardrails shut, and started the short journey across water to the island. I got out of my car like a tourist and stared into the rushing water. When I'd been with Casey on this ferry I had been landbound, seeing the water as someone with roots would see it, but now I was a sailor. I no longer saw the earth as bodies of land with water at the edges. Now it was all water, oceans, bays, rivers, waterways, with land merely here and there. I turned and watched as a lone sailor, hunkering down at the helm, piloted his sailboat through the wake of the ferry. I watched as his boat tossed, the sails luffed the slightest bit, and he touched his hand to his hat. I held very still and recognized one of those moments when time ceases, when everything comes into alignment, the whole earth is perfect, life, absolute, and then the man took his hand from his hat and sailed on.

Charlie was already there when I arrived. At first there was no answer to my knock. Next to the front door was a hanging pot draped with wonderful purple and pink flowers that I thought would look to a child like telephones for wood nymphs. The brick stoop was swept clean, and on the door was a delicate wreath of grapevine and silk flowers. I chuckled to myself and went looking for him.

Around the house, neatly shuttered, and chicly weathered, a path of slate led to the garden in the back and the view of the water. Above the sparkling and dark waters of the bay, the sky was like an illustration in a children's book—perfect with huge billowing puffs of clouds—and the blue was the same color as the rocking chair I had bought in Georgia that time when I was newly pregnant with Casey.

Beneath this blue sky, and surrounded by stakes and spindly, new tomato plants, hunched Charlie. I wanted to stand there a while without him seeing me, to watch him, to see how he was with himself when he thought he was alone. I had a friend once who always looked inside people's medicine cabinets, and swore that that was the only way to really know someone. She was wrong. The way to know is to be silent, to not add yourself, but to just watch. I knew if I waited long enough Charlie would do something so profound and meaningful that I would be compelled to say, "Oh yes! That's who Charlie is!"

I stopped in the grass, and the air about my head acknowledged and accepted without movement the heavily laden bee that labored by. Then Charlie looked up at me. "Ellie!"

"Finish what you're doing, Charlie," I said, going toward him slowly and holding up my hands for him to stay where he was. "I want to watch."

He lifted his straw hat with the garden fork still in his grip and wiped his balding crown with the back of his hand. I loved Charlie out here in the country. He had this country persona. If he'd been a woman he wouldn't have worn makeup, but being a man, he donned a straw hat.

"Roads okay coming out?" he asked.

"Fine. I flew."

I went to him, gingerly weaving through the stakes and plants, and knelt opposite him. I watched as he scraped a perfect circle around the tomato plant between us and then slipped off his work glove. He dipped into the bag of plant food next to him and pulled out a handful of white grains. "Open wide, you little buggers," he said as he sprinkled the granules into the circle and churned it into the soil with the garden fork.

I laughed, and reaching out I gently rubbed my finger over a small swelling tomato that was still hard and green, and its wilting yellow blossom dropped into my palm. Then it was mine, and like a broken fingernail that I didn't know where to put, I pushed it into the back pocket of my jeans.

"Do you do well with tomatoes out here?" I asked him.

"Last year I had tomatoes a pound and a half each, juicy as peaches and as sweet as honeysuckle."

"And I'll bet red as fire engines."

He looked at me quizzically. "What fire engines? What's a fire engine? I don't know from fire engines out here.

"To grow them so big," he said, "you have to pull off these suckers, the extra stems that grow in the crooks of the other branches." He grasped one. "They weaken the plant." When he snapped it off, it didn't break clean, but tore a long fiber of stem nearly to the base of the plant.

I cringed. "Ouch."

"Life's a jungle out here," he told me and smiled.

Suddenly a cardinal landed on the stake right next to us and we froze. We looked straight at him. He was brilliant red, twitching and making clicking sounds. Quickly he jerked his head in and out of the rising tomato branches and pulled out a fat green worm. He was startled when we laughed, and flew off in a frenzy, taking the worm.

"We all cooperate out here," Charlie said, coming up off his knees with a groan. "I provide the tomato plants for the worms to breed on, and the cardinals provide the service of removing the worms before they eat the tomatoes."

"Kind of like doormen," I quipped, and even though he had the tomato food bag in one hand and the fork in the other, Charlie put his arm about my shoulder.

"Glad to see you, Ellie. It's so good to have you out here again. It's been a long time." I touched my head to his shoulder for the slightest instant, so that we both could have pretended I hadn't.

Charlie's kitchen was his pride and joy. I've heard people talk about near-death experiences where a figure appears to them in a kind of white light that they cannot describe. That was the color of Charlie's kitchen—indescribably heaven white. And every appliance, every gadget looked like it either came from one of two places: a treasure barn or the Museum of Modern Art. I loved it, so clean and stark and so unlike anything I would have guessed about Charlie seeing him in his office. He had had the kitchen redone since I had been out there, and he basked in my sighs and gasps. "Oh, Charlie, this is wonderful. And look at this huge window. You can watch the boats on the bay."

Drying his hands, he touched a spot on the wall, *touched* it, and sunken lights in the ceiling began to glow brighter and brighter. "Jesus, Charlie! I'm impressed."

"Look at this," he told me, and touching a finger to a panel, a drawer silently rolled out, neatly organized with baking trays and pans. Then another and another. He turned to the refrigerator that was disguised as a wall. It lit up like *Space Odyssey* while he removed fresh vegetables and tossed them on the cooking island in the center of the room.

He tossed three different kinds of lettuce onto the counter, yellow peppers, cucumbers, a cluster of fresh basil, mushrooms, a hunk of turkey, and a parcel of carrots bound together by their leaves like ballerinas hung by their ponytails. He drew out a large bottle of imported water, and dropping two perfect mint leaves into our glasses he poured us each a drink. "Sit," he ordered, drawing a stool up to the island. "Tell me about your next book. Talk to me."

I did as he said, clasping my hands before me and staring at his rectangular Chinese knife as he sliced through everything. Off with stems, off with skin, off with the plastic wrap, off with the ballerinas' heads.

"It hasn't completely jelled yet, Charlie. But I feel it coming. I really do. All this stuff about a kid, a little girl and her father's boat."

"It's all so surprising to me, Ellie. I had no idea you had any boats in your background. *You Again* didn't even have a body of water. I thought about it. I went looking through it last night. Not even a glass of water."

I shrugged. "It never came up."

"Well," he said gently, "it's all different now. Your perspective, your view, probably even your voice. Now that Casey's gone. Do you think you'll deal with her hit-and-run in this book?"

Hearing the lie coming back to me, I actually put my hands over my face, hiding my eyes, my cheeks, my chin from him. I rubbed my forehead with my fingertips, remembering my vanished headache, and still feeling its pale residue along a single nerve at a certain spot on my brow. "Who knows, Charlie. Who knows. I don't even know if the little girl represents Casey."

He looked at me, puzzled.

"Maybe it's me."

"Everything we look at is 'me,'" he answered. "The universe is a mirror we hold up to ourselves, from the homeless man in the street to the mother with a child. If I can see it, it is 'me.'"

He was tearing the lettuce leaves and tossing them into a large glass bowl. "Like in a dream," I agreed. "Every part is me. But I don't know. I can't see it in this book yet."

Charlie began chopping the yellow pepper into paper-fine strips. "Well, you know what Pirandello used to say."

I stared at him. "Not only don't I know what Pirandello used to say, Charlie, I don't even know who that is. Who? Your old Latin professor?"

Charlie stopped chopping and looked at me thoughtfully. "Your ignorance slash innocence sometimes baffle me, Ellie." He went on chopping. "Luigi Pirandello, Italian dramatist. Awarded the Nobel prize for literature, I believe in the thirties. He was of the Grotesque school."

"Grotesque? As in Djuna Barnes?"

"As in."

I nibbled on some peppers. "I wouldn't like him."

"Probably not." Charlie silently sprinkled the julienned peppers over the multicolored lettuce.

"So what did he used to say?"

"He said, 'One cannot choose what to write, one can only choose to face it.'"

The hair stood up on the back of my neck and down my spine. "I would hate him."

Charlie became very still, his hands on either side of the

salad bowl. He was looking at me thoughtfully. The salad was done. In the distance I could hear a cardinal stealing worms.

Then Charlie's fingers squeaked along the glass edge of the bowl. "I know you'll choose to face it, Ellie," he said, lifting the bowl. "Good writers have to."

Later, after we had eaten, he took me out to show me the new dock, soon to be the *Nemaste*'s summer home. The wood was still fresh and unweathered. It was a nice-sized dock for a man without a boat. Already he had hung black tires over one side to protect docking crafts.

"But why a dock, Charlie? You don't even have a boat."

"I had to do something with this waterfront strip. Besides, I do have friends who sometimes come in their boats." He seemed defensive and I smiled.

I remembered the old, salty woman who came that day in a crusty clammer's boat, pulling her boat up on the dirt and bringing Charlie a basket of crabs. "Like Annie, you mean?"

"Yes, there's Annie, and a few others. Besides, a dock looks nicer and it increases the property value."

"For your heirs," I teased.

He frowned.

"Will you adopt me, Charlie? I'll do you proud. I swear I will."

"If you're good," he mocked.

We stood there side by side on the dock facing the bay, breathing the air. We grew silent, lulled the way water lulls, like a blessing that descends on a bed when a clean sheet is snapped in the air over it. All was well.

"You know," Charlie said after a while, "I really notice the weather living out here. The color of the sky. The wind on the water. The different sunrises and sunsets. In the city the only way I notice it is when I have to remember to carry an umbrella to work, or sometimes if I'm really astute I might notice the sunshine is coming in a certain window at a new angle—but out here weather takes on a kind of dignity." He went on. "It's as though for years I've known some bland, uninteresting character who barely makes an impression on me, only to discover one day that he can play the piano like a typhoon in my heart." I glanced at Charlie. He was almost handsome in an old, tweedy kind of way.

I smiled there, looking at Charlie's oddly youthful face beneath his bald head, and then suddenly out of the corner of my eye, I saw something, something wonderful. There was a huge sailing vessel, an odd classic, like a *Mayflower* or something coming around the bend, around a jut of land in the distance. "Look at that, Charlie!" I cried. "Time warp! What is that?"

"She's out of Greenport," he told me, "some tourist ride boat. She's a replica, here for the summer and comes by every day about this time."

I watched her, a yearning beginning somewhere deep inside me, and I crossed my arms to keep myself still.

"So, who's this guy you'll be sailing out here with?" Charlie asked abruptly.

"The guy who's selling me the sailboat. Max." I didn't take my eyes off the old ship.

Charlie had a dumb smile on his face. "Oh? Is this part of the deal, or does Ellie Brinkley have a love interest in her life at last? Is this a main character, or a supporting character? Or is he an antagonist? Or maybe a red herring."

Now it was my turn to be defensive. I shrugged, and turning started back to the house. "I'm not sure. I don't know him very well. He's a nice guy. Young." I wasn't sure how to talk to Charlie about me having a lover after all this time. I didn't know what he would think of me, and I realized I was blushing, embarrassed. I worried about how Max would look to Charlie. Would he think Max was too young for me? Too much of a nutty character? And then I thought of something more troubling.

"Listen, Charlie," I said nervously, turning back to him. "He doesn't know about Casey."

"What do you mean? That you had a daughter?"

"No, he knows."

"Well, what do you mean?"

"Listen, just don't mention Casey while he's here. Please, Charlie." I held his eyes. "Please."

He nodded agreement, but I could tell he wasn't comfortable with it.

"I have my reasons."

"I'm sure you do."

I insisted on washing the few dishes from lunch before leaving to get the train back home. The two of us stood before the gleaming sink, me building a pile of bubbles, and Charlie standing poised and ready with a stiff linen towel in his hand.

The bubbles reminded me of Casey. "Case and I used to wash dishes together when she was little," I said thoughtfully. "She'd say, 'Look, Ma. See the dirt? Now watch.' And then with her tiny little hands, bubbles up to her elbows, she'd swoosh around in the water and like a magician come up with a clean bubbly dish. 'Bobbity boo!'" I held up a rinsed clear dish to Charlie and he took it from me. "And I'd dry the bubbly dish while she did her next magical trick."

Charlie was quiet and let me go on. "You know, one night while we were doing dishes—we always had these deep conversations while this was going on—one night she asked me if she was Jewish or Christian or American. At school she had learned it was the first night of Hanukkah, and she was sure she was missing out on something. I told her that I guessed we were Christians, way back somewhere, and she was kind of disappointed and embarrassed, I think because she had told her friend she was an American. I had to explain to her that she was that, too."

I put a handful of silverware on the rack and Charlie dried them one at a time, placing them back singly in the quiet drawer.

"Then she wanted to talk about the word *Christian,* how it's a combination of Christ and gin." I laughed and looked at Charlie, who smiled when I turned to him. "Imagine that," I said softly. "Christ and gin.

"Then, I don't know why, but I asked her if she knew how to pray. I'd never taught her anything like that and I was wondering what she'd picked up. So she tells me, yes, she knows how to pray, and she folds her ten little bubbly fingers under her chin. 'I do this,' she says, 'and I think about God and the seasons and how they change.' Isn't that nice, Charlie?"

He was waiting for more things to dry. "Kids are wonderful."

I soaped up a glass, remembering Casey's small hand fitting in the swirling glass, remembered her asking for more soap. "And then you know what she said, Charlie?" I looked at him and suddenly felt my eyes filling as he sadly looked back at me. "She said, 'Ma, if someone comes and steals you, I'll run after them. And I'll bring you back.'

"Then she wanted to know if I was going to die, do you believe that? What was she? Five? Six? Her grandmother had just died."

"What did you tell her?" Charlie was leaning against the edge of the counter now, waiting, making me feel like I had all the time in the world to tell him these things, these little memories, like buttons that came spilling out of old pockets.

"I said that someday I'd die, but not now. 'I'll be with you as long as you need me, Casey. Nanna was sick and her body was old and she must have been glad when she died. But I won't die for a long time. Not as long as you need me.'

"God, I went on and on, blabbering at her like an ignorant adult, telling her some nonsense about how someday we'd all be in heaven and she'd meet her great-grandmother, who she was named after." Standing there at Charlie's sink, I sobbed and then laughed. "'Hello, Cassandra,' the angel would say, 'My name is Cassandra, too.'"

"She used to stand on a kitchen chair to do the dishes and I remember picking her up that night and holding her, her legs and arms wrapped around me." I closed my eyes and held very still. "I can remember how she cried, not bawling like a kid, but quiet, like an older person, with just her chest heaving and her breath heavy. I was so sure. I was so sure that night."

I heard the sound of a distant boat horn.

"Sure of what, Ellie?"

"Sure she'd outlive me."

I opened my eyes and looked at Charlie.

"Oh, God, Charlie."

*S*ometimes when I ride alone on a train, I am certain I have walked through other lives before. It becomes clear to me that I am looking through the eyeholes of a temporal mask. I become all eyes, all observer, and I will even look down at my hands to see who it is I am this time. On the train ride home from Charlie's that day, I did this and thought, this is how that replica ship must feel, hidden behind the ghost of another ship, sailing in the wind of another's spirit.

The ride was long and tiring. My whole body ached and I was ashamed that I had cried in front of Charlie. So much for professional boundaries. Such stuff seemed impossible for me. I felt stiff and sore, especially across my shoulders and down into my arms, as though all day long I had been carrying a child who had grown too big to carry. Numbly I leaned my forehead against the window and watched the flat plains and then the houses go by.

Familiar tract houses lined up along the side of the railroad tracks, their black, empty eyes looking out at me. Some of their yards had round turquoise blue pools, some had decks and flowers, a few had barbecue grills and picnic tables. They all looked neat and orderly from that raised distance, and they all seemed small, so small that if, inside, someone was hitting someone else, I was sure it couldn't have hurt very much.

During the long night before my journey with Max was to begin, I bolted upright in bed again and again. I would be nearly asleep, so relaxed in the summer heat that my skin felt like the surface of a calm pond, and then abruptly I would be sitting on the gunwale of my father's boat, feeling it jibe, feeling the boom fly too hard, and then feeling myself come loose of the gunwale and of the line that I held on to, and I would hover rigidly above the churning dark water—bam!—I was in my room, panting, on my bed, sweating, knotted in my sheets, trembling. Or I'd be at the helm and Casey'd be up at the bow. "Sit down, Casey!" I'd call. I couldn't see her through the swollen sails, and I knew she didn't hear me. "Sit down!" I'd call over and over, and then suddenly I'd see her in the water, drifting toward the outboard motor that roared behind me, and I'd see it draw closer to her like a train coming toward a damsel tied on the tracks, and yet it was the expression on her face that bolted me upright again in bed. Bam! "Case!" I shouted aloud into the empty house.

No sound came back to me. Panting, I laid back and pulled

the sheets up to my chin. So quiet. How I ached to hear some-one in a long-ago room down the hall, someone easing out of bed, someone leaving my mother and padding heavily toward me. My door would open, and his shadow would fill the door-way. " 'S that you, patootie?" he'd whisper.

When my father came home that day and told us all he'd bought a sailboat, my mother was furious. We needed a new rug, the house needed to be painted, Peter needed special shoes. We didn't need a sailboat—of all ridiculous things. But my father had been patient and kind to her. He called it a poor man's sailboat, real cheap, he said. He'd gotten it from one of his buddies at the tavern, which made my mother's face tighten another notch. But nothing could rob him of this happiness, not even my mother, and I welcomed it.

After we'd been out on the boat a couple of times, my father decided that we all needed to know first aid and emergency procedures. He taught Peter and me how to bandage a sprained wrist or a sprained ankle, and Peter and I would wrap each other like mummies in Ace bandages, secured with funny little silver tabs that bit into the skin-colored bands. He brought home a horn and showed us how if ever we were in danger to blast it five short times, like this, and then my mother would come in from the kitchen and tell us to stop. If ever Peter were to fall overboard it was my job to yell "Man overboard!" and point at him. Nothing else. I would just point and point and point and never take my eye off him until my father guided the boat back to where I was pointing and Peter was pulled safely into the boat. And it was Peter's job to point at me, endlessly point until *I* was safe, and I wondered about that, because I had seen how my brother would throw up on the boat and not pay attention to anything.

And then my father taught us what he called "artificial

respiration," and the words reminded me of the "artificial flower" shop down on the avenue where they sold wax flowers on wire stems.

"Pretend you can't breathe," my father says to me, drawing me to him. "Lie on the floor here, on your stomach, and pretend you've just been pulled out of the water. You were drowning."

I think of Abbott and Costello. My father told me once how one of them had a child who drowned in his Hollywood swimming pool, his own child whom he loved, dead, floating in the beautiful pool, and it was lucky we were poor. Rich people had big troubles. It is lucky we aren't rich. I hope having a poor man's sailboat doesn't make us rich.

"Now—" He sounds serious as he kneels by my head. I close my eyes and rest my cheek on the worn and scratchy living room rug. I am near death. "Hold your breath, Elizabeth. Fill your lungs with air, just as they'd be filled with water. And see if you can *not* breathe."

I inhale as he kneels by my head. He pulls my elbows toward him and places my hands under my face. I am nearly dead, very rich, and full of water. His hands spread on my back, a finger for each rib; I am small. I feel him rise over me and all his weight sinks into his hands and whoosh! I am startled to feel all the air rush from my mouth. I laugh. "Wait a minute! No fair!"

He sinks back and pulls my elbows, my arms up and toward him. "See how hard it is not to breathe when someone does this to you?" he asks. "Try again. See if you can hold it."

Serious again, I close my eyes. I am very, very rich. I am full of water and gold jewelry, weights that have pulled me to the bottom of my huge shimmering pool. My maids and my chauffeur stand around wringing their hands—"She's dead! She's dead! Even her money can't save her."

Then my father's hands, his weight—whoosh—against all

my will to be dead, to be drowned, he makes me breathe, but I don't laugh now. It's a battle of wills, a rhythmic—*I won't breathe, breathe, child, inhale, I won't breathe*—over and over. I fill my lungs and he pushes them empty, and then thinking not to fill them, I remain slack. He pushes, nothing, but then as he pulls my arms, he leans back, and against my will, my lungs fill with air and the smell of the gray rug.

Lying in my bed, years later—or is it millions of miles away?—I felt myself breathe, breathe deeply as if to please my father, to bring him to me one last time.

Before Max was due to arrive at the house, I checked my computer over and over to make sure I had unplugged it, in case there was a lightning storm while I was gone. In case what little was left in there would somehow trickle out the outlet while I was away. I double-checked the locks on the windows, opened the washing machine, wiped the refrigerator shelves, paced the rooms. I had never been away before. I could never remember leaving the house empty for days, with no one there but the ghosts and the recollections. I even found myself wondering what if Casey came back? and needed to remind myself that such a thing was impossible. Without wanting to, I remembered seeing her cautious face one morning framed in the bottom half of the dining room window, looking in, after a night out, after I had locked the doors and the windows against her once she was gone.

But no one was coming back here ever again, except for me. I carried out my duffel bags and then lugged the food chest down the front steps and out to the driveway. It was pale early morning, and the cicadas were already shrill in the trees above me. Within moments Max's white truck came up the street and I suddenly realized that much of my anxiety had been the unformed thought that he might not come, might not show up at all, and instantly I was awash in relief. All I could see of him as he turned in the driveway was his flashing white teeth.

He jumped out the instant the truck stopped and came after me. He swept me up in his hard workman's arms and tumbled us over the food chest. "I'm so horny the crack of dawn looks good," he said. "Have you ever done it in the driveway?"

"Not in broad daylight."

He froze. "At night? I'll bet it was that young guy, right? The one you said could do it seven times."

Face to face, hugging him, I was laughing, thinking fast. "He wasn't the only man in my life, you know."

"Then who?"

"The oil-burner man."

"No kidding. Right here in the driveway? He delivers at night?"

I pushed Max away and he stood up and pondered the driveway. "Imagine that," he mused.

"Help me with these, Max." I tossed a duffel bag at him, and looping it over his shoulder he hoisted the food chest up and carried it to the cab of his truck.

"Fair winds today. Ten to twelve knots." He tossed my bag in the back over his. "And some rain expected tomorrow night, but we might be there by then."

I handed him another bag. "I hope so, but I packed a slicker, just in case. I'm ready for anything."

He was looking at me. "You have a black smudgy circle under each eye."

"Couldn't sleep," I told him, and I touched my fingers to my lids. He took my hands away and gently kissed each one, slowly, fully with his warm lips.

"There," he said. "They're gone."

"Oh, thank you, kind sir."

We grinned at each other, with days ahead of us, with number three and an entire adventure ahead of us. "It's good luck to kiss a chimney sweep," he said softly, "especially before a long and dangerous voyage." I kissed him and felt his lips open to me.

Then, "Are we ready?"

"Aye, aye, Captain," I answered.

"Casey all taken care of?"

"She's with friends."

Then we headed out to the old boatyard one last time. The *Nemaste* would never be so close again, docked within such a quick drive. It seemed absurd to buy her and then move her far away. "They'll be good sailing out where we're taking her, right, Max? Way out there?" I asked, wanting reassurance.

"The best," he said, "a sailor's paradise. It's deep, and it's open, and you won't have a tenth of the boat traffic out there."

"Tell me I'm not out of my mind."

Max stopped at a light. He leaned over and nuzzled his face into my lap, making me smile and touch his hair. "You're nuts," I heard him mumble.

The light changed and we were moving. "Aren't you going to miss a lot of work these couple of days?" I asked. "Aren't there chimneys waiting for you?"

"Are you kidding?" he laughed. "With all this dough from the boat, I'm going to retire now. Who needs a job! I make myself rich—"

"By making my wants few," I finished for him. "Four thousand dollars will cover very few wants, for a very short period of time."

"Yes, well, I've given new meaning to the words *eking out an existence*. Actually there's not much work in the summer. It's not till the fall that all the panic-stricken people call. They'll want to build a fire on a cold and blustery night, and suddenly they'll feel something evil lurking around the hearth. That's when they call me."

I turned away from him and smiled out the window. I wanted to make love with him again. It had been a while. And I felt a stirring inside, a thirsty longing now that he was near me.

I could see the *Nemaste* gleaming in the morning sun. Waiting for us. We unloaded the car and made a couple of trips down to the dock, where we dumped everything at the spot where she was tied.

"We could have used a wheelbarrow," I muttered on the final trip.

"Like Queequeg and Ishmael," he said and I laughed.

"You know, I remember my father reading that to my mother in bed when I was little." I told him this and sort of held my breath, remembering and forgetting, like a pinwheel blowing.

"*My* mother watched it on the 'Million Dollar Movie' every night," he said. "Remember that? How they'd show a movie five or six times a day for the whole week? The same movie." Then, like a ten-year-old boy, he made crashing noises, spraying and exploding. "Storms and waves breaking over their heads, and the mighty white whale gets away."

Max took a leap from the dock onto the boat and wrapped his arm around the mast. "Now hear me," he said. "See this Spanish gold ounce? Whosoever of ye finds me that white whale, he shall have this Spanish gold ounce, m'boys!" He was peg-legged, he was hook-handed, he was diabolical. In his imagination and mine, he hammered a doubloon to the mast. Then he froze as if in terror. "Tick, tick, tick."

"Oh, stop," I laughed. "That's *Peter Pan*. Don't even joke

about confusing them." I handed over the duffel bags. And together we struggled with the food chest.

Max must have hosed the *Nemaste* down and polished her a day or so before. There wasn't a leaf or a scuff mark anywhere, and her old, dried-out teak was stained dark with oil. He stashed all our things in the cabin as I handed them down to him. Once he was up in the V berth, pushing and rearranging, I heard him mutter, "My harpoons, my harpoons? Where are they?"

Somehow all that helped. It would have been too hard that morning to have simply been my father's grown daughter — older than he was himself on that last sail — on board for my first real journey in so many long years. Laughing this way with Max was better. I was Ishmael, and he was Captain Hook. I was Queequeg, and he was Tinker Bell. The memory of an aging young man who betrayed and was betrayed one night on the phantom tail of a bottle of bourbon was far from my mind. And I gave no thought to the shadow of my own white whale somewhere in the depths of the Great South Bay, a whale who had once tasted my flesh, and was still looking for me.

*M*ax was careful and neat about his new charts. Unlike my father, he didn't roll them like an old sailor, but folded them in a special sequence that let them unfold and open in useful ways. The wind was off our stern, so the sails were far out and we were level and steady in the water.

"Who taught you how to fold them like that?" I called to Max. He was in the cabin leaning over the table, studying the current chart, and I was at the tiller, trying to keep the compass at a steady ninety-degree reading. I wavered now and then, but always kept the land off to port, always there, smooth and low.

"A guy named Patty McShay," he answered. "An Irish sailor I'd met in Newport. And a sailor's sailor he was, old Patty. Seaweed in his ears, a compass where his glass eye was s'posed to be, and once a day he wiped his arse with anchor chains."

"What a guy."

Max came up the steps from the cabin. "Yes, he was. Taught me everything I know."

"Then you must be quite a sailor, too." Max sat next to me and I pressed my thigh into his.

"Only one difference, though," he said. "Old Patty was a real no-nonsense sort, and me, well, I'm a regular old yes-nonsense kind of guy, you know what I mean?" His arms were around me and he buried his face in my neck, then down in my breasts, and I laughed.

"One odd thing though," he said, stopping in midembrace and staring out to sea. "The man couldn't swim a stroke." He looked at me. "Imagine that. A sailor all his life and never got wet, except for spray."

He looked at me and I didn't say anything, suddenly nervous and uncertain.

"You know why that is? Why Patty never learned to swim?"

I shrugged.

"Off Ireland, where the fisherman sail and work, the ocean is so god-awful cold all the time that if your ship were to go down, they say you'd be better off to drown immediately than die a slow death, freezing, trying to swim to shore."

"I can't swim."

"What do you mean?"

"I never learned."

"You grew up on Long Island, and you never learned to

swim?" Max was incredulous. "Your parents never took you to the beach?"

I shook my head.

"They never gave you swimming lessons?"

I wound the mainsheet around my hand and checked the compass.

"That's child abuse," he insisted. Then he stood and reached across the cockpit to the bench compartment. He pulled out two orange life preservers and came at me. He put my feet through two armholes and pulled it up around my legs and made me sit on it.

"Max!"

"Can't swim? Why didn't you tell me you couldn't swim?" He pushed my arms into the other one and tied it behind my back. He stood back and looked at me. "Now that's very kinky." He took a life preserver ring and looped it over my head. "Now you're safe," and sitting down next to me he clapped his hand over my knee protectively.

"Max." I squirmed out of the bottom jacket and tossed it back into the compartment. Then I turned for him to untie the other. "The boat's not going to sink. I'm not going to fall over-board. And if I should fall over," I handed him the ring, "just toss me this and come back for me."

He shook his head, and then giving up he collapsed and laid down with his head in my lap. He looked up at me, and I could feel him watching me while I watched the compass and the shore and tightened the mainsail a bit, glanced at the tell-tales.

"Even if you can't swim, you're still pretty good at this," he said.

"You taught me everything I know," I lied and smiled.

"But you're a natural." He traced the outside of his pinky

along the line of my breasts, first one and then the other. He circled my nipples, and I could feel them hardening all the way to my jaw. "Ellie?"

"Mmm?"

"How about instead of it counting as one time as long as we don't put our clothes back on, how about it's one time until we touch land? You know, for the times we do it on the boat."

He waited.

"Like it will be one continuous lovemaking until we're in port. Once we've touched land, that time is over. How about that?"

"So if this takes three days," I asked, "and we're in and out of clothes and stuff, it'll still only be one time?"

"Even if we go in the water for a swim."

"I won't go for a swim."

"Yes. Yes, you will."

I frowned at him.

"So say yes. It'll be number three, constantly number three, until we get to your editor's dock."

"Okay. Number three. For as long as it takes. Until we dock."

Max turned and slid his hands behind me, around my hips, over my buttocks, then up my back, under my T-shirt. His head went under my T-shirt, his lips, like a summer snail, melting a warm wet trail up my stomach. "I hope we get lost at sea," I heard him mutter. I closed my eyes. The mainsheet unlooped itself from my fingers, and from somewhere high above us, a seagull might have watched as we changed course, the jib fluttered in warning, and then the boom, like the pounding fist of an angry father, flew over our heads and crashed wide to the starboard side of the boat. The seagull might have heard me scream and then laugh as Max took the tiller from me and set us straight again.

It had always been a sadness for me that I couldn't swim, and I was determined that Casey would learn, that she would be more than I was. Do you remember the time I insisted that you teach her, and the three of us went to the village pool together? It was the middle of winter and the glass-enclosed pool was warm and muggy under bare towering oaks and a winter white sky. How warm the air had felt on my face, yet chilly and dank on my pale body. I was heavier then and had wrapped a terry-cloth towel around my waist to cover my legs. I sat along the side waiting for you, until you strode out of the men's locker room; you—always lean and slim, no matter what you ate or drank. You seemed playful that day, willing to splash and paddle with Casey, "teach her a few strokes," you had said in the car on the way over. And Casey, only three, as I remember it, her small legs clamped together, sat on my lap, trembling, her fear like blooming geraniums that had their roots in the bell jar of my own soul.

"Go with Daddy, honey," I had coaxed her, and trusting you, always trusting you, she had slid off my lap and gone to your side. I watched you walk away with her, you so tall, stooping to talk as you walked, and Casey so tiny, taking forty steps to one of yours.

You had left your towel beside me, and I picked it up and put it around my shoulders. I watched the two of you. Pretended I was Casey, being lifted by strong, indestructible arms, and carried down some tiled steps that disappeared under sparkling water. You held her in your arms, and as you stepped into deeper and deeper water I could see her walking up your chest. When the water was waist deep, she scrambled and stood doubled over, her feet pressed into your ribs. When the water was to your nipples, she struggled to your shoulders, bent over your head, her arms blocking your eyes, and her little pink gingham bathing suit draped over you like a hat. I could hear her squealing and laughing, until you sank—and the two of you disappeared beneath the surface of the water.

I don't even remember how I got to you. Did I leave the towels? Did I jump off the side? Did I run down the steps? Did I fly? I just knew that when Casey emerged from the water gasping and clutching, it was my neck she clung to, my hands that patted her back. I pushed the water and hair from her face and watched her choke and struggle for air.

"She's all right," you insisted, laughing, treading water where you were. "Don't baby her. She's fine."

I had hated you so much that day, but I said nothing. I just turned away from you, up to my neck in water, and went back to shallower water with Casey wrapped around me. Once she was calmed and lulled by me, under a glass sky of bare oaks and the beginnings of snow, I knelt in the heated water and let her float, her legs kicking wildly and her hands gripping mine. Some things grow faint, but this I will never forget: Casey there in the water before me, feeling safe again, her little face, glistening with water. And then like the true "Sesame Street" student she was, she said— the moment, as indelible as a tattoo on pale skin—she blew some bubbles and then she said, "Agua." Just "agua," and I knew she could learn anything. I would teach her myself what little I knew of water. Then I would send her to a summer camp. Hire instructors. I still had it in me to make her world safe for a little while longer.

All day Max and I took turns at the tiller, *terns,* I silently told myself. He would sail for an hour and I would sit next to him. Then I would sail and he would sit next to me. It wasn't till after lunch that the one who was not sailing would wander around the boat and do other things. There was no need to tack, so it was the most boring kind of sailing. Nothing was flying around the cabin at a wild tilt, no spray, just the wind steady at our backs, pushing us in our slow progress.

Sometimes I would look at the charts that Max left on the table. Other times I would take his binoculars and look for buoys, study the shore, the houses, the tanks, the antennae, the beaches, the signs of roads, glintings of light coming from somewhere deep in the shore, where a car moved silently through trees. Sometimes I just laid on the bench and slept, everything quiet except for the sound of the sails and our gentle wake.

Somewhere in the late afternoon I came back to sit next to Max. There was a quiet numbness that settled over us, a stillness that made great tedium possible. Patience is like moss, slow and still. I put my head on Max's shoulder, but he said, "Look! Look at this!"

A large cabin cruiser was coming toward us. There was no indication that the captain of it saw us. He was just barreling along, oblivious. He was alongside us in no time, too fast, too windward, stealing our wind for an instant, and then leaving us in a tumultuous wake. The cruiser's name was *The Great Escape,* and the letters said she was from Sing Sing, New York.

"Rogue wave!" Max shouted, grasping the tiller and feigning a rough struggle. The *Nemaste* bobbed and dunked and things fell in the cabin. He spread one arm across me, as though to protect me, and I silently let the powerboat's wake toss and shake me.

How often I tried to shield Casey from you, from your quirky ways that sometimes seemed so cruel to me. But as she grew older she seemed to lean toward you more than she did to me. It was as though midvoyage she mutinied and left me without a crew. And the two of you—in some sleek powerboat—would keep stealing my wind and leaving me in havoc.

When You Again *started to come to me, I constantly fought with Casey and with you for the time to write it. She was older then, I guess ten. It took me three years to write that book, not counting the short stories and articles before, so she was familiar with the closed door on the room we called my "office" from the time she was seven or eight. And how the two of you loved to torture me.*

You never understood that writing for me was like working at a potter's wheel. Both hands and my full attention had to be centered on the wet hollow clay, and if for one instant there was a tug or a pull in some other direction, the pot collapsed in on itself, or swirled off in a lopsided dance.

So many unfinished sentences were left, dangling paragraphs, cryptic notes to myself that meant nothing to me twenty minutes later. "Violin in the sandbox," I would jot down on my notepad beside my typewriter, and later, after making you both lunch and eating with you, I would wonder if I had even written that at all, or had a Rumpelstiltskin crept in and tried to spin my pots while I was gone? The words would lose their elusive meaning, and I would feel robbed.

But the joke was on me, I guess. Time passed and you were gone. Casey was gone. And in all that solitude, I hadn't written anything of worth for nearly three years. I'd had all the silence, all the peace a writer could hope for, dream of. There were no tappings on my door, no hell-raising downstairs, no unanswered doorbells, no stereo blasting, no doors slamming. Just silence. Emptiness. Like the dark inner chambers of a conch.

So when the stillness became unbearable I began to copy other writers. Not to plagiarize, but in an attempt to stoke my fire, to prime my pump. I would put on Melville's leather boots, shaped to his feet after months of walking, and I would don his hat, slip my arms into his jacket, measure the weight of his harpoon in my hands, and paragraph by paragraph I would walk in his shadow. Where he had written "Call me Ishmael," I wrote "Name him Mordecai." Noun for noun, verb for verb, article for article, I would poorly match him, rambling on for pages, till nothing made sense, till it read like a beat poem. Only then would I toss him aside and take down Faulkner and look in my dictionary and thesaurus to see how many other words he could have used to express "endure," yet never did. Over and over his landscape endured, and his characters endured. Like me. They lasted, held out, were ever the same, cheated death, hung tough, held to their course.

How many people do you know who have ever wept over a thesaurus? Certainly not you. Not any of your chums. Why, you probably think that's as silly as mistaking the sun for the moon.

*O*n the first morning of our journey, anchored near the shore, I woke up in Max's arms. The light in the cabin was pale and soft. We were still sticky from each other and bound like mummies in sheets. I kissed his neck, beginning where I woke up and on up his throat, his ear, his cheek.

"Don't make me kiss you," he said. "My mouth is like a subway toilet in the morning."

I laughed and ignored him, kissing him more, his nose, his chin, closer to his lips, and he fought me off. He rolled over me, fighting fiercely, and from outside it must have looked like we exploded from the cabin, only I stayed there naked on the deck and he leaped over the side with a splash.

The sun was barely up. There was even one or two bright stars still in the west, and the pink sky in the east softly brightened the furled sails with an almost unnatural light.

"Come in," Max called to me.

I sat on the gunwale and shook my head. "Patty McShay, remember?"

He ran his hands over his head and his hair flattened and pulled away from his wonderful face. He shook his head wildly and went under. When he came up he said, "Impossible. Birds fly. Cows shit, and people swim. It's natural. It's our element. Hand me my toothbrush and the paste there, will ya?" He swam close to the side. "In my case inside."

Rummaging inside I heard him swear to himself. "Jesus. I didn't even put the ladder on. See what you make me do?"

I found the toothbrush, a small paste, and five condoms and brought them all outside. "What are these for?" I asked, waving the condoms in one hand.

"My dick."

"You never use them with me." I was startled to hear myself whine.

"You never asked me to. I will if you want."

I handed down his toothbrush and paste into the water.

"Set the ladder up, will you? And come on in."

Setting the condoms on the bench, I pulled the ladder out of the cockpit compartment and tied it securely off the stern. Then, "What if I'd gotten pregnant?"

His mouth was afoam with brushing. He spat and gargled and carried on like a playful walrus. He shrugged. "Why would you get pregnant? You're a big girl. I figured you knew what you were doing."

"What if I'd tricked you?" I picked up the condoms again.

"How?"

"If I'd gotten pregnant so you'd stay."

He was very still in the water, suspended there, not even treading. "I think that would have backfired on you."

"I see." I turned to put the five condoms back in his case. I suspected with Max there was nothing I could do to make him stay once he didn't want to anymore. I felt poised on the peak of some terrible pyramid. I knew I could tumble down one side into some awful kind of blackness, or with some effort I could tumble down the other side into laughter and once again turn my back on pain.

"Come on, Ellie." Max's voice was gentle. "I won't let anything happen to you." I looked at him and realized he meant he wouldn't let me drown there in the water beside him. *I won't let anything happen to you.*

What could happen to me? We were anchored in a tree-lined cove, with not a single boat or soul around. The water looked deep and dark and had taken a lot of anchor lead. "Can you touch bottom?" I asked him.

He disappeared briefly and popped up again like a cork. He shook his head no.

I stood on the bench, feeling as naked as I was. Vulnerable, mortal. "Is it cold?"

"Cool. Refreshing." He came closer to the boat.

I crept onto the gunwale. Hung my legs over the side. He held up his hands to me. "Come on."

"I'm afraid."

He closed his eyes, understanding, and his hand beckoned me.

I worked my way to the edge of the gunwale, gripping the edge with white fists, my rigid toes already aching from the anticipated cold. "Oh, Max," I called as I went off the side and sank faster and faster, straight down. My feet never touched bottom, there was nothing to kick up from, and in a panic I kicked and paddled and arched up into the brightness over me. Max was waiting.

I clung to him like a monkey to its mother. Sputtering and choking, I would never let him go. He was laughing. "You won't sink, don't worry. Look at all the padding you have. Women have wonderful buoyancy." He sank and I clambered to stay on top of the water. I pressed my hands fiercely onto the top of his head while he nestled his bubbling face into my submerged breasts. I shuddered from cold and from some leftover lust.

Then he held me level with him, our chins in the water. We held still and our lips dipped in and out with a gentle movement. There was a splash some distance away from the boat and we both turned to it.

"Morning fish," Max said.

Another splash, closer, over Max's shoulder. Again we turned to it, but we were too late. They were always gone before our eyes found them, leaving ripples, teasings. It was a quiet morning. Just our heads were above water, and below in the darkness our bodies were entwined. The *Nemaste* loomed above us, and the sight of her from that angle made me uneasy. I felt we could be drawn beneath her hull, as though a current would take our bodies under, against our wills.

"Why do I feel like we're being pulled under the boat?" I asked.

"We're not," he said, and one at a time he tossed the toothpaste and then the brush into the boat. Perfect aims. "Maybe you were keelhauled in a past life."

Yes. Maybe. He paddled out away from the boat into the open water with me clinging to him. The new sun was making everything sparkle and glimmer. The fish kept jumping, always out of range. Once we were away from the boat he unhooked himself from me. "Now watch," he said. He held my hands. That's all that connected us, my hands in his hands. I kicked furiously, I ground my teeth.

"Relax your body," he said.

I couldn't. I kicked to keep myself afloat. I kicked to run away. And I kicked to keep away the jellyfish and the sharks and the ticking alligators. "I'm trying to," I said.

"Why are you so afraid?"

Max's face was full of concern as he watched me, but it wasn't him I saw. Suddenly the *Little El* looms above me in the dark night with my father silent and now vanished from the deck. Only the mast light shines, not even a star. I am in the water, alone and freezing cold, the heavy sweatshirt weighing me down and my teeth chattering so loud I think my father will yell at me to be quiet.

Clutching the still propeller of the outboard motor I reach out and hold the stern anchor line as well, a line whose untied end dangles sloppily into the water. I hang there, terrified and cold, until I can't stand it any longer.

"Daddy?"

Not a sound.

"Daddy, I'm sorry." I start to cry. "Please, Daddy, help me up. I'm sorry."

Max's face was close to me, studying me. I could see every bead of water in his hair. The skin along his cheekbone glistened and I could see a scrawny reflection of my adult self reflected in his dark eyes.

"Ellie? Let's go back up. We'll take this slow. We've got all the time in the world."

All the time in the world. I doubted it. There is never all the time in the world. There's the moment things begin and the moment things end, and with people you lose, there never seems to be all the time you need, to get over fears, or to say what needs to be said.

There had been a swimming pool in the institution where they finally put Casey. There was another place first, a halfway house while they were preparing a place for her, but I never saw it. Casey told me, though, that they took the girls' shoes from them and forced them to smoke standing up. I was surprised when I first drove up to Our Lady of the Shepherds. There were sloping lawns, manicured shrubs, and circular drives, one of which led to a grove of trees where there were line after line of modest, identical tombstones. Ex-inmates? I wondered blackly. Escapees?

The main drive led right to the impressive stone building, not at all institutional. Graceful columns, wide and inviting marble steps, and huge spotless glass doors. The waiting room was pristine and softly lit with a painting of a woman standing in a field of sheep with a sanitized human heart held gingerly in her upturned hands.

"May I help you?"

A receptionist sat expectantly at a switchboard in an alcove off the waiting room.

"Yes, my name is Ellie Brinkley, and I'm here to see my daughter, Cassandra."

"Who's her counselor?"

"Umm, I'm not sure. I'm new at this."

"Well, who set up your appointment to see your daughter?"

"Dr. Phelan."

She began plugging and unplugging wires into a wall, and I looked back at the woman in the field of sheep. "Dr. Phelan, Cassandra's mother is here." Turning to me, "Have a seat, please, Mrs. Brinkley. Someone will be right with you."

I sat obediently beneath the painting and looked out the

doors. I had expected chain link fences and barbed wire, barking dogs, and watchtowers. I'd give Casey a week here, maybe two, to figure this all out, and then I'd bet she'd be gone. This tender, gracious place could never hold her.

"Mrs. Brinkley?" A tall black woman stood in the doorway. And I swear she actually had a ring full of keys hanging from her belt.

"Yes?"

"Come with me, please." Again I obeyed. She led me into a small office with corny posters on the wall. *Hire a teenager while they still know everything. I need a hug* under a sleepy kitten. "Sit down, please."

I did. And she sat opposite me. We looked at each other.

What was this about? I was here to see Casey. "Who are you?" I asked.

"I'm sorry. I'm Dr. Phelan. We spoke on the phone."

I thanked her.

"So, tell me, Mrs. Brinkley—"

"Call me Ellie, please."

She nodded, closing her eyes. "Of course, and you can call me Mattie."

I shrugged. "I don't mind calling you doctor. You're a doctor. I'm not a Mrs."

She looked at me shrewdly. I sat very still, trying to block whatever body language I was sending out.

"You're very exacting," she commented.

"I'm very single."

She shuffled papers abruptly. "I don't want to spar with you, Mrs.—uh, Ellie. We're both here because we care about Cassandra and we want her to be able to go home again."

My whole body tensed. "I'm not sure that's what *I* want. If I wanted her home, I wouldn't have taken her to court, I wouldn't have taken it this far. I don't know about you, but I don't want her home."

"Of course, you don't want her home under the present set of circumstances, but hopefully we can help you set new ground rules, maybe discover where you might be able to change, maybe areas where you might be ... let's say ... too exacting with her."

I felt my mouth set. "So Casey's told you about me."

"What do you mean, Ellie?"

"She's told you how I'll no longer tolerate her taking money from my purse? How I don't let her roam the neighborhood till dawn on school nights? How I'm so *exacting* I insist she not smoke marijuana in her room, or leave her bong in the bathroom?"

"You sound very angry."

I nodded, and when tears threatened to spill over I stared at the bulletin board behind her.

"Would you like to talk about it?"

"I'd like to see Casey, like we said, and then I'd like to go home."

"Well, in the next weeks, hopefully the three of us can meet together and work out some things. After all, Mrs. Brinkley, the best place for any child is in her own home. And that's what we strive to do."

"But the judge said she'd be here for the next six months."

She nodded. "That's correct, and during this time we work with the girl and her parents with the intended purpose to create a good home environment for the girl to return to. Then hopefully she'll be back with you by Christmas." She smiled and I thought of the holly that would wind around the banister, holly that never worked.

"Will her father be called in?" I asked.

"He's not in your home any longer, is he?" She shuffled her papers and searched for something, some words written that would say the father was gone, no longer an item on her agenda. She found it. "No, it doesn't seem that it will be necessary to bring him in."

"He buys her cigarettes," I informed her.

She stared at me blankly.

"And when she goes to see him, she comes home smelling like a tavern."

She scribbled on her paper. "Then we will have to make sure she doesn't visit him during this time."

"So it's just me you'll be working with," I said flatly.

She nodded once more.

"Then it's me who's the problem."

"Mrs. Brinkley—"

"How about Mizzz Brinkley? That would be closer."

Her eyes hardened. "Miss Brinkley, we are not pointing a finger. There is clearly a problem and we are willing to work with you and Cassandra in whatever way we can."

"Fine." I rose. "Can I see Casey now?"

"Well ..." She was suddenly soft and sheepish. "Casey didn't want to see you, and she didn't accept the pass to get her out of gym. She said she wanted to go swimming, instead."

I set my jaw and began moving toward the door. "Where's the pool?"

"Do you think that's wise, Miss Brinkley?" She rose too.

"I just want to say hello and then I'll leave. I have a right to see her, don't I?"

She hesitated, then "Yes, you do. All right, I'll walk you over there."

"Just point the way, please, Dr. Phelan. I'd rather see her alone."

"You're a very difficult woman."

"I've had a very difficult time," I told her. "I'm not feeling real cooperative, or hopeful, agreeable, or sociable. I just want to see Casey's face and know she's really here."

She bent over her desk and scribbled on a pad. Then she handed me a note that had her signature on it. "Follow the walk outside to your right. Once you get past the building you'll see the pool through the trees straight ahead of you. If anyone stops you show them this and tell them you're just saying hello to your daughter."

I took the paper. "Thanks," and left.

I began to tremble once I was out the glass doors. I stopped for a minute on the steps. I hadn't meant to be like that with her. I hadn't even said good-bye. It was just that I felt so responsible, so much to blame, and I didn't want anybody poking through me as though I were a smoldering pile of autumn leaves, looking for the fire, for the spark, the place where everything begins and ends.

I turned right and headed toward the pool. Three girls in plaid uniforms came around the corner of the building and passed me. They looked like normal kids, like kids off the Catholic school bus. Would Casey look like that here? Like just another young girl?

I heard a whistle, and then voices as I stepped onto the lawn and followed the sounds and the light glinting off water through the trees. The pool was surrounded by a low fence with two entrances. As I opened one gate a group of girls in bathing suits were leaving out the other without seeing me. I would have called to them, but at the last instant I saw there was still a figure in the water. A small girl doing a frantic crawl diagonally across the pool. Her face jerked over her shoulder with every other stroke, her eyes were scrunched closed, and I could tell Casey wasn't breathing, just stroking wildly.

Slowly I went to the corner of the pool where she was

headed and waited for her. Reaching the edge she clung to it with one arm bent at the elbow, her arm pale but muscular.

"Hi, Casey."

She still hadn't opened her eyes, but she froze when she heard my voice. At that moment a woman came to the gate. She was wearing Bermuda shorts, a whistle around her neck, and a nun's short headpiece on her head. She looked as if she were about to call Casey, but then saw me, and instead she smiled, nodded, and backed away as if she were trying to be very quiet. To not disturb this mother and child reunion. This tender moment.

"What are you doing here?" Casey was looking at me, and when I turned back to look at her, I was startled by her hair. It looked as though she had put a basket over her head and tugged her hair out through the weave and cut it randomly. I didn't say anything about it, which must have disappointed her.

"Just wanted to make sure you were settled in." I crouched down by the edge of the pool and looked around. "This place looks pretty swanky," I commented.

"It sucks." She pulled herself out of the water, carelessly splashing me and turning as she came out. She sat at the edge of the pool with her feet still in the water. I noticed a couple strands of her hair that were still long, and there were spots on her head where I could see the skin of her scalp. "And I can't get any sleep here. They check on you all the time. There's a fucking goddamned window in the door to my room and they check on me all night long."

I nodded. Good. Then I noticed the backs of her wet hands and her four fingers. Between her hand and her first knuckle, there was a scab on each finger. I reached out to touch one with my own finger. "Casey, what happened—"

She pulled her hand away.

The scabs were peculiar, too neat, too symmetrical. "Casey?"

"Cigarette burns," she answered.

Cigarette burns? I had seen cigarettes turn the insides of fingers orange, even seen cigarettes burn too short and singe the skin a little, but these were four, identical, intentional, hold-the-cigarette-to-the-backs-of-my-fingers-till-I-smell-flesh scabs.

I stood suddenly, feeling as though I might throw up. Pressure swirled in my head and I moved away from the edge of the pool.

"And if you don't get me outta here, I'll do something worse."

"I'm glad you're here," I said faintly. "At least you're safe here." I wanted to believe that.

"Safe! Ha! I'm getting outta here whether you help me or not. I'm gonna run."

I backed away toward the gate where I came in, wondering, knowing, that she probably could. "I have to go, Casey. I'll be seeing you." I hurried back to where I had parked my car, and I never looked back. I started the engine, the foot on the gas pedal still wet with pool water, immediately backed up and drove out the circular driveway, past the little graveyard, out to the road.

Where had my baby gone, the one with the little lopsided grin and bluish-white milk running over her chin? From then until now, exactly when had things begun to turn so bad? And if I had known just when, and if I had known precisely where, would there have been anything I could have done to stop it? I suddenly knew the answer was no, there was nothing. Casey, for whatever reason, had taken the stuff of our lives—with its particular shortcomings and inadequacies—and with her own characteristic double helix of DNA and her inner soul, she had tried to make sense of it, and to come up with her own answers. And her answers terrified me, like burns on a child's fingers.

I got on the entrance to the expressway and began to cry from the loss I felt, a cry that drained my whole body and left me empty.

$\mathcal{M}$ax and I set sail soon after our early morning dip. My confidence had returned to me once my feet were on the hard deck and I had chores to do, a purpose. Just before noon, the *Nemaste* drew near the entrance to the Shinnecock Canal, the short cut into the Peconic Bay, and Max stopped her in the water. He turned her dead into the wind and gave me the tiller. Standing at the bow he peered into the canal's distant locks and tide gates. We both watched as other boats motored right past us and entered them. Max pointed and called back to me. One sailboat had stopped not too far from where we sat, and we could see the crew lowering the sails, and then peculiarly tipping the mast back and lowering it to lay across the cockpit.

"Low bridge," Max called. "We can't get through with the mast up." I could see the railroad bridge that passed over the waterway right before the entrance to the locks. Max nervously rubbed his chin and watched as the sailboat motored past.

"Only eighteen feet, Skipper," one of the crew warned us as they passed.

Max went to the base of the mast and stared at it.

"So we'll take it down?" I asked.

He didn't answer.

"Max?"

"I don't know *how*." He looked back at me and shrugged, holding his palms up to the sky. "And if I *did* know how, I don't know that just the two of us could get it up again."

I looked around. The sails were luffing and I had to hold the boom steady above my head with my hand. "So we'll go the long way. That's all," I said, as if I knew these waters.

Max stood and thought. I had never seen anyone else think the way he did. He had to hold very still and be very quiet, as if some great clock workings were churning and laboring in his head. I smiled and looked away from him out to the canal.

When I looked back at him he was staring at me. "Around the tip then?" he asked.

"Around the tip!" I echoed.

He pointed east, toward the distant end of the island. "Up helm then, men. We'll bring the wind aft and head for the Guinea Current! They shan't keep us from the gold-filled waters of the Peconic Bay. On *Niña!* On *Pinta!* On *Santa María!* To the top of the wave! To the crest of the swell! Now dash away! Dash away! Dash away, all!"

Slowly the *Nemaste* responded to her rudder, slowly she

turned away from the tide gates, and like me, just like me, she went blindly forward into the unknown, with a sort of madcap faith in charts, and puffs of wind, and Max.

Going around the tip was uneventful, but it added hours and hours to what we had anticipated. And even more so when the wind died. We wouldn't make it all the way to Charlie's that night, so we motored into Montauk Lake, exhausted and eager to anchor. The sun was beginning its setting show, streaking the clouds like a cheap painting—a gaudy warning that we'd soon be left in darkness. Max said he knew a cove deep in the salt lake, but when we got there, there were already a few other boats anchored, and water-skiers were buzzing around like mosquitoes. In the center of the cove they had erected a ramp, and they took turns motoring around it, and then approaching it full speed on their skis. The boat would pass it by, and then the skiers, at the end of their ropes, would fly up the ramp, then off the tip, one-handed, one-legged, whooping and hooting, and land expertly back in the water.

Max put the motor in neutral and looked at me. "They won't be here much longer. They can't ski once it gets dark." So he put the anchor down temporarily and we waited until, one at a time, the skiers and their boats took off for their slips under a tacky pink and orange sky.

Then we moved in. I knelt at the bow and held the heavy anchor suspended by a chain over the surface of the water as Max motored noisily into the silent cove, and once there, as close as we dared be to land, and as far as we could be from other boats, I lowered the anchor for Max. He backed the boat gently to tug its Danforth teeth into the sandy bottom and then turned the motor off. Such quiet. Such total stillness. Why is it the motion of water in darkness is somehow even more calming than total stillness?

Without speaking to each other we settled in. I got towels and soap from below, and Max hoisted the shower bag high onto the mast, its little nozzle within easy reach. Still in his bathing suit, Max wet himself down with the sun-warmed water and began to soap up. I looked around at the other boats. There were no lights, no signs of life, so in an act of abandon or bravery, or pure foolishness, I stripped off my bathing suit and let Max aim the nozzle where he would.

Without a single word, we moved like one creature preening itself. Dark, strong hands soaped breasts in round, tender circles, and lighter hands soaped the backs of long, hairy legs in gentle strokes; two trunks slipped and slid against each other in slow motion, the nozzle squirting hot water into both thirsty mouths, then through long, straight hair and dark, curly hair. The creature bubbled with laughter and panting.

I was sure there had never been an erection quite like Max's. So eager, so ready, so firm that it stood straight up against his belly. I slid smoothly down his body, leaving him alone and leaning against the mast. Then I took him into my mouth, my smiling mouth, while he made it rain on me with hot fresh water. I kept my eyes open. I kept watching the darkening orange and black clouds against the fading horizon, through the drizzling water, and when he whispered quietly from somewhere high up on the mast, "This is still number three, right?" I nodded. Then like losing my place in a book that is caught up in a light summer wind, I let him slip from between my lips, and sat back on my haunches, grinning and then laughing into the surrounding darkness.

I fell into a fitful sleep that night, snuggled against Max, deep in the cabin on pillows of extra towels and life jackets. I could hear the rope ladder Max had put out tapping against the side of the boat, and although it annoyed me, it wasn't enough to make me get up and silence it. I drifted in and out of sleep, always aware of the sound of the ladder and the touch of Max's breath on my face.

But suddenly I was fully awake in the dark. The *Nemaste,* usually so calm and still, was being tossed about. Things were dropping from compartments and shelves in the cabin. I could tell by sounds that the mast was swaying wildly from side to side. Just as I reached out to touch him, thunder crackled the night sky outside and Max bolted from sleep and sat up.

"Shit." Max quickly climbed over me and made his way out the hatch.

"Where are you going?" I stood in the companionway and called after him, grabbing a sweatshirt and pulling it on. It had grown cold, and the wind tore at me.

Max stood motionless for a minute in the center of the cockpit. He didn't answer me. Then he dove into one of the compartments.

"Max? What? What is it?"

"We'll go aground if the anchor doesn't hold." He cursed and pulled some line and then lifted the extra anchor into the darkness. "I'm so stupid. I should have done this last night." He spoke into the wind, forgetting I was there.

"What can I do?" I asked.

But he didn't answer.

I glanced at the shore. We were very close to it. Closer than last night? I couldn't tell. All we could see about us—the near beach and dunes, the tree-lined shore, the other boats, were all black silhouettes lit by flickers of lightning against a green-gray sky.

"What can I do?" I repeated, now feeling panic rising in my throat.

"Nothing," he mumbled. "Just stay here."

Stay here? Where would I go? And then I watched him

untie the dinghy and lower the second anchor into it. Lightning flashed and I could see his naked body. Quickly, wanting to do something, I ran below and came out with my yellow rain slicker. "Here," I shouted. "Put this on. Where are you going?"

He flung his arms into the slicker and tossed the hood over his head just as the fat drops began to hit the deck. The hem of my slicker cut across his bare ass. "Shit," he said again as he jumped over the side into the dinghy. I stood by helplessly as he edged his way along the side toward the bow and then began paddling furiously away from the boat.

I clapped my hands over my ears as another crack of thunder exploded right over us. I began furiously to put the slats in place to cover the hatch and thought how it would not be good to run aground. I remembered the times my father had run aground. But at those times the sun had been shining and the tide a little too low and his knowledge of local sand bars and unyielding tides just a little wanting. The *Little El* would burrow her keel into the bottom like a shovel scooping into earth. And she would stand suddenly still, slightly atilt, like a gymnast poised at a breathless angle before she topples. On those few times, my father had let himself down over the side into the water, a wreath of line around his shoulder that was tied to a cleat, and from the stern, I would watch him as he'd wade out into the deep, but not deep enough, water and tug and strain to pull the *Little El* loose. But that had been in daylight.

I began to tremble as I kept my eyes glued to Max's yellow shape in the stormy shadows of the water. *Man overboard, man overboard.* Farther and farther out, the wind and waves tossed him, until I could see his yellow arms toss the anchor over.

I suddenly remembered the one other time the *Little El* ran aground. There on that stormy night with Max, I shuddered from somewhere deep inside me. Deeper than my bones. Deeper than a dagger in some barnacled treasure chest.

It is so gruesomely dark that the night hovers about me like an evil presence. I am alone at the tiller, sobbing and gasping, wiping my nose and eyes against my sopping wet sleeve as I steer back blindly to what I hope is my father's slip. The sails are full of night wind, and I am at a terrible tilt, moving on the cusp of what is too fast for me to control. And nothing is familiar around me. Everything is different in the darkness. I cannot tell if a particular dot of light is as far away as the distant shore or as close as the end of my arm. My mother was right. I never should have come this time.

But I sail on, my legs extended over my father, who lies motionless in a dark puddle along the floor of the cockpit. My small bare feet are jammed against the opposite bench, my arms straining and quivering as I pull the tiller toward me with all my childlike might. Then suddenly, somehow, the sails buckle above me. I am thrown away from the tiller, against the outer wall of the cabin, and my ear cracks against the compass floating there. The *Little El* is still, motionless, her centerboard gouged deep into the shore. We are no longer afloat, but the boat sits clean and erect, her mast perfectly perpendicular to the beach and totally solid. Still. The sails break free and flap like towels hung to dry on a backyard line.

After what must be hours, I am no longer crying, but shocked into silence. I cover my father with a blanket and wait. I don't know what it is I am waiting for until I see the flashing Coast Guard boat coming toward me in the moments before dawn. And then I know. I try to talk to the man who leaps aboard. I try to tell him I didn't mean it. But there are no words. He wraps me in a blanket and hands me over the side to another man. I try to tell this man, too, but he just holds me tight against him while a terrible shuddering wracks my small body and silences any explanations I try to make.

Max came paddling furiously back to the *Nemaste,* and I was horrified to see the blue dinghy oars curve almost to snapping, horrified to think he may never make it back, but be swept out into the lake and then out to sea, forever lost to me. When Max was close enough, I leaned over the side and held on to the dinghy with all my strength until he was safely on board.

Once Max made sure everything was tied down and double secure, we climbed back into the pitching cabin together and drew the sleeping bags around us and held on to each other. His body was cold against me, his thighs nearly icy. And I responded by trying to cover him, to warm him with myself. I could feel his heart pounding against my breast and realized he must have been afraid.

"My hero," I whispered.

"Aw, shucks," he said.

Then, smiling, I ran my hand down his chest and stomach and wound my cold fingers around his soft penis. He lurched. "Cold, lady, very cold."

"Sorry," I whispered. I held my fingers to my mouth, huffed on them, rubbed them together a few minutes and returned.

There, deep in the womb of the tossing *Nemaste,* who was double-anchored in a summer thunderstorm, I reached beneath the warm sleeping bag and tried to make Max hard. Like a grateful rescued damsel, I caressed and stroked and fluttered and pressed, but nothing happened for Max. I wasn't sure what to say, but after a while he turned on the small bunk light and threw back the sleeping bag that covered us. He began searching for something in the dim light.

"What is it, Max?" I asked.

"It's gotta be here somewhere," he muttered, feeling under the cushions and along the shelf.

"What? What's gotta be here?" I looked with him.

"Kryptonite," he said. "I know it's here."

"Oh, stop," I told him, pulling him to me, laughing, pulling the sleeping bags over us again. "Let me just hold you. Just be still," and he quieted in my arms then. Even his heart quieted to near stillness. He slept before I did, and I lay there a while, secure, double-anchored, listening to the storm.

I love sleeping on a boat. Sometimes on land, when I cannot get to sleep, I pretend I am lying on a berth, wrapped in blankets in the womb of a sailboat on a gentle sea. And when that doesn't work I imagine I am in the womb of a sailboat on a tossing sea in the arms of a man who loves me. His arms hold me close to him and his one palm cups the back of my head and holds my cheek against his neck. And when this doesn't work, I am alone again, this time on deck, stretched out on the bench in the cockpit, wrapped in blankets that I have brought out with me. Imagining myself lying there, staring wide-eyed into the dense and powdery stars, I listen to the sounds all around me. For even with its shrouds and halyards secured and the sails wound tight and held with bungees, there are hundreds of sounds on a sailboat. So I count them. Warm as a worm in a cocoon case I count the sounds.

First there are the gentle lappings of the water against the hull, so soft and unobtrusive I never notice them until I grow quiet. At first the lappings seem irregular, but then, gradually, a pattern sets in—like an infant at my breast who breathlessly suckles and suckles and suckles and then pauses to breathe and lets my milk trickle down into the creases beneath her chin before she suckles again.

Then, inside the mast, swaying with the motion of the boat, are wires that lead to the head of the mast, where the antenna and the mast light are. Tap. Click, clank. Tap-bink. Ka-chunk. Clickclick. They sway and click against each other without pattern or music. I never hear this during the day, but at night it startles me with its variety.

Sometimes a breeze kicks up and forms a flute of my ear, a hollow note that blows from its emptiness and makes me snuggle deeper into my cocoon.

I grow tired and heavy. Neither adult nor child, I no longer move, and I struggle to keep my eyes open. Then a childhood memory comes of a night when there is a rattling that is not familiar to me. A constant gnawing rattle-rattle that keeps me on the edge of consciousness. In my sleepiness I think it is a beaver gnawing on our anchor line. He goes on and on, chewing and crunching, nibbling to cut us loose. And then I hear a stirring in the cabin, blankets swirling, bare feet touching the floor. Slowly he comes out of the cabin, stumbles sleepily on the companionway, and passes me. I hear him fumble with something at the stern, and then I realize the rattling noise has been the little flag in its holder. Suddenly the noise stops. The flag is tossed on the opposite bench, and then, before going back into the cabin, he stops and places his hand on my head. "You warm enough, patoot?" My head and his hand nod and he goes back down to the cabin.

Gently then I am drawn again to sleep, my eyes closing against my will, even though I can't bear to miss a moment of the celestial procession above me. I can feel the great weight of it, the great heaviness and the night sky's vast mission to draw away the darkness and bring day. Nothing is slower than the night, I think, unless perhaps it is my own body. And then within my deep tunnel of blankets, my hand stirs and moves sleepily to my rib cage, where my searching fingers touch my flat breasts and the still, innocent nipples that lie there like buttons on a baptismal dress. My body is slower than the night.

But there are other nights, restless, sleepless nights. It was a month or so after a couple of sessions with Dr. Phelan and me that Casey ran from Our Lady of the Shepherds for the first time. I got the call in the middle of the night.

I heard the phone from some deep place and sat up abruptly and numbly pressed the earpiece to my ear. "Yes?"

"Mrs. Brinkley?"

"Yes?"

"Mrs. Brinkley, this is Sister Gregory, and I'm so sorry to bother you at a time like this, but we do have to notify you immediately. Casey has run away. Apparently she ran with another girl. Two of them are gone."

She waited for me to say something. But there were no words to describe the despair and nameless fear that washed over me.

"We have notified the police and there will be a missing person's report out on both of them. And of course we'll call you the minute we have them back."

"All right," I said to her. "You do that." And I searched for the phone base to hang it up.

In those earlier days, when Casey had first run from home, I had always been pretty sure she was somewhere in the neighborhood. The police had found her once sleeping on a rooftop in town. Another time she'd stayed with school friends. Now she was in a strange county, a distant place, with maybe only the expressway as an exit out. Two young girls hitching, holding out small cigarette-burnt thumbs to truckers and dark vans.

I slipped out of bed. Always before when she had run away from home, I had locked her out. Double-bolted the doors, secured the windows, and stuffed cotton in the doorbell chime. This time I went downstairs and made myself a cup of tea.

I poured water in the old red pot and set the flame under

it. I took down a mug and a chamomile tea bag, like Peter Rabbit's mother would make for him when he was bad, and forgiven. I made myself a cup of chamomile tea and stood shivering near the stove. I thought of a book I used to read to Casey when she was little. About the little bunny that was always threatening to run away, and his mother would say that no matter where he went, no matter how far he ran, she'd always go after him and bring him back.

My water boiled and I dunked the tea bag up and down and added a little honey. I turned out the light, and in the darkness I checked to make sure that each door was locked. I bolted the house against her, yes, but this time I didn't stuff the doorbell with cotton. I hoped that in my sleep I would hear it ring, and she would be there, contrite and remorseful, a Casey who would come into my mother-bunny arms and be good.

The police picked her up a few days later a couple of states away. And they brought her back to Our Lady of the Shepherds.

Sleepless and remembering other sleepless nights, I rose before Max did the morning after the storm, and being careful not to wake him I wrapped one of the sleeping bags around myself and stepped out into the dull morning light. The entire earth seemed still and peaceful. The calm waters extending away from the cove toward the lake went from a gleaming sparkle to a flat dullness the color of worn blackboards in an old school. And the trees along the shore looked hard and brittle as though they would crackle beneath my fingers.

A light breeze wound around my head and mussed my hair as I looked over at the other boats. Silence. They floated there in the water on slack anchor lines, going nowhere. I watched the silhouette of a person appear and then disappear on the deck of one of them. I heard someone knock over a cup onto a cabin floor as though they were right beside me. And then I saw a solitary woman standing along the shore. I watched her as she watched two swans glide away from her, making an ever-expanding double-V in the still water. All about me everything was swept clean. I could sense the aftermath of a great storm. I was sure the air almost had a hum to it as though a great chime had been struck just moments before I awoke. Even my body felt charged.

And then I noticed the rest. The ramp for the water-skiers was gone. Simply gone. I scanned the horizon all about me and couldn't find it. Then, instinctively, I checked that our dinghy was still there. It was, tied securely at the stern, but the bright blue aluminum oars were gone. Without making a sound I crept into the cabin to get the binoculars and then I scanned every bit of the shore. I saw them.

Far from where the woman walked on silent bare feet along the sand, I could see one and then the other oar lying along the waterline a short distance from each other. I lowered the binoculars and saw their faint foolish blueness in the sand. When Max got up he would jump in the water and brush his teeth and fling the sleep from his curly hair. And then he would swim to shore and bring the oars back. My hero, I thought. I'd learned to be grateful for even the littlest of life's rescues.

J showed Max on the chart where Charlie's house would be, and when we drew near and I looked through the binoculars, I could see it, the light wood of the new dock and the sloping garden, lush and rocky.

"There it is!" I called back to Max. He was at the tiller, and I had been sitting up on the deck, in sun, then in shade, as we tacked along across the bay. "We made it, Captain," I called. "We really made it!"

Max stood in just his faded cutoffs and took a full bow from the waist. "What do you think?" he asked, looking down at himself. "Are we presentable? Are we shocking? I could put on my full parade dress, you know."

"You're fine," I said going back to the binoculars. There, there were the tomato stakes. And I could see Charlie—a round form in a pale blue work shirt digging in his garden. I cupped my hands around my mouth and sang out, even from where we were, "Char-leeee!" But he didn't hear me. Excited now, and anxious to touch shore, I made my way back to Max.

"Know what I want, Max? More than anything else in the world right now?"

"One more orgasm."

"Max, number three is officially over and complete—"

"—when we hit land," he corrected. He wound his arm around my waist and pulled me to him. I heard the sails fluttering, but as always, until we were blown in careless circles, we ignored them. His mouth covered mine, and I wondered what it would be like to have him forever, for seven hundred and eighty-three more times, or for endless times, until we didn't want each other anymore.

How many times do you think you and I made love, while you were still here? Over a thousand, do you think? While Max's soft, warm mouth covered mine in some sort of delirious suspended moment, I thought of you and tried to multiply our fourteen years times fifty-two weeks, give or take, more in the beginning, less as we grew familiar and ordinary to each other. I was glad Max and I had decided to count and to keep it to just five. Because imagine if in your whole life you were only allowed to make love five times. I know I would've really made them count for something. I would have performed them with great care. You may find this hard to believe, but the one time I would have absolutely made sure I had would be the morning we made Casey.

I know exactly which time that was. It was a sunny Saturday morning with nothing else to do, and Maria Muldaur was singing "Midnight at the Oasis." I was your Scheherazade, thinking myself into silk scarves and flat, shiny bangles, and rolling in the sand. I have never had such breasts before or since, never felt so keenly aware of every inch of my body. I felt as though our souls were no longer inside our bodies somewhere, but rather above us, swollen and ripe. The clock radio clicked on and that's when Maria Muldaur found us wound in each other, wild and wet with a seasoned yearning—our souls hovering over that old bed like storm clouds, and while we panted and tasted and sucked and ached, there was Hollywood lightning above us, and somewhere in the universe, a giant hand snapped its fingers, and Casey burrowed her single-cell being into the walls of my womb and held on for her life.

And I would have kept her there like that had I been given the choice. I would have kept her just like that.

Max pulled away from me as if he had just asked me a question. My head was on his shoulder, I had turned sad.

"What?" I came back to him.

"So what were you saying? What do you want more than anything in the world?"

"More than anything in the world?" I paused. "I was thinking I'd like a cup of hot coffee."

Charlie came walking down to the end of his small dock when he finally heard my call across the water. I was so glad to see him. Just the sight of him made me think of my word processor at home, made me itch to get some paper, to write. He helped guide the *Nemaste* to a spot alongside his tire-padded dock, where he then took the lines Max tossed him and tied us to the upright posts. Leaving the boat as she was, still opened and with nothing put away, Max and I both leapt ashore and sighed. I felt stiff.

"Charlie, this is my friend and captain, Max Turkel. And Max, this is the greatest editor in the world, Charlie Jaspers." They shook hands, Charlie in his work shirt and muddy knees, and Max naked except for his cutoffs. I was suddenly shaken, seeing them together like that, as though I had thought all along Max was an imaginary friend who would somehow disappear when we got to Charlie's. I thought how I should have insisted he get dressed when he offered. "And this," I said, looking nervously away from them both and sweeping my arm in the air over her, "this is the wonderful, the fabulous, the magnificent *Nemaste,* my muse, my inspiration."

"A beauty," Charlie admitted and climbed aboard. Max was suddenly acting like a little boy eager to please his teacher. He climbed after Charlie and began showing him all her little details with ardent politeness and a sort of flustered silliness.

"The cabin's small, but with the pop-top up you can stand up in her, and she's got a retractable centerboard." I could hear him inside cranking it up.

I looked back up at the house and around at the garden, and even though I was standing on the stationary dock I could feel the trees drift and lurch. Three days on a boat, and it would take awhile for me to get my land legs back. I took a deep breath to steady myself.

"Why don't you two make yourselves at home," Charlie was saying as he and Max stepped off the boat. "If you want to take hot showers or make phone calls, whatever. There's a fresh pot of coffee in the kitchen."

"Oh, coffee! Such luxury!"

"I'm just going to finish up in my tomato patch," Charlie went on. "That storm last night played havoc with my stakes. Even lost a couple of plants, broke right off at the dirt. How did you two make out through the night? I was thinking of you."

"We were okay," I told him. "We were anchored in

Montauk Lake, nice and safe. And Max was a real hero, rowing out into the wind and breakers to put out an extra anchor."

Max lifted both his bare brown arms and flexed his muscles, grinning. While ordinarily it would have made me laugh, Charlie and I glanced at each other and I was embarrassed.

"I forgot to check the weather before we went to sleep," Max explained. "Otherwise I would have known ahead of time. I'm all stiff today—"

He went on about his heroism, while I, remembering why it was we had forgotten to listen to the weather, flushed, climbed back aboard the *Nemaste*, and ducked into the cabin to get a clean change of clothes for myself. Thinking quickly, I grabbed a T-shirt for Max. I could hear their voices, Max's young, exuberant, thoughtless monologue, and Charlie's patient, mature response. They were walking up the hill when I came out, and I watched the two of them ahead of me. I couldn't reconcile myself to their being together. It had been easy to have them in separate compartments of my life, but together? When I was with Charlie, I was the Ellie he knew, with a past and a history that held certain half-truths, and with Max I was a very different Ellie, an Ellie embroidered with different lies. So who would I be now? I felt as though I might need mirrors and smoke to pull the day off.

Max and I went into the house, leaving Charlie puttering in the garden. In the gently lit living room, there were bookcases along one wall, a low sofa with large, soft pillows, and a writing table before the window with a few cut wildflowers floating in a bowl. I could smell something wonderful and indistinguishable. Maybe it was Charlie's copy of Proust, or maybe it was the butterfly wings his cat had carried in on the pads of her feet. But no sooner were we in the door than Max was kneeling before the fireplace, his head in its opening and his face turned up into its gullet.

"Max!" I said in a stage whisper. I felt like we were two bad kids.

"What?" he stage-whispered back.

"Behave."

"I'd better check out his chimney," he explained. "You can't possibly trust the man with your writing when you don't even know what sort of chimney he has, can you?"

I sat on the edge of the chair by the writing table and watched.

"Now there are good chimneys and there are bad chimneys," Max was saying. "Kind of like witches."

He twisted to look at me and I could see his forehead was already smeared with ashes. "Max—"

He held up his hand to hush me. "Now I don't know if you know this, but some chimneys will suck smoke into the house if there's the slightest breeze while others will pull smoke only if there's a wind from the north."

He crouched, blew across the hearth, and dust and soot rose as he talked. I could see a barely visible cloud pulled into the fireplace and dragged up the chimney, as if the fireplace had inhaled. "A chimney is the soul of the house," he went on. "The very soul." He was quiet and still, and then he turned slowly to look at me. "But you know, Ellie Brinkley, famous, illustrious Ellie Brinkley, once or twice in my chimney career, I've been called out for a very difficult chimney condition." His eyes widened. "Chimney possession," he whispered hoarsely. And I found myself smiling at him again.

"People will call in a panic and say their chimney is spewing forth noxious black soot and smoke—" his words grew louder and thickened with importance, "—right into the house, and then they tell me that a terrible voice rumbles from deep within the darkest depth of their chimney. And it says—"

He had me laughing.

He thrust his head up into the chimney where his voice resonated and echoed, and then he roared, "YOUR CHIMNEY SWEEP SUCKS SOOT IN HELL!"

I jumped from my seat. "Shhhh! Jesus, Max! Charlie will hear you!"

He sat back down and looked at me. "Since when are you so proper and well behaved?"

"Charlie isn't like you," I stammered.

"But you are. You're just like me."

"Maybe not when I'm here." I looked around the room as though I were looking for some clue as to who I really was.

Max stood and brushed his hands off on his cutoffs. He seemed disgruntled as he wandered over to the bookcase, frowning and perusing the titles. I was the one who felt scolded somehow and I grew quiet. Max tapped at one book. "Why, here it is," he said, "In the flesh, or rather in the binding. *You Again*." He pulled my one and only novel off the shelf, held it as though he were weighing it, "Fairly hefty," and then opened it to the title page. He read aloud. " 'To Charlie, with much love and gratitude for all your patience and kindness. Ellie.' " I had forgotten I had written that, but not how grateful I had been for Charlie's softness and encouraging words when we began the revisions together on the manuscript. Charlie had known things weren't going well at home, and he'd been gentle with me.

"And what's this?" Max asked.

I looked over his shoulder, and saw Casey's handwritten scrawl next to mine. I remembered how she had insisted on signing it as well and Charley had gotten such a kick out of that. She'd written "Charlie, it's me again. Cassandra Tina Brinkley."

"Casey," I told Max and I smiled. Tears bit my eyes.

"Does she ever come out here to see Charlie anymore?" He asked and he was looking hard at me.

"It's been a while," I said softly.

Max turned back to the bookcase, walked slowly along its fullness, touching titles, brushing a heavy fern Charlie had set on the shelves, and then he picked up something in his palm. He stared down at it.

"Well, look at this," he said softly.

I walked over to him and looked. He held a small acorn in his hand. I looked at it and up at him.

"See what this is?" he asked.

"An acorn."

"No, it's a carving of an acorn."

I looked closer and saw that it was.

"Amazing, isn't it?" he asked me. "It looks like an acorn, smells like an acorn. I'll bet it's even made out of oak. Everything's there, right?"

He was studying me.

"But you know what, Ellie? Even with all that going for it, there's no little oak tree inside."

"What are you getting at, Max?"

He shrugged. "I don't know. It's just sometimes I get the feeling that you're not at all what you seem to be on the outside. That maybe you're just a chip of oak carved into the shape of an acorn, but there's no oak tree inside you."

I held very still. I met his eyes and felt a flicker of something old and familiar there: I knew Max would eventually leave me, as everyone had. Max turned then and put the carved acorn back on the shelf.

Charlie insisted we stay for dinner and accepted my quietness as exhaustion from the heat we suddenly experienced now that we were off the water. He told me to lie down on his bed for a while and he'd call me when dinner was ready, but I slept lightly and woke on my own. When I padded out into the hall, Max was deep into what appeared to me to be a monologue and Charlie was chopping and cooking.

"I could probably write about my sailing adventure in Washington state," Max was saying. "The Pacific is a whole other experience—"

"Ellie!" Charlie said. "You're up." He seemed relieved to see me. "And I was just about to call you." He handed Max a bowl full of salad and beckoned me to him. "Here you go, my dear, you carry this," a dish of cold salmon steaks, "and I'll bring the wine."

I followed Max out the back French doors that were open onto a wide patio of pale woods and tubs of vibrant geraniums. A glass-topped table was set with glass dishes and crystal wineglasses. It was nearly transparent but for the food we placed on it.

"There!" Charlie said. He was pleased and motioned for us to sit down. I squinted out at the water, sharp with the brilliance of sunset.

Max began serving himself immediately out of the salad bowl, talking all the while. I glanced at Charlie, but he didn't seem to notice. He served me a salmon steak, then Max, and then himself.

"I have this great idea for a story that I told Ellie about," Max was saying, "but I don't think she's too keen on it, so who knows—maybe I'll write it myself." Charlie stood and pulled the skewered cork from a pale bottle of wine he held under his arm. I couldn't tell if he was listening. "It's about this woman with a sailboat. You see, she puts a personal ad in the local paper, maybe say *Newsday,* and all these guys show up to sail her boat with her. Only she murders them all. I can see it now. All these bodies of swinging single men with their toupees and gold chains and money clips washing up on Jones Beach."

"Wine, Max?"

Charlie held the bottle over his glass, and Max nodded.

"She's gotta be this sort of incredible woman who's capable of great tenderness, but also violent passions. Maybe Meryl Streep would be interested. Or Cher."

"Ellie?"

A pure drop of wine hung from the lip of the wine bottle. I nodded and watched it flow into my glass.

"But can't you see the setting for this? Boats, maybe some singles bars where she meets them, a police precinct, a beach with dead bodies. This story has it all."

I lifted the glass and brought it to my lips. I watched Max over the top while the wine flowed through me like the tide over a jetty. I drank it quickly, willing it to flow into all the gullies and furrows of my mind. I thought that Max was beginning to seem truly ridiculous, and maybe I hated him. I ate the salmon, which melted in my mouth like cool sherbet. I had another glass of wine.

"This is wonderful, Charlie," I said softly to him, as though I didn't want Max to hear, but Max didn't seem to notice.

"It's just the ending I have to figure out, that's all," he was saying. "I'm not sure what the best way to end this should be. Should she get caught, maybe even murdered herself?" Max stared up into the trees, a hunk of pink salmon stabbed on the end of his fork. "Or should she fall in love with the investigator who's trying to solve the mystery of the single men being washed up on Jones Beach?" He chomped the salmon. "Other than a few minor things like that, I think the story's got every-thing."

"What about symbolism?" I asked. I moved slowly, taking the wine bottle and pouring myself a third glass of wine. I wanted to show Charlie I could squash Max under my thumb, right there at the table.

Max looked up from his dish with a blank expression. I could feel Charlie sit back in his seat as if he anticipated that something was about to fly.

"Well, to tell it real simply, Max, so you can understand, let's say there's this woman. What shall we name her?"

His eyes met mine over my wineglass. "Cookie," he answered. "Name her Cookie."

"All right. There's this woman named Cookie who had two grandparents who were both killed in automobile accidents. It was on two separate occasions, but each time they were driv-ing a yellow Volkswagen Bug. Then Cookie's seven aunts and uncles all died—remarkably in yellow Bugs. Now Cookie's fa-ther'd been driving around in a yellow Bug for years saying he wasn't superstitious, even though sometimes for no apparent reason he'd put it in the garage up on cinder blocks and refuse to drive it for weeks at a time."

I took a bite of my salad while they waited. Drank the wine. I patted my lips with the napkin.

"Following me so far?"

Max nodded, and when I looked at Charlie he just blinked slowly.

"Well, the story goes on that one day Cookie got married. A very nice man, mind you, but you know what he drove."

I made a circle with my hand and ended palm up toward Max as though he were a tap dancer and I had just challenged him.

"A yellow Volkswagen Bug."

"Nope. It was a blue one. But he told her, he said to her, 'Don't you worry, sweetie pie. It's blue and I know how to drive it, unlike the rest of your family.' Well, she didn't worry until one day he was in a terrible accident and crippled for life. She couldn't bear to look at him, and he couldn't stand her self-righteousness, so he moved away."

I took a long cool swallow of the wine, and, trying to set the empty glass before me, it crashed loudly but harmlessly against the edge of my plate.

"Well, it wasn't long before Cookie's only child got herself a job and a driver's license. Soon she was ready to buy a car. 'Don't buy a Bug,' her mother warned her. But the daughter came home with a Bug just the same. They fought and the daughter moved out. Months later Cookie saw that old rainbow-colored Bug wrapped around a pole on the expressway. So she went on in life, and of course she drove a red Ford. The funny thing was though that she was always attracted to men who drove Volkswagen Bugs."

That satisfied me totally, but Max and Charlie were waiting. I looked from one to the other. They *both* seemed ridiculous now.

"So?" Max said.

"So what?"

"So what about the symbolism?"

"The Volkswagen Bug is the symbol," I said.

"The symbol for what?" Charlie asked patiently, but clearly troubled.

"For booze!" I laughed. "Or poker games! Some kind of mental obsession. It's just that I happen to know that drunkenness ran through Cookie's family like widow's peaks or a perfect pitch runs in other families!"

"Aren't you really talking allegory, Ellie, and not symbolism?"

"Oh, Charlie, nitpick, nitpick. Jesus, keep at it and in a few more years you can get a job as a copy editor somewhere."

I bent over my plate in earnest and cleaned up the last few bits of salmon with great concentration. We three ate quietly, and I did not look at them. When Max finally spoke I realized the sun was down and night had eased its way onto the patio. Max said, "There's a wonderful buoy on the way here, out by Gardiners Island, I think it was. Wasn't it, Ellie? It has these clanging bells that ring like church bells on the slightest swell. Other kinds of buoys are set up to howl in the wind."

And it wasn't till that instant that it suddenly occurred to me that I was drunk.

*C*harlie and Max both insisted that Max be the one to drive the car back that night. Max assured Charlie that I would sleep it off on the way and be able to drive myself home once we got to the boatyard and he picked up his truck.

"Why don't you follow her home anyway, just to be on the safe side," Charlie suggested.

"Absolutely," said Max.

"Oh, you two," I muttered, climbing into the car. Then, remembering, I climbed back out and kissed Charlie on the cheek. I couldn't see his face, just his silhouette framed in the light over his front door. There was cricket song in the darkness and a frog or two. "Thank you, Charlie, thank you, thank you, thank you. I'll be back out real soon. And I'll take you for a sail. And you'll see. I'll start writing again. Like you won't believe."

"I'll believe it," Charlie said, and nodding he guided me back into the car. "Drive carefully now, and call me during the week, Ellie. Let me know what your schedule's going to be."

"Right," I said.

Max got into the car on the driver's side, and as soon as he had the motor started and the lights on and was backing down the long rutted drive, I dropped like a felled tree, landing with my head on his thigh. He drove on without a word into the warm summer night, until I recognized the familiar sounds of driving up onto the ferry ramp, and then I heard Max roll the window down and buy a ticket from the ferryman. "One way. Two of us," he said softly. I started to feel gentle toward him again.

Max turned the engine off and I could feel the movement of the ferry and the braked resistance of my car being carried across the water. His hands dropped from the wheel and he put one hand on the crown of my head and the other along my neck. Slowly he stroked my skin, slowly, thoughtfully. I could tell he was looking down at me. "So did you have a good time on our cruise, Captain?" I asked, really wondering, needing to know.

"Perfect cruise," he answered. "Pretty good sailing, good planning, decent food, a little stormy adventure—"

"Good company," I added for him and immediately wished I had waited. I studied the underside of the steering column.

"Good company," Max echoed absent-mindedly. "I like Charlie."

"Charlie's the best," I agreed. "He's really been there for me over these last few years."

"You have such soft skin," Max said. "I've never felt such silky skin." His fingers skimmed from my ear to my breastbone over and over. "What are you? Swedish? Norwegian?"

"Irish."

"Irish," he said. "I should have known."

"Why should you have known?"

"That's what Ferrari uses for their car seats."

"Uses what?"

"Irish girls' skin. Now I know why."

I smiled sleepily, savoring the touch of his fingers along my neck.

"So how has Charlie been there for you?"

"Oh, you know. When my husband left. And with Casey."

"What with Casey?"

I felt way off guard—placid, horizontal, and still a little drunk. I pulled myself upright, slapping my cheeks and straining my eyes. The ferry was drawing close to its dock. I watched as it bumped and bounced against the tall pilings and slid roughly into its niche. "Oh, you know. Kids are hard when a parent leaves. It was a rough time. For all of us. And I was working on rewrites of *You Again* when it happened. God, I'm so tired."

"You shouldn't drink," Max said. The gates of the ferry opened onto the darkness of the land, and under a glaring spotlight the ferryman waved us off.

"I hardly ever," I told him. "I just about never drink."

But you remember the time I bought all that champagne, don't you? When I got the grant for those first early stirrings of You Again? *It was a brilliant summer morning when I got the call, and*

I had immediately gone out and bought six bottles of the best stuff I could find.

"Having a celebration?" the man behind the counter had asked me.

"Yes!" I had told even him. "I just got a grant! A state arts grant to write a novel!"

"I'm impressed," he had said. That's exactly what he had said, kind of deadpan, like this: I'm impressed. I can still remember him, and I watched as he carefully put three bottles in each brown bag and put cardboard slices between each bottle to protect them.

Then I had gone home and called some friends you and I had. "Now for sure I will be able to find a publisher," I had told each one. "Come around seven-thirty, and we'll celebrate."

You had come home late that night like a pouting child, after everyone was there. We had all held off on the champagne, waiting for you, and when you finally came in the front door with your attaché case dragging and your tie tugged loose, the corks had popped and the laughter began. "The next Virginia Woolf," someone had called me and I felt awkward because I knew you probably didn't even know who she was, and I had watched you nod and smile as if you did know, but I could tell when you looked into my eyes over the edge of your glass that all was not well. I saw the muscle clench along your jaw when Nick began reciting James Joyce from memory, and I watched you switch from champagne to Scotch when someone asked me how much money I'd be getting with the grant.

They had left after a while, and the two of us had stood out on the front steps, batting away moths and waving good-bye. "Don't any of you call me before noon anymore," I had called. "I'll be writing!"

"Writing for money at last!" one of them yelled back, and I laughed, hugging myself, but you had turned on your heel and gone inside, leaving the door open, letting the moths in.

"Hey!" I complained. "The bugs!" I shut the door after me. I locked it and turned off the hall light.

You were collecting glasses, tucking an ashtray under your arm, wiping a corner of the coffee table with your sleeve.

"Hon? What's wrong?" I followed you into the kitchen empty-handed and watched as you filled the dishwasher.

"Why'd you have to invite all of them?" you said.

"Why? They're our friends."

"None of them care about your writing."

"Of course they care about my writing. They're my friends."

"Then where were they when you needed someone to take Casey for the day so you could write? Where are they when this house gets like a pigsty and you're off somewhere typing?"

"Off somewhere typing? Jesus Christ, I'm right here! All the time! I don't expect my friends to clean my house for—"

"But you expect me to."

"You're my husband. My partner. We do that kind of stuff for each other."

"Just the two of us? Doing those things for each other?"

"Yeah. I've done it for you." Hadn't I? Hadn't I? Typing out reports for you? Running your errands? Fielding phone calls?

"Then just the two of us should celebrate," he said.

The house felt too bright, like some sort of harsh beacon shining randomly into the night. You must have felt it too, because you began shutting off all the lights as you made your way through the house and up the stairs. All the lights were out and I stood there woodenly, the couple of glasses of champagne beginning to pound in my ears.

And it was that night, that night that worried me into not inviting anyone the next time I had something to celebrate, the time Charles Jaspers from Heaton and Clark Publishing called to tell me my manuscript was a gem, and that he would consider it a joy to work with me. I had literally bounced through the house all day: a joy to work with me. I find myself wondering today if that had been true for Charlie, if he had indeed found me a joy to work with. I've never asked.

So I called you in the city that day and gave you the good news. You seemed happy for me, and you didn't have to ask or remind me; I didn't invite anyone to come. I just went out and bought two bottles of champagne, real good stuff, expensive, and I stopped in the cheese store and bought hunks of imported cheeses and fancy crackers. I had everything laid out that night, waiting for you.

Casey was about eleven then, beginning what I now know was to be the start of her tumultuous time, but there was no hint then of how tumultuous it would get. We still had our gentle times together and that night she had helped me put everything out. You were late, so I covered the cheese and went upstairs to help her get ready for bed. She was curious about my excitement.

"What kind of book?" she had asked.

"My novel, the book I've been working on in my office for so long." As the tub filled, she undressed with a new shyness and with her back toward me. I gathered up her dirty clothes and took them to the hamper in the hall closet, listening all the while for the sounds of you arriving downstairs.

"What kind of cover will it have?"

"Oh, I don't know. What do you think? It'll be for grown-ups, so it might not need an illustration. Maybe it'll just be letters." I watched her getting into the tub and noticed her body. Her legs were growing long and straight, and though she was delicate and fine boned, there was nothing curvy about her yet that hinted at the woman she was meant to be. She knelt in the clear hot water and slowly eased herself down.

"Does your book have a title?"

"You Again."

"Me again?" I had knelt beside the tub and was beginning to pour water from my hand onto her back. "Don't do that!" she said, squirming. I leaned my chin on the edge of the tub and stared at the tiles.

"You. Again," I said. "You is the first word. Again is the second word."

"I like Me Again better."

I smiled and poured water from my hand over her knee. "Maa! Stop!"

"Want me to read to you?" I suddenly asked out of my restlessness, and her face brightened.

"Oh, yeah! Like you used to when I was little. Get Wind in the Willows."

"You got it," I said, getting up from the floor. Out in the hall I listened for you. "Is that you, honey?" I called over the banister. Nothing.

"Is Daddy home?" Casey called to me as I shuffled through her bookcase.

"No, Daddy's not home yet."

I sat on the floor that night next to the hissing radiator with my back against the warm tiles, and I loved how my voice sounded bouncing off the walls. I hadn't read to Casey in the bathtub in a long time. I thought how here I was—a soon-to-be-published author, my words between hard covers, just like Joseph Conrad and Dickens, like Faulkner, even, or Joyce Carol Oates, or how about John Updike? I wondered if Jimmy Breslin had ever done this. Or Anne Tyler.

I let the words fill the echoing bathroom. Casey soaped up quietly and let me be the mother, the modest, unpretentious mother, doing a motherly job of reading, and all the while there was this joyous scream in my throat that could barely be contained. I would be a joy to work with. And I couldn't wait for you to get home.

It was your hand on my shoulder that woke me. I turned stiffly on the sofa cushions, turned to face you and to see you in the dim light. The windows were black. "What time is it?" I asked groggily, not yet remembering what scene I was in, what was about to be played out.

"Two-thirty," you answered.

I sat up and sleepily stretched the skin around my eyes. I looked at the coffee table before me with the cut-up cheese nearly gone, the cracker crumbs, and one bottle of nearly empty champagne. And then it all came back. Along with the fine thread of a headache slicing through my eye.

"Why are you late? We were going to celebrate."

You lit a cigarette. "Had to meet Riley downtown. The time just went." A balloon of Scotch grew around us as you spoke and breathed and blew smoke across the table. Your face was slack, as though the bones had been removed and replaced with foul air. I stared at the match you tossed into the cracker crumbs and then I turned back into the sofa cushions. You were drunk. I pulled in my head and my legs and my tail and left only my hard shell for you to knock at. But you didn't knock. I listened as you walked heavily across the rug and then the wooden floor. I listened as you hung up your jacket in the closet and started up the carpeted stairs. I counted your sluggish steps. A tear rolled over the bridge of my nose and into my other eye. I bit my lip to keep from crying, to keep from hating you so much I would kill you.

It was cold on the sofa and I curled in on myself, tucking my fingers under my armpits and jamming my feet under the edge of the cushion. I listened to every move you made upstairs, every step, imagining slicing you up with my sharp carving knife, beginning from the bottom, a slice off your feet with every step you took, then your calves, up your body till I got to your head, until you were just a series of tiddledywinks disks throughout the upstairs rooms. I waited for the sound of your step in our room above my head, and the creak of our bed as you'd take your shoes off.

But there was silence. An awful silence. I sat up, alert now and *rigid, like a panicked dolphin sensing a net drifting down through the waters over the unsuspecting head of her youngster. I stood. Oh, no. I was across the room to the foot of the stairs, listening. But upstairs something dropped softly, squeaked. Casey's old tattered monkey. I took the stairs two or three at a time, stumbling, scraping my shins, banging my hand hard against the banister, all without making a sound. I wouldn't wake Casey. Sleep, Casey, sleep, please, sleep.*

I flipped on the hall light and froze in the doorway to her room. "Get out," I hissed.

You were kneeling beside her bed, one arm curved around her pillowed head, and your other arm over her, drawing her to you. You ignored me. I had no choice.

At first I pulled frantically on your sweater and your shirt, and when you resisted me and they tore, I dug my nails into your hair, your shoulder, your pants, wherever I could get a hold. Through gritted teeth I hoarsely whispered, "Get out, get out, get out, get out," over and over as low as I could.

"Get the fuck—" You grabbed my wrist and twisted it until I knelt on the floor beside the bed. "Are you crazy?"

"Get out of here, get out of here, out, now." I grabbed for your leg, and when my hands weren't strong enough my teeth were all I had. I went after you with my mouth, to tear you and shake you and leave you for dead.

Now you were yelling. "GET! THE! FUCK! OFF!" Casey stirred in the dark shadows of her bed.

"Shhhhh, oh shhhh, Casey. It's just Mommy, honey, get back to sleep now."

"Daddy's home?" she said groggily, sitting up.

"Yes, yes, Daddy's just going to bed now." I pushed past you to her side and patted her back down under her blankets. I picked her monkey up off the floor and tucked it under her chin. Her eyes closed. When you reached past me to touch her I was as fast as a

snake, grabbing one of your fingers and cranking it back on your hand. But you have always been stronger than I, and with two hands you had me by my wrists, up on my feet, and you dragged me out into the hall. All this with barely a sound.

You shook me hard, till my head cracked against the wall outside Casey's room again and again. And I lied to myself that she never heard. Never heard a thing. "You crazy bitch! What is it with you?" you growled.

"Stay away from her," I said. "I don't care what you do. You can fuck Riley for all I care. You can move out. You can glue your ass to a bar stool for the rest of your life." You kept shaking me, banging me up against the wall as if you were shaking those words out of me. "Just stay away from her."

Suddenly you were very still, staring at me. I had never seen your face like that: transformed. Where there had been no bones before, now there was steel, where there had been glassy eyes, now there was fire. I often wonder if I had pushed you to this awful place with my own inexplicable fears. Hadn't they colored everything I looked upon, not only you, but Casey as well?

"Are you out of your mind?" you whispered. You tossed me away from you, and I crashed into the wall, crumpled in a heap thinking you would come after me, but you went into our bedroom and slammed the door.

I stayed where I was, quiet and still, listening for Casey's sleeping breath, but I couldn't hear it. I leaned back against the wall and listened to my own sounds. My breath. Casey's breath. My father's. Her father's. It was all mixed up for me.

I touched the back of my hand to my sore lip, and rubbed my swelling wrists. So there I was, potentially famous, or at least soon to be mentioned in the New York Times Book Review, and I was sitting in my upstairs hallway at three in the morning. I wanted to be a joy to work with, an unpretentious mother leading a charmed life. And really, who would have guessed I wasn't?

I don't know if you saw it, but You Again *got more than a mere mention in the* New York Times Book Review. *It made the coveted first page. The headline said "Frequently, ever not ..," a line lifted straight from the protagonist's revealing journal, and then in the upper left-hand corner:*

> *You Again*
> By Ellie Brinkley.
> 422 pp. New York:
> Heaton and Clark Publishing. $19.98

There was an editorial sort of illustration of a man standing at the head of a line of other men who all looked exactly like him. It was very clever, but I didn't see this until a week after it came out, because when Charlie called to tell me, on the Thursday before it was to appear, his call interrupted the policeman who was still at the house asking questions. When I anxiously and hopefully answered the phone and heard his gentle voice, I said, "Casey's gone, Charlie. She's run away." That was the first time she'd run, and that more than any other time after carried the threat of danger and imminent disaster. But it wasn't till that very moment that I finally broke down and cried. And of course Charlie wasn't about to tell me about the review then. Even though it was wonderful.

It's strange, but I keep thinking it was my mother who had tried to teach me that everything in life balances out in the end. It was unlike my mother to be philosophical. That was more my father's style, yet still, everything balancing out in the end carries the faint coffee taint of my mother's breath. It all balances out: the more good you have in your life, the more bad you have in your life, and you've got to take them both.

For some reason that reminds me of the decorative balancing scales she kept on the coffee table in the living room. It was a colonial wooden thing, a post that had two wooden dishes hanging by chains from each end, dishes that were forever crooked and tipping over, spilling out pinecones at Christmastime and plastic grass and eggs in the spring. I used to try to get them even, to balance them. Ten of Peter's toy metal soldiers could lift the TV Guide in the air. One empty beer can would weigh the same as seven pinecones and a candle. And now I could put my front-page review on one dish and in the other Casey, and you, my father, my mother, the Little El, and the scale's chains would come loose and spill all over. Nothing balances. Nothing at all balances like she'd promised.

———

My mother sits in the kitchen at the table reading. It's the afternoon and I think it's a magazine she's reading or else a novel she's gotten from her book club. She's sipping a mug of coffee and absentmindedly reaching into a bag of potato chips torn open on the table.

My father comes into the kitchen and tosses a duffel bag on the chair, and pulling his wallet out counts out some bills and puts them on the table. It's then that I notice his fishing poles standing in the corner.

"Where you going, Daddy?"

"Fishing, sweetie, out on the *Little El.*"

I look at the clock. Three o'clock.

"Night fishing? You're going night fishing!"

"That's right," he tells me. And to her, "Here's some cash till I get back. Probably tomorrow night or the next morning."

She turns the page she's reading.

"Can't I go with you, Daddy? Please?"

My mother's voice, hard like a stone: "No."

"Oh, why, oh, why? I love to go night fishing. Can I get to hold the big flashlight, Daddy? Can I shine the light into the water?"

"Why can't she come?"

My mother folds the bills and puts them in her apron pocket without looking at either of us. "Because she can't. That's all. I don't want her out on the water all that time. At night."

"Why, Mommy, why?" I am near tears.

"Because I say so!" She's looking right at me now, and when our eyes meet my tears spill over. "And don't give me that."

I lower my head, wanting to cry and run away, but I stay, hoping he'll win this one, hoping he'll persuade her it's okay for me to be out this one night on the boat. I reach out my hand and loop one finger in the pocket to his pants, an unspoken covenant between us, and he tries.

"She's good on the boat at night, Tina. She's a careful sailor. And I may need a matey for this cruise after all." He has reached out and placed his hand on top of my head. His fingers flicker in my hair.

My mother stands up. "Listen," she says in a menacing voice, "she's been up late every night this week. She's just getting over an earache. And I said no."

I feel the hesitation in my father, feel the pause and the hopelessness run through his hand on my head. "Well, maybe next time, patootie. Why don't you go upstairs for me and get——"

And as he says this he lifts his hand to point into the dining room, and at the same moment Peter appears at that very spot, sees my father's hand raised, and as if he's been shot by a machine gun Peter flinches and hits the floor. The three of us stare at him, horrified.

"Peter!" my father says. "What is it?"

Peter's face is perfectly round. His eyes are round, his nose, his mouth. All round circles, and he says, "I thought you were going to hit me."

My mother pushes past my father and me to get to Peter. "I guess you're happy now!" she snaps. She cups her hands under his armpits, and even though he is eight and gangly she picks him up and holds him to her. His legs hang down along her sides and foolishly he puts his head on her shoulder.

My father seems stuck. I look at his face and I am afraid he might cry. "Happy?" he whispers. "Do you really think that makes me happy?"

"Get out of here," she says. "Go fish on your goddamned boat."

My hand is firmly looped in the back of his belt now and I can see the side of his face, flushed and tender. He waits and then very quietly he says, "Come on, patootie. Let's go night fishing."

"Don't you dare," my mother warns. I think she is saying it to me, but she is looking at him. The kitchen floor is suddenly buckling and churning beneath me like a floating dock. I take a step. He hoists his poles and his duffel bag and they glare at each other.

"Ellie—" my mother says.

But I follow my father from the kitchen, through the dining room, the living room, out the door, down the front porch steps.

"Get back here, Elizabeth! Right this minute!" But I don't look back. She doesn't understand.

Neither did you. Do you remember saying the exact same thing to me in court that day with Casey? That's where I'd heard it! "I guess you're happy now," you had said, just like my mother had. My mother looks out at me accusingly from my childhood, and you look out at me from our marriage. God, how right you both thought you were. And yet neither of you really knew how I would have to live with both their deaths, how I would live believing I was somehow guilty, as surely as though I had held them suspended over a torrential river's bridge and let them go, one at a time.

I kept putting off taking the *Nemaste* out by myself. A few times I persuaded Max to visit the *Nemaste* with me for just an afternoon, for some day sails during the early hot days of August. It wasn't the best winds for sailing, but usually in the late morning, once the fog lifted, there would be enough breeze for us to maneuver out in. Max was one for always using the outboard motor whenever we were leaving or approaching the dock. My father never would have done that, and remembering this I encouraged Max to leave the dock one morning under just sail power.

"What's the big deal?" Max wanted to know.

"It's no 'big deal,'" I told him. "I just hate the noise. Why don't we try?"

"It's not good to be so close to land here without having the motor ready to pull us away."

"But we're tied up," I reminded him. "We won't cast off until she's pulling out."

So I left him at the tiller, risked looking like I knew too much, and while he watched, doubtful and sulky, I scrambled around, hoisted the mainsail until it filled with late morning air, and once the *Nemaste* was straining to go I tossed off the lines onto the dock and smiled back at Max. "See?"

Max gave me the thumb's-up sign and looked away. "You're the captain," he said.

I went and sat by him, circled my hand beneath his bare thigh. "*You're* the captain," I corrected him. "Aren't you? You're *my* captain."

"You're good enough at all this. You don't need me here all the time anymore." I thought nervously of maybe coming out alone, oddly paralyzed at the thought of leaving the dock with no one on board but me.

"But we still have two more times," I said softly. I felt like a paratrooper must feel when the doors slide open in the belly of the aircraft.

"Then let's do one of them."

"What do you mean, 'let's do one of them.' Jeez, Max, you sound like you've been married to me for centuries already."

Thank God he laughed.

"I mean it. That's awful. Maybe with you I should have said just three times. Maybe five is too much."

He suddenly held me in a headlock, forcing me to my knees in front of him, between him and the tiller. "Get off it," he teased. "Three times would never be enough for you. You'd spend the rest of your life pining for me. Searching the streets of Long Beach. Calling my name in dark alleys."

We were heading out into the bay, a gentle wake kicking up behind us. "You mean you want to just use up one now, here? In one afternoon?" I asked.

He looked at his watch. "Well, my wife and kiddies aren't expecting me home till dinner."

I nuzzled my face against the front of his cutoffs. He cupped his hand behind my head, ruffling my hair as I rubbed my face back and forth, my forehead, my nose, my lips against him. "It's not enough," I said.

"I'll make you come," he promised.

I shook my head no.

"Thirty-seven times," he begged.

"No." I ducked backwards under the tiller and sat across from him. "That's too depressing to use it up in one afternoon, so quick."

"So quick? Thirty-seven times is so quick?"

"But then there'll only be one more time together, and it will almost be like we wasted number four."

Max clasped his hand over his erection and squeezed his knees together. "Oh, no, and look what you've done. You have to help me, Ellie. You can't leave me like this."

"You'll live." I stood and looked ahead thoughtfully in the direction we were sailing. I needed Max. I needed Max most of all to keep sailing, so I could be on the boat and start the writing soon. "Let's try to make it all the way around the island today. Do you think? Do we have time?" I looked back at him.

"Around the island?"

"Once."

"On one condition," he said, and he waited.

"Name your price, Captain."

"We set the date for number four."

I stared into the sunny glare of the water and counted up the empty days ahead. "How about sometime during the last week in August?" I asked. "For a couple of days. We'll sleep on the boat." The bay sparkled and shone.

"What about Casey?" he wanted to know.

"What about her?"

"What will you do with her?"

In the distance wind rippled the dark water like illusory schools of fish. "She has camp that week."

"Camp?"

I remembered the camp she had gone to once right on the island, the camp Charlie had told us about.

"Yeah, right here on the island. By Jennings Point, as a matter of fact. She goes there every summer for a week." I felt the lie settle over my face like a vinyl mask. I peered out at him through the eyeholes.

"Okay," he said, smiling. "It's a deal."

We sailed around the island that day and on into the night. It took longer than I'd originally thought, and when it grew late and he didn't want to tack forever through the stretch past Dering Harbor and Pipes Cove, Max insisted on using the outboard.

Unlike my father. My father never would've used the outboard. He prided himself on his tight tacks, and on how he could inch his way along into the wind. What a sailor he was. I remembered the incredible way he had stopped the *Little El* that last time, when we'd gone night fishing and he had wanted to find a sheltered spot to spend the night.

———

The sky is purple and peach above us and the sun so precise and defined that I can look right at it. My father is sailing along under this canopy of sky and color, and me, I'm wearing his sweatshirt and I've pulled its hood tight around my face and tucked my hands up into the sleeves. I stay close to his side, pressing against his warmth as he cruises along the dark and wild shore.

"Hmmmm. There's a mooring," he says aloud, but I know he is talking to himself. "Wonder if it belongs to anybody who'll be back tonight."

He sails past it closely, straining to see, looking all about us. There is no one, no one about, and as the sky continues to darken, lights begin to dot the shore.

He turns to me and offers me the tiller. "Here, Ellie, you steer while I get the sails ready, and when I say now, turn her into the wind, right into it, you hear?"

I nod and look up at the telltales. And I sail on into the night. He goes up ahead and I catch glimpses of his black silhouette taking down the jib. I hear him toss the sailbag below. And then he begins to let the mainsail down, only partially, as though he is going to reef it, but he leaves it up soft and wavering. He comes back again and stands by me, steering himself for a moment, and then he again presses my own hands to the tiller. The boat is moving ever so slowly through the water.

"All right now," he says. "Turn her into the wind." And I slowly push the tiller with my eye on the shrouds until the telltales stand straight back, like ribbons on the braids of a little girl, and as I turn into the wind, my father moves slowly forward, with each step pulling handfuls of the mainsail down. It is perfectly choreographed, his steps, the lowering of the sail, the telltales, the water, so perfect that when his steps finally take him to the bow, with the sail white and limp behind him, the

Little El comes to a complete stop in the water and all he has to do is reach down with one hand and clasp the mooring. I can see him etched in purple with a lavender aura, against the tail end of the sunset. He kneels to tie up to the mooring.

Oh, how I loved my father, with such a deep, fierce love. I would have steered wherever he told me. My love was so deep, so fierce, there was nothing I wouldn't have done for him, no hardship I wouldn't have endured, nothing, until that night, until he showed me what else there could be.

*T*ime and again as I stood alone on the deck of the *Nemaste,* I would ask myself, why have I so little courage left in me? I would go to bed the night before, braced and determined to get up the next day, to drive out alone and take her out on the bay by myself. Such was my tenacity that had my car broken down on the parkway, I think I would have just gotten out and continued walking in the direction of Charlie's dock. But once I was on board the boat, once I had stowed my stuff below and prepared the sails, I would stand paralyzed, unable to cast off from the dock. Even if the wind had tugged me away, even if I'd been able to leave without the motor, I didn't have whatever it took to let go of the lines that kept me locked to shore.

I would stand motionless, immobilized, so glad that Charlie wasn't there watching me, pitying me through his kitchen window. My strange paralysis reminded me of the day after Casey was born, when I stiffly took myself to the hospital bathroom, sat gingerly on the toilet, tender from my stitches, aching all over, waiting, and nothing happened. My bladder felt ready to burst, and still nothing happened. Not a drop. I even laughed at first, thinking somehow I had forgotten how to release my own water. How was that possible? Yet whatever network of communication had been between those tiny muscles in my urethra and the willful cells in my brain, it was traumatized by the birthing, and in time the nurses had to bring a sharp and bitter tube to empty me.

But now there was no solution. There was no one to unknot the lines for me, or to tell me I was strong and capable, and to "go on ahead." I touched the compass that was suspended from the cockpit wall. I spun it and the universe twirled about me.

The only other times I could remember when I'd had to muster such an enormous amount of courage were those times in family court, when I had walked through steel traps, over burning coals, through quicksand, and under crumbling bridges. I was like the chap in an old Buster Keaton film who stands before a collapsing building that tilts and falls directly on top of him to crush him, and when the dust clears, there he is, standing exactly where he was, in a window opening. I stood there before the judge, trembling.

"Why won't you take your daughter back into your home, Mrs. Brinkley?" the judge says, his head cocked way forward, his chin pressed into his chest, so he can look down at me from his lofty perch, look down at me over his glasses.

"I don't think she's safe there," I answer, not sure whether to say Your Honor, Your Highness, sir.

"Why is that?"

"We've tried it," I answer, and here my mother's palm would slice through the air and sting my cheek for the tone in my voice. "Isn't it in the records? Didn't you read what happened?"

The judge glares at me, no doubt deciding that Casey's gotten her lousy attitude from me, but he hadn't been there with me during her home visits, no one was, no one drove with me through the streets of town, stopping in the delis, the 7-Eleven, the deserted basketball courts. "Have you seen Casey?" I had asked the group of boys sitting on a bench by the railroad station. They looked like the same group I'd watched sitting on my front stoop that afternoon, laughing and smoking while Casey strutted and flashed for them.

"Who?" one of them asked.

"The Brink," another answered him, and they all shrugged.

"Haven't seen her. No. She hasn't been here." One of them smiled.

"Well, if you happen to see her, tell her her mother's looking for her and she's got to get back to school."

"Right," they answered. "If we see her."

And when I drove away I watched them in the rearview mirror, so sure they were laughing at me.

I came across Casey by accident, once I'd given up and headed back to the house. I was ready to call Our Lady of the Shepherds and report her as a runaway. But she was walking up the front walk as I turned in the driveway.

I put the car in park and flung open the door on her side. "Get in," I ordered.

"I have to get my stuff," she snapped, pointing at the house.

"All your stuff is in the car already," I told her. "Get in."

She got in the back with her bag that was tossed on the floor and slammed the door shut. "How do I know you got all my stuff?" she asked. "Did you put my tapes in here?"

I ignored her, grateful she had sat in back, out of my range. I scattered gravel as I backed out the driveway. "I was supposed to get you back to school hours ago," I stated. "You'll probably lose your next weekend privileges now."

She didn't answer me.

"How can I keep letting you come home if you don't follow the rules when you're here? First of all, you and Dr. Phelan and I had agreed on 'no boys' during these first visits—"

I was at a stop sign and I abruptly turned and looked at her. Her eyes met mine and I just stared at her. I couldn't go forward.

"What's the matter with you?" she asked.

"You've been drinking," I whispered.

"I have not," she answered as though I was boring her, tiring her out with my accusations.

"Not only were you were drinking," I said quietly, "I can tell you were drinking rum."

Silence. She looked away from me.

I opened the window. I gripped the steering wheel and took deep breaths. Someone behind me beeped and finally went around. It made Casey nervous.

"What are you doing? Why are you stopping?"

Slowly I put the car into gear and eased through the intersection. I accelerated and imagined myself going faster and faster and then hitting a tree, one of those sidewalk sycamore trees with the peeling bark. I could even see the bark sprinkled all over my car as they pried our dead bodies out of the crushed seats.

"That's it," I said calmly, realizing my arms were numb,

that my hands were growing hotter and hotter. "No more home visits until you've had a lot more treatment."

"So what. I'll go to Dad's."

Over my dead body, I thought, but didn't say. After that day I never said another word to Casey. We rode in silence back to the school and she got out without a word to me. I left the car doors open and went into the foyer. A young woman was at the switchboard.

"Excuse me," I said, "I've left my car running, but I just wanted to report, I want someone to know that Cassandra Brinkley is back, three hours late." I hadn't looked but I heard Casey slam the door behind her as she disappeared down a long hall. "And someone should know she's been drinking. Maybe you'll want to do a urine test or something."

"Oh, we can't do that without the girl's permission, ma'am." The young woman looked at me innocently.

I stared at her. "No. No, of course not. How foolish of me. Just make sure someone knows she was drinking, okay?"

"What was her name again?"

The judge clears his throat and I look up at him. "Excuse me?" I say.

He looks down at his papers. "I said if you won't have her in her house, we have to have some place where she can go on home visits, some place that we can use as a reward."

I wait.

"It says here in our records, Mrs. Brinkley, records which I have read carefully—" a glance over his glasses—"that you won't give permission for her to go to her father's apartment in the city. Why is that, may I ask?"

"Maybe I wouldn't object if Casey went to her father's *apartment,* but the fact is she goes to her father's bar. There have been times with him when she's spent the whole day in one bar or another."

"Yes, so you say in the records here, but have you personally witnessed this? How can you be so sure?"

I feel like the walls are closing in on me. The floor is rising, the ceiling lowering. My voice is a whisper. "Because I know," I say. "Because she's told me."

"Where is Mr. Brinkley?" the judge asks the social worker.

"He couldn't come today, your honor. He had a work commitment."

I smile. "If you call this little tavern on Second Avenue, 212-560—"

The gavel pounds like gunshot. "You're out of order!"

My face grows hot.

He continues. "From this date forward, home visits will be with Mr. Brinkley—"

"But how will she get there?" I ask, everything blurred now by my tears.

The judge looks to the social worker. "What's your answer to that?"

Her hands are clasped before her as though she's handcuffed. "We've arranged for Cassandra to take a train into the city alone and be met by him at the station."

"But she's run away on trains before!" I cried. "She was picked up once for buying drugs in the station—"

Again the gavel pounds and pounds and I am silenced. The judge shuffles his papers and makes his declarations while I feel the foundation tremble, watch the great wall tip forward and collapse on top of me, but this time when the dust clears, I am gone. And I will never go back to family court again.

It took tremendous courage for me to go there, and I'm still not sure whether or not my decisions to ignore future summons were acts of more profound courage or acts of monumental cowardice. Whatever it was, I would live to say I had been right; *I told you so* could have been my banner. Yet how unproductive and futile such words are, like pouring a cup of water on your house when it has already burned to ashes.

But years later it seemed I'd grown so lacking in courage that I became paralyzed at the thought of sailing my own boat. So I decided to go out to Charlie's alone with no intention of sailing the *Nemaste* at all. I would just write on board her. That was all. I took along some deli chicken, soda, chips, plenty of white typing paper sealed in plastic, and my old manual typewriter that I'd had since high school. I brought a sleeping bag, too, promising myself I would sleep on her that night, right at the dock, sleep on her alone and see what inspiration came to me.

It was an unusually cool day for August, with high puffy white clouds in a blue sky, and I was comfortable in my jeans and a T-shirt. I'd brought along a thermos of coffee, and I poured myself a solitary mug. I sat in the cockpit, feeling strangely at peace. When I leaned my head back and closed my eyes with the mug held warmly between my hands, I tried to feel how far away the surface of the sky was, the way a blind person can feel by the air on her face how far she is from a wall. I never even unwrapped the sails that day, noting to myself that there was nothing in the world more still than a stored sail, an old sail secured and wound by worn and twisted bungee cords.

And when I finally set up the small table below and placed my typewriter on it, I stumbled and bumbled my way through the first sentence, "There is nothing more motionless, more lacking motion, stiller, nothing in the world more subdued, more still, than a stored sail, an old, worn sail, a worn sail secured and wound, held by old, worn, stretched-out, twisted bungees, bungee cords." After writing on a computer for a few years, using an ordinary typewriter felt like making my way through buffalo grass with a rattling lawnmower.

But I wrote. I wrote descriptions of the interior of the boat, its redness, its whiteness, where the dirt collected, where the charts were best rolled or folded. I would stand outside and stare at the boat from the position of the tiller, and then as though I were balancing a huge basket overflowing with fruit I'd hurry below and try to write down everything I'd seen, popping back out again and again for more cherries, more pineapples.

As it grew late and my fingers started to cramp from the manual typing, I took a seat on top at the bow with my back against the cool mast and I silently watched the sun begin to descend. I had brought along a pen and a pad, but it lay empty and clean beside me. I wished instead I had brought a sweater, but I was too lazy, too mesmerized to move. I don't even remember the sound of Charlie's footsteps on the dock, maybe it was the breeze over my ears, but when the boat rocked softly, I turned and saw him come aboard.

"Ahoy, Captain," he said and laughed. I knew he thought no one had ever said that before, and I smiled.

"Welcome aboard, landlubber."

"Stay where you are, Ellie. I'm coming your way."

"I didn't know you were coming out here today, Charlie." He was still wearing suit pants and a dress shirt, but the tie was gone and he was barefoot. I noticed his pale white feet with little ghosts of paler corns on the knuckles of his toes.

"I didn't know either, but there was a bomb scare this morning in the Heaton and Clark building, would you believe, and it's Thursday, and tomorrow's Friday, so I thought what the hey."

"*You* thought, 'What the hey?'" I leaned back against the mast and laughed. "I can't imagine."

"I ate a late lunch," he said, "and I don't have any food yet to offer you—"

"Oh, please, pretend I'm not even here. I have some chicken left, and a thermos of lukewarm coffee, and a whole bag of sour cream chips."

Charlie grinned stupidly. "Sour cream chips? A whole bag?"

"You like sour cream chips, Charlie?"

He nodded and held up a small case. "And look what I brought for us." I felt warm and glad he was there.

"What have you got?"

"Cribbage. I'm going to teach you," he said, and he stood and started back to the cockpit. "It's an old sailor's game."

I glanced back into the sunset and smiled. I gathered up my pad and pen and said, "I know how to play cribbage. My father taught me when I was little." The boat rocked beneath my weight. "But you'll have to refresh my memory, Charlie. It's been a long time."

The little lights in the cabin worked, shining a warm glow over everything. Charlie and I sat opposite each other on the makeshift table, the cribbage board between us and the bag of potato chips on its side and opened like an origami lily.

"So have you taken her out yet by yourself, Ellie?"

I shook my head and put two cards aside for my crib.

"How come?" he asked, dropping his two on top of mine.

"I'm afraid," I said, "plain and simple." I fanned my cards open to see them. Then I held them to my chest and looked at him.

"Of what?" he asked. He held a small red peg poised to count.

"Of not being brave, I guess. Have *you* ever had a time when you've had to show tremendous courage, Charlie?"

He leaned back against the red cushion and closed his eyes. He opened one eye to look at me. "Would you be terribly disappointed if I told you my life has been pretty much devoid of courage and adventure?"

"Everybody has to be brave at some point," I insisted.

"I don't know." He put down a seven of hearts. "Seven."

"A pair for two," I said, putting down a seven of diamonds.

He glanced at me. "I thought you said it had been a while."

"It's in my blood." I smiled at him and counted off my two points on the board. "But tell me. Can't you think of any time you've been brave? Any time at all?"

"Does going to see my endodontist count?"

I shook my head.

"What comes to mind," Charlie said thoughtfully, "when I scrape my memories for scenes of heroism or bravery, is a dim memory of my father's Doberman, Duke."

"Your father had a Doberman?" I said. "Jeez, that would scare *me* too."

"Oh, no, he was a great dog, very gentle. I wasn't afraid of him at all. But I was thinking about how Duke would go insane with fear in a lightning storm. It was fascinating. I used to wonder what he could have been thinking. I was about eight or nine, I guess, and here was this bold, strong dog, who probably weighed more than I did, and as soon as the slightest hint of distant thunder would rumble, he was under the radio, shaking."

"Under the radio?"

"Mmm. My father had this huge mahogany radio that was like a piece of furniture." His glasses were on the very tip of his nose. He rearranged his three cards. "You know, kind of an early version of today's entertainment center.

"Anyway, it was on decorative claw-feet legs with a crossbar between them. And when the thunder would crack, old Duke'd cower under the radio in complete and total abject fear. Soon he had the crossbars broken, which really infuriated my mother, but there was no comforting Duke. I can remember on a sunny afternoon climbing under the radio myself to see what it was like under there, to kind of experience what Duke was feeling." Charlie shrugged and picked up his cards again. "I don't know. It never felt especially safe to me."

"Whatever happened to Duke?" I asked.

"Happened? Huh, I don't remember. I guess he just got old and died. Probably while I was away at boarding school."

I thought I knew. "Maybe he got struck by lightning."

Charlie burst out laughing. "Oh, Ellie, that's good."

I stared at him.

"Ellie!" He laughed more and popped a big chip in his mouth.

"What?" I insisted. "Maybe he knew something you didn't know."

Charlie shook his head and wiped a tear from his eye. "Oh, that's good. That's very good. I wish my mother were alive to hear that. She'd scream."

"You really haven't experienced fear yourself, have you?" I asked him.

Charlie smiled at me and dropped a seven of spades on the pile. "And another seven for six. I love you writers," he said, counting off his points and smiling. "You have such crazy minds."

"Crazy minds, ay?" I snapped down a jack of clubs. "Thirty-one for one and his nibs for another. Take that, Mr. Smee."

Right before the time Max was due to come sail with me again at the end of August, I went out with the single intention of cleaning the boat up thoroughly, as though cleaning it would make it less formidable and help it feel more like something I commanded. I thought that maybe if I touched every spot on her, I would trust her more, trust her and myself more.

I arrived at Charlie's with my car's trunk full of cleaners, sponges, scrub brooms and brushes, polishes, duct tape and rags. I wiped her down inside and out, even the storage compartments. I polished her teak, the teak along the side shelves and along the hatch, and also the darkened post beneath the mast. Once that was done I knew the hardest part lay ahead.

I searched the rear storage for the long-handled broom I had noticed there, and taking it with me, I stepped out onto Charlie's dock. From there, on her port side, I scrubbed the green growth on her hull beneath the waterline. The sun was warm on my back and I was soon perspiring. I worked my way slowly forward, watching the water grow cloudy with simple life. I should have put on my bathing suit, but I knew I wouldn't have gone in the water, not alone, not without Max there, and certainly not with all those living cells that would stickily cling to my skin and make me itch.

When that side was done I lowered myself gingerly into the dinghy. Then, keeping myself loosely bound to the *Nemaste,* first to this cleat and then that, I worked my way around the boat, from the bow to the stern, scrubbing the starboard side. I had to hang onto the gunwale with one hand and scrub the broom back and forth with the other.

It was a mindless task, and I thought things like "a household task, a boathold task," and I idly wondered if there was such a word: *boathold.* Then I worked myself around to the stern. My arms were weary and my mind grew quiet. I tossed the broom behind me into the dinghy and touched the carefully stenciled letters with my wet fingers: *Nemaste.* It made me wonder if Max had named her, or someone before him. I had never asked. I eased along the stern, reaching for the brush again, knowing there was just a little more to do.

The outboard motor hung heavily off the back, cranked up out of the water. I touched its blades, and like a certain scent can stir a part of the brain that hasn't been stirred in years the touch of it on my fingers stirred me and I grew very still.

This was so much like the *Little El.*

For some reason my father has lowered the engine tonight, saying earlier that the shoreline isn't too safe here, and just in case we drift before sunrise we'll be ready to move away from it quickly. But he's not making evening preparations now. I can't see him anymore. He's not answering me. And I am floating in the dark water off the stern under a starless black sky.

"Daddy, I'm sorry. Please help me up. Daddy! Answer me!" The water is cold and I am trembling. I look out to the dark shore, but it is so far away that the lights that dot it may as well be stars.

My father doesn't come for me. I wait for him to appear, to reach his big, strong hand over the side, to help me back in, to pull me up by one hand the way I've seen him hold Peter out at his side.

"Daddy?" I whisper.

I cling to the locked blades, and when it seems he will never come and my feet are growing numb I try to climb up the back of the motor. I get a foothold on a blade while my hands are scrambling for a better, higher hold. But it all slips, and my ankles slice along the blades, my hands and wrists tear on the bolts that hold the motor to the boat—and I am dropped deep into the water, screaming.

Again I try, gasping for breath now and panicked, feeling sharp pains in my feet like strings tied around them too tightly.

I get a foothold on the blades, knives slicing now, my fingers locked onto the bar and bolts, only this time I grab the loose end of the stern anchor line. In this way, I make my way up the stern, until I claw and clamber my way over the edge. Breathless and crying, I tumble on top of my father, who is lying facedown on the floor of the cockpit. By the illumination of the mast lights, I see the black puddle that his head lies in. His eyes are open as though he's looking at the cockpit bench, past it, I think to the compass. I look at the compass too. It's steady at 340 degrees. I look back at him. I stare at his chest that is very still. His lips that are closed. I know there is something I should be doing. Some artificial respiration, maybe, but I know without trying that he is too heavy for me to move. And I know, without being told, that I have killed him.

In a peculiar awakening, a shift in time and place, I heard Charlie's cardinals clicking up the path in the vegetable garden. By the time I had pulled the dinghy to the dock my whole body was trembling. Somehow I hoisted myself out and made my way back to the boat's cockpit. I was grateful to find it empty, clean and empty, and I sat there on the bench until the birds quieted and until I had convinced myself that what I was feeling was just a child's memory, and that it was from too long ago to matter.

$\mathcal{T}$he boat was clean and ready the day Max and I finally got out for our August sail. We got to Charlie's in the afternoon, getting a late start, we said, to get past the hottest part of the day. As I look back on those last days out with Max and try to recall the good parts, I smile to remember how I drove my car out with Max beside me, and it was so hot we kept all the windows rolled down, and on the parkway our heads were like frenzied riots of brown and black whipped hair. It stung my face and neck, and we played the radio real loud. Max cracked open a bottle of chilled mineral water, and while I kept my eyes on the road he poured streams of water on my legs and smoothed it over my thighs. Then he sprinkled it across my shoulders and down my collar under my shirt.

"Know what smoreplay is?" he shouted over the wind and music while trickling cool water on my neck and smoothing it in.

"What?"

"SMOREPLAY!"

"I can't imagine!"

He poured more water down the front of my T-shirt and patted my nipples with a lazy affection. "That's what smurfs do before they smuck!" A passing trucker beeped and pulled on his whistle, and we laughed.

It all seemed so right again, so tight and lasting, like I could be with Max forever, easily for the rest of my life. So maybe I did hold on a little too tight those last days out. I let myself forget, or maybe I just refused to remember that there were only two more times.

If we had put up the mainsail and the genoa right there at the dock, and pulled in all the lines, we would have sat motionless in the back of Charlie's quiet and empty house for days. There wasn't the tiniest puff of wind, not a breeze to be had. So to be funny, Max did raise the sails, did pull in and wind up all the lines that had held us to the dock. He stood with his hands on his hips. "I know," he said suddenly. "I'll tie her to the dinghy and we'll row for a wind!"

"Right," I said, "and I'll blow on the sails and we'll fly." Ignoring him, then, I lowered the motor and got it roaring. The sails did nothing but make shade for us to sit in. So we motored lazily for over an hour out into the waiting bay. The water was a dark and shimmery mirror. No wind. No current. The fish were probably barely moving, hot and still at the bottom, on a sandy bed.

We were soon out of sight of Charlie's, at an unexplored place in the bay, surrounded by a glassy plate of motionless water. Not a soul was around, and we were equally distant from all shores when Max turned the motor off and we sat opposite each other in complete silence. The dinghy floated behind us with no tension in its line, and the sun was going down in a muted sky, just pale pink streaks to the west.

"We won't even need an anchor," I whispered into the empty air.

Max was quiet and I watched his face, absorbing and memorizing him so thoroughly that even today, all this time later, I can recall it in great detail, the sharpness of his cheek, the curls around his neck, the cool flawless rise of his forehead, and his dark eyes that turned on me. Suddenly Max tensed and hunkered down strangely, his face crafty and twisted. "Ah," he whispered, "that white whale tasks me, HE HEAPS ME!" Max leaped up onto the bench, animated and taut. He shaded his eyes. "Aye, like a corkscrew he's stuck full of harpoons, men, and his spout is a big one, like a whole shock of wheat, and he fantails like a broken jib in a storm." He pointed at me, glaring, and came slowly toward me. "Death, men, you've seen him." His voice grew deep and low. "It's Moby Dick."

Max wound his arms slowly around me. Everything was so quiet, so still, we could have been in a padded room. His breath wound down my neck, and his fingers brushed over me in places of uncertainty and I chuckled from a deep and open place. Then—he released me and sprang to the bench. "Thar she blows off the starboard beam, m'boys!" And in an instant Max was overboard.

I laughed and leaned over the side after him.

He was swimming furiously and disappeared around the bow.

I sat grinning and waiting, pushing down the wings of panic that flickered inside me as the time stretched on. He'd be back. "Max?" He wasn't there. I moved to the other side of the boat and looked down into the still water. "Ahab? Captain Ahab?"

Nothing.

"Max?"

He suddenly shot up into the air about four yards from the boat. "HE BREECHES!" he shouted and he slapped his body into the water and sank.

"Jesus, Max," I said, kneeling on the bench and feeling my heart pound. How would I have gotten home? I found myself stealing a glance at the motor, the sails. "Don't ever do that again," I scolded when his grinning face finally bobbed up to the surface. "You scared me nearly to death."

"And what were you scared of?" he teased. "That you'd never see my handsome face again?"

"No. That I'd be all alone here."

He laughed. "Nice! I could just see you calling the Coast Guard to come get you, and once they tied you safely to Charlie's dock, you'd say, 'Oh, yeah, by the way, I think my friend drowned out there.'"

"You know what I mean," I said weakly.

"Do I?" he muttered playfully. Then, "Come on in. The water's soup."

"We're not anchored," I reminded him, pointing up at the sails.

He made a face like I was ridiculous and maybe I was. If anything the stillness was deepening. I hesitated. I was suddenly trembling. The thought of sinking into the water at that moment was more than I could bear, but I started to take my clothes off. Mechanically, deliberately, I removed my T-shirt and folded it on the bench. I stepped out of my shorts, my underpants, I slid my bra down my arms and hung it by its two straps from the tiller. Then I pulled the inflatable dinghy close to the side.

"Coward," he taunted.

Awkwardly, knowing he was watching, and feeling very naked, I eased myself over the gunwale and lowered myself down, my foot pressing deep into the floor of the dinghy and my hands gripping the sides of the *Nemaste*. Then I let go and tumbled into its padded warmth. Max swam up alongside.

"The oars in there?" Max asked.

And I nodded yes, thinking I felt their hardness beneath me. So he unwound the line to the boat and began to spin me. Slowly at first, then faster and faster. I laid back and looked up at the sky, watched the streaks and the early stars twirl about my head. Warm water splashed in on me and I could feel and hear Max's hands touching the side of the dinghy. I imagined myself creating a mighty whirlpool, an eddy of escape, as the *Nemaste*'s sails passed pale and limp from my vision and back, over and over.

Then, like a leaping dolphin Max propelled himself from the water and tumbled into the spinning dinghy, bringing along buckets of warm water. We clung to each other and laughed. With our behinds in a puddle of water, we arranged ourselves with our heads on opposite sides, with each of us having our legs open and running along each other's body. I pressed my feet into the rubber on each side of his shoulders. He pressed his feet on the raft behind mine. We settled in quietly, the spin growing slower and slower, and our crotches meeting innocently in the center.

"Do you remember in *Last Tango in Paris* when Brando tried to come this way?" Max asked.

I remembered. "Yes."

Max grew quiet. Then he began grunting and straining. "Shit," he said. "I can't even get a hard-on like this."

I laughed. "I don't think he had a bathing suit on."

"Okay, okay, wise guy," Max said. He tossed about in the dinghy and finally got his bathing suit off. "All right," he said. "Let's try again." He settled back in. I felt his heavy penis there resting on me. I kept my eyes closed. I felt it twitch and tried not to laugh.

"I think this is how lesbians must do it," he said thoughtfully.

"In dinghies?"

"No, butt to butt like this. Don't you think?"

"I wouldn't know."

"I kind of feel sorry for women," he said then.

"Why?"

"You can't get hard-ons."

"It's not all bad," I told him. "There are compensations."

"Like what?" he asked.

"We get wide-ons."

He lifted his head and I knew he was smiling. I looked at him and his teeth flashed bright in the dusk. I smiled back. "You're wonderful sometimes, Ellie, you know that? A 'wide-on,' the lady says. A fucking wide-on!" He began to laugh, stomping his feet into my end of the dinghy. When I felt his penis growing lighter and standing up away from me, I reached down to hold and stroke it. Then Max came toward me, over me, clasping my shoulders back and making me arch up into his chest. His mouth found mine, and when I heard water pouring into the dinghy I bolted from him and saw his knee pressing the edge of the dinghy below the water level.

"Max!" I shouted. "Be careful. You'll drown us both. And look how far we've drifted from the boat."

It was growing darker and we hadn't lit the lights on the boat. She stood like a shadow farther away than I could ever try to swim.

"All right," he said, running his hands down my sides and pressing his thumbs into the softness before my hipbones. "Hand me the oars and we'll tie up. But tonight we're doing it in the dinghy. Number four will begin with a walloping—"

I reached behind me to get the oars for him and pulled out the long-handled broom. We stared at it.

"The oars?" he asked, taking it from me.

"I thought I was sitting on the oars," I said.

He stared at the broom and dipped it in the water. He began mumbling to himself, "Well, what do I expect from somebody who gets a wide-on?" He knelt up and began rowing awkwardly with the bristles of the broom. The water inside the dinghy was deep now, but my laughter spun out across the water like skimming stones. The dinghy reeled in half crescents, making its way slowly back to the mother ship. And Max's voice, "Aye, and I'll follow Moby Dick around the Horn, men, around the Norway Maelstrom, and around perdition's flames before I give him up. Hill and gully rider, hill and gully." The broom dipped in and out of the water beneath a canopy of pale and brightening stars.

No one else could ever make me laugh like Max could. God, he was wonderful. He made love to me that night in the deep and warm puddle of the dinghy, calling me "baby, baby, baby," and when he had made me come over and over, with his fingers, his mouth, and his gentle teeth, he sat back and waited. He waited for my breath to fall even and steady. And then he reached out and cupped his hand on the side of my face. "Now," he promised, "now I'm going to make you come."

I didn't count the times I came that night, or count the number of our kisses, hungry open-mouthed kisses or tender searching lip kisses, but because I didn't count them doesn't mean there was not a certain finite number that would define it. I think now that I could have made a chart that would have taken note of how many times the fingers on his left hand touched my right nipple, and how often his nose smoothed past my navel. The exact number of ejaculations. The number and intensity of tremors that went from my teeth to my clenched toes, making me buck and rise beneath him. How many times did his finger slip into my mouth? And how many times when I ran my hand along the side of his face did his lips turn to my warm palm like a baby turns to an offered nipple? I am sorry I did not keep count. If I had counted maybe now I would be able to remember every single movement, every breath.

I remember thinking, I never should have said we'd only make love five times. For now there was only one left.

*M*y dreams are usually so real and easily recalled, yet that morning on the *Nemaste* when I woke up on the red cushions we'd laid out in the cockpit under the stars, it was as though I had quietly stepped out of a noisy room and closed the door after me. On waking, I'd left all parts of the dream behind.

"Where did you say your daughter's camp was?" Max was asking.

I opened my eyes and held very still. Max wasn't beside me. He was in the cabin. "Where's what?"

"The camp where Casey's staying this week?"

I heard him rustle the chart and I heard a morning fish slapping its body against the surface of the water. Even at that early hour, the sun barely up over the trees, I could feel the heat pressing down on us.

I raised my head so I could see the water. "Jennings Point."

He was quiet a moment and then, "Aha! Here it is. That's not far. Why don't we head over there this morning, for something to do, some destination?"

"But Casey'll be busy. She won't want to see me."

He stepped up the two steps from the cabin and sat across from me. "What do you mean, 'won't want to see' you?"

"Don't you remember what it was like to be sixteen? You didn't want your mother showing up on you when you were with your friends." I kept my back to him and stared out at the water. At that very instant, exactly where I was looking, a fish as blue as the water leapt up, twisted himself once, twice in the air, and fell tail first back into the water. "Did you see that?" I asked.

"What, are there—boys there or something?" he asked.

"Yeah. It's coed. But even when it's just girls, she doesn't want her mother hanging around." I sat up and tried to run my fingers through my tangled hair. "God, my hair gets awful on the boat."

"We won't hang around. We'll just stop a minute."

"No, Max."

"What if we just sail by?" he persisted.

"Why?"

"Just for somewhere to go." He shrugged. "I don't know." He slapped at a fly on his ankle. "Why are you so against it?"

I watched as two flies landed on my knee. "What's with all these flies this morning?"

He shooed them away. "It's because we're sitting still and

it's hot. Come on." He stood and began pulling on the bungee cords to prepare the sails. "Let's get moving. We'll just sail past. That's all. We won't stop. But we've gotta get outta here. We'll be eaten alive."

And so we set out that morning with Max's half-cocked plan to sail past Casey's camp, a place on a chart where she'd been—when was it?—four, five years before? The wind was across our beam and soft, so it was slow going. A small part of me removed itself from the boat and watched from a safe distance to see what I would do. I saw myself sitting there on the bench scanning the shoreline. I watched as I lifted the binoculars to my eyes to identify buoys and match them with the markings on the chart.

"The coast there at the camp is rocky," I said and I held out the chart to Max there at the tiller, my finger on the little asterisks along Jennings Point.

He looked closely and hummed his agreement. "Is there a dock there?"

"No. I remember there's a gazebo that sits on a rock at the edge, but no dock, no moorings. It's too rocky. I remember now."

"Shit," he said. "We won't be able to stop. We'll only be able to cruise by."

"Lucky for Casey," I said. Lucky for me.

We sailed slowly past Paradise Point jutting out of Great Hog Neck on the North Fork, and two young windsurfers whipped past us, needing less wind than we did to carry their small crafts. I lifted a hand to them, but they didn't return my wave. It made me feel lonely, the loneliness of not having Casey in the world.

"Is this it?" Max was calling and I looked across to the shore and saw the white gazebo pressed against the dark trees. Behind the trees I knew there were cabins and a building where the business of camp meals and rainy-day crafts was carried on. I nodded. This was it. We watched together with the wind easing, and we couldn't have passed more slowly if we were sealed in a floating casket.

"Call her," Max ordered.

I looked at him.

"Go ahead, just call her. See if she comes. Hold this."

He handed me the tiller and ducked into the cabin. Call Casey. I looked at the shore and thought of calling her, calling across the backyards of the neighborhood to let her know dinner was ready, calling from the bathroom to let her know her bath was full. Calling her in the night, my head thrown back, calling pathetically into the darkness of an empty house when Sister Gregory called to say they had put Casey on the train in Farmingdale earlier that day, and that after following up on her whereabouts once more, it turned out that she never showed up at the other end at all. Calling her. Calling her.

Max was beside me with a blast can, a can with a little megaphone at the nozzle, so that when you pressed its release, it would let out little or long loud blasts to signal to other boats. "Here, use this."

I was silent.

"Go on." He nudged me. He had no idea.

Mechanically I climbed up the bench to sit on the cabin roof with my feet supporting me on the gunwale. I could see the gazebo and the huge rocks jutting out of the water beside it, and through the trees there were glintings of the windows on the cabins.

There I sat, poised on the gunwale of the *Nemaste,* not naked, but nearly so, and barefoot, holding a little blaster over my head and calling for my only child, a child who was not even living, yet I felt her presence there that day as though she were still some sweet-smelling infant I could call back to me. I held the little blaster over my head in two hands, gave four sharp blasts and called her name, Cassandra, long and slow like the tail of a dragon lunging and swooping through the waters. Her name was made for calling. It wasn't like Emily or Barbara, names that get tripped up on the lips when you try to call them across waters, but Cassandra—it calls like the wind itself. Her name was like a primal wail that came from somewhere deep inside me. Tears came and I began to weep silently as again and again I pressed four blasts and called. Cassandra!

Max came about, circling the boat in place, reluctant to get too close to the rocks at the shore. Blap. Blap. Blap. Blap. Cassandra! I felt like a character from a Greek myth. I was all women, all mothers. I was on all waters, beneath all skies. Blap. Blap. Blap. Blap. Cassandra!

Then a young boy appeared in a purple sweatshirt in the trees, holding up his two arms. He had a friend with him who waved, too. My eyes filled with tears of startled disappointment.

"Who's that?" Max asked.

We were sailing by a third time, and I stopped calling. I just watched the two boys disappear into the trees, leaving me behind, sitting on the gunwale of an old fiberglass sailboat. Leaving me alone with a man who might understand about Greek myths, but who would never understand about the bindings of motherhood as thin and transparent as spider threads and as strong and as demanding as steel.

Max stood dumbfounded at the tiller. "Ellie! What is it?" as I held onto the shrouds with both hands and sobbed with a great longing that threatened to swallow me up and drown me.

Max wanted to hear about it. He wanted to talk and make sense of it all, but I couldn't speak. My forehead felt like it was going to explode, and pressing my hand to it I made my way into the cabin and crawled into the womblike **V** berth. I laid my head on the damp coiled line of the anchor and cried.

"Can I get you something?" he called after me. He was at the tiller, his brow furrowed with concern, or was it another uneasiness? All that day he would treat me with a gingerly held regard, but looking back on it now I can imagine that on some level it must have been then that he began to mentally pack his duffel bag and abandon ship. And who could have blamed him?

I didn't answer him. I just laid there crying like I'd cried when I was a child, like I hadn't cried since Casey's funeral.

Somewhere toward the end of that hot day, I felt the anchor line begin to uncoil from beneath my head and I moved and watched it disappear, inch by inch, into the hole above me. I listened to Max's bare feet overhead, and I heard the anchor splash into the water. My father would always lower the anchor without a sound; Max threw it wildly, senselessly away from the boat. I didn't know how long I had slept. There'd been no dreams, only the sound of water passing along the hull, only the occasional sound of the sails taking the wind on a new side. I moved and discovered I was sweating and stuck to the red cushion. I changed position and closed my eyes. I listened to Max come into the cabin and open the ice chest. He would want to eat.

"Ellie?" His voice was quiet and near. His fingers went around my ankle.

I didn't respond.

"Ellie, sit up a minute."

I stirred, moved around so I could see him. My body was a road to him, ending at my ankle, which he held in one hand. In his other hand he had a cup. "Sit up a minute."

"Where are we?"

"Coecles Harbor. A little place called Shanty Cove."

I sat up slowly, sticking to the cushions, every joint stiff, and the pattern of the coil line making my cheek rough. Max rubbed the side of my face with the back of his hand. "You okay?" he asked.

"I don't know."

"Here. Have this."

I looked in the cup and smelled the wine. I held the cup to my lips and sipped it.

"You scared me. You've been out of it for hours," he said and I met his eyes, embarrassed.

"Sorry."

"Hey, don't be sorry. Christ. It's just that, I don't know — what the hell was that all about?"

I took a deeper sip. "There's just some stuff that's hard for me to talk about. It would be like opening Pandora's box to tell you. I can't talk about it. Don't ask me."

"Is it about Cas —"

"I just asked you not to ask me."

He drew me close to him. "Okay, okay." In the circle of his arms I held the cup to my lips and drained it. Already it had begun to run in my blood, warming me and creating a comfortable distance that separated me from myself. Max pressed my head against his neck and stroked my hair. "Whatever you say," he whispered. "It's okay with me."

Then, on his own, he began to set up the boat hibachi that hung over the side. I sat in the cabin trying to pull myself together and gather enough strength to move about. I watched as Max lit the briquettes into a small orange fire and began digging in the ice chest for the chicken cutlets. Getting up and reaching into the ice chest after him I pulled out the bottle of wine and poured some more into my cup. I held it out to him and cocked my head.

"Okay," he answered, holding out his cup. I poured. Then I stepped out of the cabin and looked around.

"This is pretty here," I said, seeing the trees, the one house set back from the water, and two or three boats moored and seemingly empty a distance from us. I screwed the top back on the bottle and sat down next to him. I leaned my head on his shoulder, but he stood right away and stirred the briquettes. I never feel safe when someone leaves me. And each time Max moved away to turn a cutlet or adjust the hibachi I felt a certain foolish panic building from those little leavings. I was as limp and as weak as a telltale indoors and I couldn't get close enough to his body. But I didn't want to talk.

We ate in silence. I kept my thigh along his thigh, and my arm behind him without actually touching him. I ate with one hand. When I was finished I asked him, "If I fell overboard right now, Max, would you save me?"

He looked at me and then went back to his eating.

"Would you?"

"What kind of question is that?"

"If I fell over and called you to pull me in, would you do it?"

"Of course I would."

"Make love to me, Max."

"Mind if I have another cutlet first?" There was a tremor of impatience to his voice.

"Let me feed you the cutlet," I said, taking his fork.

"No. Don't." He took the fork back.

"You don't want me anymore." I hated myself as I said it.

He didn't answer.

"I know," I said, straining to be playful. "Let's say you're a pirate, captain of this small ship, and you've just pirated some fancy yacht. You took on all its money and jewels, champagne, maybe some recreational drugs, and you even kidnapped the captain's young, nubile daughter." I began stroking him, leaning into him like a cat.

"Ellie, let me finish," he muttered, eating his cutlet.

"She's an undergrad at Sarah Lawrence, a virgin, but she's done some modeling, mostly for stocking ads, and one spread in *Penthouse*. She's got these incredibly great legs." I draped a leg over him and slipped my hand inside his trunks. I closed my eyes and rubbed my lips up and down his neck until my lips tingled and ached. I felt him put his plate down and turn to me. He didn't kiss me but took me hard into his arms. He lifted me to face him, straddling his thigh.

"Shut up," he said softly.

"Even though she's a virgin, when she saw you, masked and armed on her father's boat, she wanted you. She wanted you to take her and you knew it. You slipped a finger into her straining halter top and released one of her breasts. 'Get in my dinghy,' you told her, and—"

"Would you shut up!"

Max ground his mouth into mine then, not a kiss but something fiercer, something more raw and dangerous. I pressed harder against him, reaching for some kind of pain that would block everything out. It was as though I was trying to stay afloat by holding my breath. As long as I held my breath I was okay, floating atop the water like a bubble, but the minute I needed to breathe, the minute some vague consciousness flickered, the air would escape me and I would begin to sink, and then I'd gasp for air again, grasp for oblivion.

"So you get her back to your ship and she begs you not to kill her. She says she'll do anything. She'll be your slave, your—"

"Would you shut the fuck up!"

Max reached down and grabbed my bathing suit bottom and with one movement ripped it off me. I struggled to clasp the waist of his trunks, but as I did he slipped his hand between my legs and discovered how dry I was. I started to sink again, as he stroked me and rubbed me, breathing into my mouth, groaning, calling "baby, baby, baby." But suddenly I knew it was no good. I couldn't make it up to the surface again. I grew still and limp in his arms like something drowned, and I felt him crumple. He quieted and sat like a stone with the top of his head pressed into the part of my shoulder where I would press a rifle butt. He withdrew his dry fingers from me.

"What?" he whispered. "What is it?"

"It's no good for me right now, Max. That's all."

"Then why'd you start it?" he accused.

"I know. I know. I'm sorry."

I'm sorry.

I can remember a time when I was very young. I was about four years old. It was pre-Peter, and I must have done something that made my mother or my father very angry. It's odd how I cannot even remember which of them it was, but I do remember being in warm water, in the bathtub, and whatever it was I had done, whatever word or movement or puzzling gesture, it earned me a stinging smack to my bottom. Then, left alone in the tub to my sobbing tears and my uncertain regret, I twisted in fascination to see the imprint of a flat red hand with five distinct fingers stamped there across my wet buttocks.

Isn't it sad the way we touch each other? And sadder yet that some touchings are last and final touchings? I sometimes get to wondering if I have made love for the last time, or if I have written my last book. It's probably a good thing we don't know which are the endings—a thoughtless word, a resounding denouement of clear delicacy and packed strength, a well-crafted metaphor, or an uneasy step off the side of a boat into dark waters. Sometimes I wonder, what part of me was the last part to touch Max and what part of him did I touch?

It's lost to me. And what about you? Do you ever wonder about the last time we touched?

I guess it's good that we forget. But with my father I remember. I later looked for the shadow of his hand on me, and it hasn't been till now, till I am so fully alone, that I can finally see the rim of it branded on my soul.

Max and I were courteous to each other the rest of the night. We slept side by side between two light sheets spread out upon one red cushion without touching and without speaking. I guess we both knew that the next morning we'd go back to Charlie's, and that it was the end of number four.

I felt Max wake up in the morning and step over me. I could hear him attach the ladder off the stern and then I heard the splash of him diving over the side. I sat up and pulled off the T-shirt I had worn during the night. After I folded the sheets and tucked them under the cushions, I stepped out into the morning sunlight. There was a nice breeze. I wasn't sure I knew how to ask Max to stay near me if I dove in, so I hooked my arm through a life ring and climbed down the ladder without looking at him. The cold was a shock, but I kept getting lower and lower in the water until there were no more steps and I let myself fall into it, gripping the ring. Max swam around the other side of the boat where I couldn't see him and I was content for the moment to be alone there in the water with the sun so new and tiny fish slaps around me. I ducked my head under the water and came up in the center of the ring. I smoothed my hair away from my face and hung motionless, suspended in time as well as seawater. I watched the telltales fluttering and the light clouds floating overhead.

Max dove and splashed and backstroked into view. Without speaking he approached the ladder and clasped it. Then he turned to look at me.

"We'll head back now," he said.

"Okay," I answered.

His eyes skittered away across the water and he pulled himself up the ladder and left me there. I stayed a long time, longer than I knew he thought I would. I thought he would look over to see if I was still there. I thought he'd call to me or tell me to come back on now. But he was silent except for the sounds of knocking around in the cabin. Then I saw him fling the gennie in its sailbag up on the roof of the cabin. I watched as he climbed after it and began to rig it.

I wondered idly if he would leave me there, floating naked in my little ring lifesaver. I wondered if he could do such a thing—pull in the ladder and never look back. What it would look like from the water to see the *Nemaste* tilt and soar away with Max at the tiller, eyes straight ahead? I shuddered, grabbed the ladder, and climbed on board.

I used my damp towel, the one he had used himself and left on the bench. "Can we get some sailing in?" I asked. I wrapped myself in it and patted myself dry.

Max didn't hear me and went on attaching the genoa to the front stay without looking up.

"We've got a good breeze today," I said. "It would be a shame not to take advantage of it."

"It'll get us home," he said.

I hung the towel neatly over the life rail and stood there naked. He wove the jib sheets down the sides and wound them once loosely around the winches and left them there on the bench without noticing me. I could have been a parking meter. I didn't dare touch him.

"Want me to pull the anchor up?" I asked.

"Can't sail too well with it down," he said, busying himself with his lines.

"Can I get dressed first?"

He didn't answer.

"Jesus," I said under my breath. "One time I don't get a wide-on and look at you. I hope you get treated better next time *you* can't get it up, Max."

He finally stopped and looked up at me. "I think it's a little more than a wide-on we're talking about here. I get a feeling we're dealing with something else, something a lot bigger, and there's no way for me to understand when you don't let me in on it."

There was nothing I could say. I went into the cabin and got dressed.

Max had pulled up the anchor himself and was sitting at the tiller by the time I'd dressed and packed up some loose things. The breeze was brisk and we were kicking up a nice wake. We sat across from each other in silence. Suddenly the towel caught my eye. It flickered up beside Max, seemed to wave good-bye, and dropped behind him into the water.

"Max! My towel!" I stood up and pointed at it as it floated away on the surface, towel blue on water blue, and then, as the *Nemaste* put more and more distance between it and us, I felt it sinking.

"Wanna go back for it?" Max cupped his hand over his eyes and squinted back into the bright waters.

I didn't answer at first. Of course I wanted to go back for

it. I hated anything to leave me. But Max made no effort to slow the boat or turn her around, and I wasn't so sure I knew exactly where it was anymore. I loosened my fists. "No. Forget it. That's okay."

Max turned forward and forgot it instantly. I thought of it sinking deeper and deeper, rocking in the darkness until it covered a small patch of the bottom, got caught in old fishing lines, and was walked on by crabs. I said nothing and the *Nemaste* made her way home at a decent clip.

As soon as I could see the peak of Charlie's roof I announced, "I want to see if I can bring her in by myself."

Max offered me the tiller and slid over to make room for me. "I'll lower the motor."

I shook my head. "I want to sail her in."

"You can't."

"I once knew someone who went a whole season without ever getting his outboard wet."

"I said *you* can't."

"I can try." I stood. "Stay there. I want to take the gennie down and just go in with the mainsail. You'll see."

The wind wasn't quite right. The docking would have been perfect if the wind had been clean from the north so that I could have turned right up into it and brushed up against the dock. But it was from the east, whistling over the planks, and even though I had lowered the mainsail enough, and even though I felt strangely confident, Max started to yell "Jesus Christ!" as we drew close, and I couldn't get her to slow down enough, couldn't get her to approach the dock gently, and suddenly I could sense how fast we were going, how fast the dock was upon us, and how out of control a boat on water can be. When she hit against the dock it knocked me off my feet and I smacked my shins with a sharp pain against the bench. Max had leapt to the cabin roof and jumped onto the dock. I watched him strain as he grabbed the bowsprit and pushed with all his might to keep her from running past the dock and running aground. I saw Charlie come running down from his garden. I could see the small shovel in his one hand and thought for a minute that he meant to dig the *Nemaste* out of the beach.

"It's okay! It's okay!" Charlie was yelling. "You got it! You got it!"

Letting go of the tiller, I pulled the rest of the mainsail down in handfuls, letting it hang from the mast around my knocking knees.

"What are you guys doing? Sailing into the dock?" Charlie helped Max pull the boat close to the dock.

"Throw us the lines to tie her up," Max barked at me. "Just an experiment, Charlie," he said. "Another day in the life of Evel Knievel."

Once we had tied her up and had unloaded all our stuff onto the dock, I put the hatch slats in place, and with trembling hands I threaded a lock through the door latch without locking it.

"I thought you'd be gone longer," Charlie said, picking up a duffel bag in one hand and a plastic bag of garbage in the other. "I was thinking what great sailing weather this was."

Max hoisted the ice chest and followed after Charlie. "Well, I knew I wouldn't be able to stay too long," he was saying. "I've got some chimney jobs coming up, and Ellie's gotta get back for Casey."

Charlie stopped in his tracks. He turned and looked at me. The three of us were standing there on the narrow dock, Charlie blocking the way, and I couldn't get past either of them. I felt so far from shore. I took in only enough breath to fill my throat, shallow, shallow breaths. *Suddenly I think of Casey and remember that night in the backyard. I'm thinking it's gotten so dark out and the flashlight doesn't hold its light so I have to keep shaking it. But I know my way to the garage, even in the dark. Without stumbling I step over the roots of the old pine tree and make my way back there. I can hear the wind way up at the top of the pine tree.* I could feel Max looking from me to Charlie and back to me again.

"What?" Max whispered. "What is it?"

"Ellie?" It was Charlie.

I hung my head and let the bundles of towels and sheets spill out of my arms and back onto the dock. *The flashlight goes out again as I am approaching the yawning garage door. I am calling into the darkness, "Who's here? Come out." And I'm wondering why I didn't carry a broom handle with me, or a kitchen knife. Suddenly the flashlight shines out. Oh, it shines. It shines.* I couldn't move or say a word. And Charlie must have known it.

Charlie spoke soothingly and evenly, like a doctor would speak to a nervous parent as he snapped a child's twisted shoulder back into place. "Casey died, Max. It'll be three years this fall. It's three years, isn't it, Ellie?"

A cardinal swooped overhead clicking at us. We were all three motionless and silent, and then I did what I'd always done to bring me back. I heard myself saying, "It was a car accident. A hit-and-run right around the corner from our house. A guy from the ambulance crew told me she must have died instantly. Her head hit the curb." I looked at Max, whose face was drained of color. I needed to know that he heard every word and felt the pain as sharply as though I were pressing a thorn into the tip of his finger. "I didn't see it myself, but you know how head wounds bleed, and it didn't rain for a while after the accident." I wouldn't let Max look away. "So after about three days, I finally walked over with a bucket of water and Clorox and a brush and scrubbed the street so I wouldn't have to look at it anymore."

Max's eyes were red. "Why didn't you tell me?" he whispered.

I shrugged and picked up my bundles. "I told you I was a writer, a born liar. Besides, what does it matter? The stain came out. It's over."

I drove and it was a long ride home. Max didn't speak. By the time we got on the parkway and headed out across the Long Island plains, I could tell he was asleep in the passenger seat beside me. I glanced at him. His breathing was deep, and now and then he'd click somewhere deep inside.

I passed the exit marked Pinelawn and took note of it that afternoon, just like I always did. I don't know what I was thinking three years ago, to have let Casey been buried there in your veteran's plot. I guess I just never thought it through. But so many times since then I've realized that just the two of you will be buried there someday and that I will never qualify. Maybe if you marry again, there will be a different wife with you, maybe even more children.

So I will insist on being buried at sea, and the starfish will eat all my memories of you. The tides will pull the recollections and remembrances from the soft matter within my skull and you, you and your grave, you and your sharp breath, and the years we spent will be forgotten.

Thinking this, I felt Max stir. I continued on, past Levittown, Bellmore. I could have found my way home blindfolded. But to make it interesting and to keep awake, I stared into the grilles of oncoming cars.

When we got to Max's truck I touched his shoulder. He woke and stared out the front window.

"We're home, Captain Ahab," I whispered.

He glanced at me and then away. "I feel so bad, Ellie."

I reached out and touched his arm, but he didn't respond. He was staring straight ahead.

"I can't believe you didn't tell me."

"I'm sorry, Max. When I first met you, it didn't seem like you had to know. It's not something I chat about. And it was easier to pretend Casey was here than to explain why she wasn't."

He shook his head and opened the door. "Well, thanks for the ride."

Max got out of the car and went around the back to get his stuff. I jumped out after him. "You'll call me when the chimney business slows down and we'll do number five, won't we?"

He pulled his duffel bag out and hoisted it on his shoulder. He looked me full in the face, his familiar, dear face. "I don't think so, Ellie. Four was enough for me."

"Oh, Max, don't say that. Please don't say that." I held his arm with both hands. I started to cry. "Is it because I lied? Because I told a story? What if I tell you the truth? The real truth, the truth even Charlie doesn't know?"

He frowned, but my panic had me. I would do anything to keep him there. Even tell him the truth. "She died of a drug overdose, Max. They told me she was mainlining heroin. I found her in the garage late one night and it was too late. She never saw those open doors, Max. She never turned around and saw the way out. She never made it." I was sobbing. Max's duffel bag was in the grass and he was holding me.

After a long time, he finally pulled away and ran his hands up and down my arms. He brushed the hair off my forehead and studied my face.

"Please stay," I whispered.

But he shook his head. "No more."

I lowered my chin and he kissed the top of my head.

He backed away from me and walked to his truck. I followed slowly at a distance, drained of all urgency. He got in and started the motor, cranked down the window.

"Ellie?"

"Yeah?"

"Tell Charlie."

I didn't answer.

"Tell him, you hear me? He should know. He's your friend."

I nodded and lifted my hand in good-bye.

Good-bye, Max.

*I*t had been a bitter cold weekend in November when Casey finally ran for the last time. When the phone calls started, I had begun to get a peculiar gut feeling that she was somewhere in the neighborhood. There were phone calls from unfamiliar people who were asking for her. Strange voices of kids who didn't sound like kids, voices too deep, too churlish for my taste. Yet for a while I fooled myself into believing that she couldn't have been anywhere in the area; she was safe at Our Lady of the Shepherds. And then I thought again. On the second day of these unusual phone calls, I knew she was somewhere on the streets again.

"Hello, Dr. Phelan, this is Ellie Brinkley, Casey's mother."

"I'm afraid Dr. Phelan isn't in today. She's gone for the weekend."

"Well, can I speak to someone in charge?"

The voice was whiney and small. "Well, we're minimum staff right now, Mrs. Brimley. Maybe I can help you."

"Actually I just want to check to see if my daughter is there this weekend. I have a feeling she's not."

"And what's her name?"

"Cassandra Brinkley." I spelled out each word slowly.

There was silence and the sound of papers shuffling.

"Mrs. Brinkley?" she asked, coming back.

"Yes."

"You're correct. Your daughter is not here this weekend. She's with her father in Manhattan."

Somewhere deep inside me a dam opened and molten lava churning with bits of broken glass spilled into my gut. "Has anyone checked to make sure she arrived there?"

"We don't do that, I'm afraid. I'm sure her father would have called if she hadn't arrived."

"I think you'd better check with him. Our Lady of the Shepherds is legally responsible for my daughter, and unless you want me to disturb the judge's weekend—"

"Please, Mrs. Brinkley. Why don't you just call your husband—"

"Casey's father is not my husband. And I will not call him. *You* will."

"Then I am afraid—"

"What's your name?"

"Why?"

"So I can tell the judge when I call him at the golf course."

"Mrs. Brinkley, my name is Alison McAyer and I was just going to say that if you will give me Cassandra's father's phone number I will call him myself right now and confirm that she's safe and exactly where she's supposed to be."

I gave her the number of the apartment, but I knew it wouldn't be enough. I gave her the tavern number as well and told her I would wait beside the phone for her to call me back, and in thirty minutes I would call the judge.

In five minutes the phone rang.

"Mrs. Brinkley, I was able to reach Cassandra's father at the second number you gave me, and you are right, she's not with him at the moment. He says she went to visit friends."

"Would you please make official note of this somewhere, Alison? Note that she's not where she's supposed to be. That her father was finally reached in a tavern. And that he is not supervising her."

"I'm writing this down right now. I will give it to Dr. Phelan on Monday and you can be sure that—"

"And now please call the police, Alison, and report her missing—"

"Mrs. Brinkley, that's rather severe. She's not a runaway. Apparently her father expects to see her this evening."

"Was she there last evening?"

"I don't know, Mrs.—"

"Please call the police."

"It's really uncalled for—"

"Would you please make note that I *requested* you call the police? It's 5:35 P.M., November 19. Got it?"

"Yes. And thank you for calling—"

I hung up.

Remember when Casey was little how she loved to swing in the park? How crazy she was for me to stand in front of her and you to stand in back, and for us to push her so high, for what seemed like hours. I would watch her face coming toward me, her little hands gripping the chains and the bottoms of her sneakers turned up to the sky, and I would grab the seat on either side, sometimes needing to jump in the air to send her back to you. I remember the scrape of her sneaker once along my cheek when I wasn't fast enough. And then the swing would go back to you. And it was almost as though all I could see was the top of her small head and her tight little fists, and you jumping, stretching in the air, to touch the bottom of her seat and send her back to me. To me, back to you, to me and back. Who would have guessed that one day she would swing in your direction, and that the swing would come back to me, twisting and reeling on limp chains, and empty, as empty as a milkweed pod in November?

Once Max was gone my loneliness and grief took the form of endless scribbling and writing. Whole pages were beginning to come. There was no shape yet, no direction, but the visions and the sounds of the words that were coming to me were intoxicating. I had already jumped out of the shower a number of times one morning, dripping and soapy, to jot down bits of monologues that were coming to me like real voices speaking from somewhere outside myself. I carried a pad everywhere I went, and I watched as things began to weave themselves together and I began to recognize a true story in the darkness of my imagination.

It wasn't cool enough to build a fire yet, but at night I would lie on the rug in front of the fireplace and read what I had written so far—pages and pages, some typed, some scrawled—and I would read books. I brought home piles and piles of nautical books from the library. I read through indexes of sailing books and each word resounded with the remembered voice of my father.

"Facing this way," he tells me, turning my shoulders forward so my face is lit by the dim mast lights, "left is port and right is starboard. You remember that because *starboard* has two 'r's in it, so it goes with *right*."

"And *left* has four letters," I tell him, "and so does *port*."

I imagine that he is proud of me, proud that I come up with my own way of seeing things. He gathers me into his arms and I sit on his lap with my back against his warm chest. He rests his feet on the bench opposite and my legs straddle his legs as though he is a horse.

"Can you find Orion's belt?" he asks.

And I point all over the heavens, searching, searching, until I find it and run my finger along its stars. My head is back on his shoulder tucked in the crook of his neck, and together we lean back and watch the stars. I am looking for a shooting star and I try to open my eyes as wide as I can and see the entire sky at once. Then I hear his voice through the thickness of his throat pressed up against my ear, and I have this sense of my father that he is somewhere deep inside himself, and I have my ear pressed to the door of his body.

"This is such a good little boat for you to learn on, Elizabeth," he says. "She's very forgiving."

"What does that mean?" I ask, and I place my arms and my hands over his arms and hands that rest across me. I feel how big his arms are beneath mine and gently pat the curly hairs that cover them. I think our arms are like the leaves of a corn husk, woven loosely in layers around a hidden inner core.

"Well, when a boat is forgiving, she lets you make mistakes and she still holds true to her course. Some boats are such slugs that if you don't know how to set everything exactly right, they flop off course, or else they'll take a knockdown too easily. But with this beauty, you set the sails the best you can, and she never wanders off course. She loves the wind with all her heart."

"She's a beauty," I agree.

But then he says, "Your mother could learn a thing or two from a good boat."

I balance in a still silence and then, "Oh! Look!" I cry.

Three shooting stars flare and vanish above us. And in pure joy, as though we have been brought back to an innocent pin-point of time, we tighten our hold on each other and I smile up into the night sky. I think how *we* could be a constellation. They'd call it Ellie and Her Father, and it would be a straight vertical line of bright, mast-light stars, and low down in the east, just over the ocean's horizon, there'd be a swirl of powdery stars like a universe and that would be us, indistinguishable, plaited and laced together with light and sea air.

"Greetings, Citizen. Chim'man here. I can't speak to you right now, so if you'll leave your name, phone number, and a brief message, I'll call you back as soon as I get in."

Beep.

"Hi, Max, it's just me. And it's Monday night. I didn't want you to think I'd forgotten about you. And I'm planning to go sailing this Friday and Saturday, so I hope you'll come."

I took a breath and covered my closed eyes with my hand. "I don't know, I thought maybe we could do number five, or whatever, whatever you want, we can even just go sailing for the day. But I wanted to let you know. Call me, Max. Let me know, okay?"

I waited a second as though the machine would give me its answer.

"Oh and Max, I have to tell you about this great book I just read about a guy who spent seventy-six days lost in the Atlantic Ocean in an inflatable raft. He was followed by a school of dorados who tortured him. You'd love it. Anyway, I'll give it to you when I see you. Okay? Try to call before Wednesday if you can.

"I'm writing again. Not a book about my Atlantic crossing or anything, but—" I wanted to start all over, erase the message and leave a different one. "Well, that's enough outta me. I'll tell you all about it when I see you, Max. Good-bye."

Then, a few days later, when I still hadn't heard from him:
"Greetings, Citizen. Chim'man here. I can't speak to you right now, so if you'll leave your name, phone number, and a brief message, I'll call you back as soon as I get in."

Beep.

"Max? It's me. Are you there?"

I listened to the hum of the recorder.

"Listen, it's Thursday night, and I haven't heard from you. I'm thinking maybe you didn't get my other message. I'm taking the boat out tomorrow for a couple of days, and I was hoping you'd be around to go with me. I'm going to go to bed now, but call me if you get in late, or anytime before seven tomorrow morning. I'll be leaving early. But listen, if you don't get me and want to come out, just come and meet me out at Charlie's. I'll probably take off around noon, you know, and just go sailing around the island."

There was a knot in my stomach the size of a moon crater. How could I go sailing around the island by myself?

"Did I tell you I got some more money for my book? Charlie liked what I showed him. He was asking for you, too, Max. He asked how you were ..." And he probably wondered why

I had lied to you. I leaned against the wall, holding the phone pressed against my ear. "I haven't told him yet, Max, but I will."

I spoke quietly, intimately into the phone. "Max, remember how you told me that day on the boat that I was your assignment?" I waited as though he might answer, strain to remember. "Well, your term paper's due." I felt myself laugh an empty laugh. "I hope I see you, Max. Maybe I'll meet you out there. Bye."

I started out early the next morning. There wasn't much traffic and I kept glancing over at the trees along the parkway to see how much they were blowing, to see what kind of wind I'd have that day. I didn't let myself entertain the thought that Max might not show, because then I'd have to think about possibly sailing out alone. I knew that I couldn't put it off any longer. This time I would do it, one way or another. But still I clung to the hope that Max might show, that he'd drive up in his truck as I was readying the sails. I could see him running up the dock and leaping onto the *Nemaste* as she eased from the shore. For an instant I even let myself imagine what it would have been like if my father were still around and if he could have come out with me for a sail. But the very thought filled me with a terrible regretful longing.

The doors to Charlie's house were opened when I arrived, and I pulled my car down the dirt drive. I parked over to the side where I'd be out of the way. Charlie's old wreck of a car, the one he used for trips back and forth to the ferry and to the market, was by the back door with the trunk open. He was just coming out.

"Hello, Skipper," he called. "Good to see you!"

I went over to him and we touched cheeks and patted each other's arms. "Need some help?" I asked.

"Sure," he said. "Grab a bag."

"What is all this?" I asked as I lifted a bag full of tomatoes from the trunk.

"I can't resist a roadside stand," he sighed. "I tell myself, just say no, just say no, but it never works."

Inside, a bag tipped over on his counter and I stopped the rolling tomatoes with my arms. "But you grow tomatoes yourself, Charlie, don't you?"

"Yes, yes," he agreed, "but this weekend I want to put up some tomato sauce for the winter and it's a good idea to have some extra and make as much as I can. One can never have too many to-mah-toes."

I followed him out to the car while he sang, "You say to-mah-toes and I say tomaters, you say po-tah-toes and I say pota-ters, to-mah-toes, tomaters, po-tah-toes, potaters—" Then in his best theatrical voice, reminding me of James Cagney, he finished, "Let's call the whole thing off," and handed me a bag of cantaloupes.

"You know, Ellie, I had a grandmother who used to talk funny. She'd say ferl for foil and poils for pearls. I remember I'd make her say, 'Olive Oil has a string of pearls.' "

"Olive Erl has a stwing a poils," I said. I followed him inside and watched as he emptied the bags and filled baskets that he pulled down from the wall.

"She never would have said 'stwing,' " he corrected me. "Do you think I come from a line of total illiterates?"

"I would *never* say that of you, Charlie. You could only have come from a pure line of literary princes and verbal pedigrees."

He nodded. "That's right, but you know what? Because my own grandmother talked the way she did, I still have moments of intense mistrust of the spoken word. To this day, I will stake my reputation only on the written word."

"As in what?" I asked.

"As in Boynton Beach," he told me. "The first time I heard

that, I wouldn't say it myself until I had seen how it was spelled. How embarrassing it would have been if it were really *Bernton* Beach."

"How about Spuyton Doivill?" I asked.

"Oh, that was the worst. I stay out of upstate as much as I can, unless I have a map in hand."

"And Newboigh? Have you been to Newboigh?"

He laughed. "Only in my dreams, Ellie."

When everything was put away, Charlie offered to help me load the boat, but I said it was okay, there wasn't much to carry. And, besides, I wasn't in a hurry. He walked down to the dock with me anyway, each of us holding a handle on the ice chest. It was heavy and we carried it together. It reminded me of my lie and the truth I must tell him, like a heaviness between us.

"I was hoping Max could have come out today," I told him. "He still might show, maybe, but I don't think I'll wait. If he's not here by the time I'm ready to sail ... well, you tell him, 'next time,' if he shows up."

"You two still talking?" Charlie asked.

I climbed on the boat and avoided Charlie's eyes. "We're not really. I haven't heard from him. He doesn't answer my calls." Charlie stood there, serious and still while I pulled out the hatch slats.

"Because he found out about Casey from me?"

"Yeah, well ..."

"There's something I've been wanting to say to you about that, Ellie."

I ducked down into the cabin. "Yeah? What's that?"

"Ellie?"

I would have to organize the food compartment to make more room. I'd brought along more canned goods and packs of charcoal briquettes.

"Ellie?"

I held still. "What?"

"Come out here a minute. I want to talk to you."

Reluctantly I came up. I felt like a small child called to the principal's office. I sat on the bench and he came aboard. He sat across from me and ran his hand down the peeling wood of the tiller.

"I'll have to take that home," I said, touching the tiller too, "and strip it and revarnish it." I saw my hands were trembling.

"Ellie, you know how sometimes when you write something, I tell you there's something about it that doesn't ring true? Remember when I said that in *You Again* about the scene in the living room with the man from Belgium that she'd met on the bus?"

"Yeah. You weren't sure what it was, but you said it lacked truth."

"Right. And you fought me at first, but then you realized what was wrong."

"You called that one right," I agreed.

"I feel the same way about what you told Max."

I looked in his eyes and wondered what parts of me he could see. How much would Charlie be able to understand about me? And how much could I bear for him to know about me before he would see me as less than he'd seen me before?

"What I told Max and what I write in a novel are two entirely different things."

"I never heard the part about you scrubbing the street."

My throat tightened.

"Ellie, if you had told him you never rode down that block again, or that you went out of your way to avoid that place, knowing you, Ellie, I wouldn't have had a doubt about that. But all of a sudden—I don't know what it was—but when you talked about the bleach and the bucket—" Charlie shrugged and lifted his palms before him, "it didn't feel like truth."

I hung my head, my hand still on the tiller.

We sat there without saying a word. The water lapped against the hull of the *Nemaste* and a sweet, inviting wind whisked through the trees and the rigging.

"It's not the truth, Charlie. But does it matter? It's just something I've built for myself to make it less painful."

"Truth matters. You know that. In a story, even in a fantasy when you construct your own network of reality, there still has to be truth."

"This isn't a story," I whispered. "It's my life."

Charlie reached out and touched my knee with two fingers. "I think you and I both know that for you the line between those two things is very thin. And there's something that's not lying flat here for me, something that sticks in my craw, so to speak."

I smiled at him despite myself. "And where's your craw, Charlie?"

My eyes filled with tears when he touched his heart. "Oh, Charlie." It seemed I just breathed, waiting until I could speak with a full and strong voice. But when I did speak my voice was small. "She was a drug addict, Charlie. Casey did drugs. That's what killed her. Not a car. Not an accident that left blood in the road." I looked at him. "I wish it had been that. I wish it *had* been instantaneous and at the hands of some total stranger. Then maybe I wouldn't feel so guilty, as though there was something else I should have done, some way I could have loved her that would have made a difference."

Charlie and I sat there holding hands across the cockpit of the boat. I remembered doing this with Casey when she was little. My hand on the bottom, then hers, then mine, then hers, and then I would move my bottom hand to the top, and on and on, whoever had the bottom hand always switching to the top until we accelerated into wild hand slapping and laughter. Without meaning to I moved my bottom hand to the top to cover Charlie's. He just sat there looking at me.

"You were right, Charlie. You're always right, but there's been a part of me that's needed to believe that it's possible to just scrub a curbside somewhere with a bucket of bleach, and be clean. You know what I mean? Like it's sort of a metaphor for what I wish I could do." I shrugged. "Was it so bad, Charlie? That I lied?"

He shook his head. "Who knows, Ellie? Who's to say why people do things? I think even the worst mistake can lay a path for great achievements and victories."

I smiled, laughed, even, and tears spilled down my cheeks. I pulled my hands from his and wiped them away. "You talk good."

"And you talk like a dockworker." We laughed, Charlie and I. Or me and Charlie, maybe that would make him laugh again.

"So will you come sailing with me today, Charlie? Max looks like a no-show."

He stood and stretched, gazing around at the bay. "I think I might like to someday, Ellie, but today I have some canning to do."

I nodded. "Your to-mah-toes." I stood, too, and began uncovering the sails.

"Where are you off to?" he asked.

"Oh, I don't know. Thought I might shoot past the Spertin Dervil and head on up to Newboigh."

Charlie stepped off the boat and onto the dock. He stood looking at me, smiling and shaking his head. "You know I always thought you were a wonderful mother. I saw how you loved her. I saw how difficult she could be." He paused. "Thank you for telling me the truth, Ellie."

I didn't have to look away. I didn't have to lower my eyes. Oh, but I swelled in gratitude for his forgiveness.

"You'll be all right on your own?" he asked.

"You bet. I brought my typewriter, two reams of paper, and an empty bottle, so if I get into any trouble, I'll write you."

"Sounds good," he said. He started up the dock. "And maybe when you return, we'll play a few rounds of cribbage."

I watched him walk back to the house, feeling how much I loved him and how grateful I was.

I tossed the sail cover into the cabin and glanced nervously at the flapping telltales. I wasn't so sure I could do this at all. I felt as though Max had taken me this far and had left me to finish something. I was like that dog Duke, trembling at the first flickerings of lightning. Only now there was no old console radio for me to hide under. There was only the windy, open sky.

efore leaving the dock that morning, I'd been putting things away below and I'd come across Max's bottle of wine that was still half full. I'd weighed it in my hands, the pale green of the bottle and its deep red liquid. For a while I had left it on the table in the cabin as I rearranged and set things in order. But it had made me nervous there, the way a loaded gun might trouble some people, so I had moved it outside, promising myself to deal with it later.

When I came up and got ready to untie and cast off, the bottle was waiting for me. If Charlie'd still been there I would have given it to him to take up to the kitchen, but when I looked up at the house the trunk of his car was closed and he was nowhere to be seen. I imagined him hovering over dozens of his steaming glass jars, carefully pressing swollen tomatoes into them.

I had sat down and held the bottle between my hands. My father's old taboo came back: no brew on board. Not that it had mattered to him eventually. The taboo had been broken, and now I could have kept a hundred bottles on board if I wished. The bottle was cool in my hands and I tipped it on its side to see if its cork would leak. Then I remembered something I'd read recently in one of my nautical books—that some sailors offer a drink to the gods before they set sail, so that the gods will not be angry at them and will treat them kindly.

I pulled the cork out and the pungent fragrance of alcohol and all its myriad allusions filled the cockpit. Kneeling up on the bench and leaning far out over the side I poured the gods a drink. The red swirled into the deep green and tiny guppies scattered, their little fins, barely the thickness of promises, burnt and tender. I leaned out further and with one hand I submerged the bottle and let it fill with bay water. It glugged empty once more and the gods were sated.

Then in the cabin I typed out a note to Charlie.

To whom it may concern:
Please see this message gets to Charles Jasper at Heaton and Clark Publishing, New York City.
Dear Charlie:
Having a wonderful time. Wish you were here.
Weather is fine. Wind is right. And the writing goes well.
If I am not back by mid-December please send the Coast Guard after me, as I will probably have

snagged my anchor on a sunken pirate ship or some
such thing.

I paused and pressed my fingers into the softness of my eyes.
For some reason I felt like crying. I wrote:

> Hope you are well and the tomaters all fit in the
> jars. I love you, Charlie. Thank you for believing in
> me. Love, Ellie.

I had shaken the last drops of water out of the wine bottle,
and rolling my letter into a tight rod I poked it inside. With
the cork intact, I set the bottle by the tiller and prepared the
Nemaste to sail. It turned into a sort of sweet ritual for me. I
did all the things I normally did, plus the things Max would
have done. I prepared the sails, rigged up the jib. I cranked
down the centerboard. I loosened all but one line to the dock. I
felt the shrouds and made them thrum beneath my fingers. Balancing myself by holding onto the mast, I reaching out and
freed the twisted telltales. I made sure there was plenty of gaso-
line in the storage compartment. I glanced at my charts. I
brought the binoculars up and put them near the message in a
bottle. I looked up at my car and at the driveway where Max
wasn't appearing. And I took a deep breath.

The wind was right. I was able to sail away from the dock
and never put the motor in, so I knew I left quietly; if Charlie
had glanced away from his tomatoes for a minute expecting to
see the *Nemaste* nestled at his dock, he would have discovered
me gone. Then he would have wondered how I had left so
quietly, and it was my hope that he would have come down to
the water and would have seen the bottle floating there, the
green wine bottle that I had tossed over as I saluted my final
farewell to the land.

Charlie eventually did get that message, but not that summer. He got it in his mail at the office late the next December from someone who'd been staying at a retreat house in Sag Harbor across the bay. A short note said the bottle had been found bobbing on the rock-bound coast. By then I had learned fully how messages and secrets can stay locked inside, bobbing along in a protected bay until finally coming to rest and to clink against the sharp rocks.

I made a plan for myself to sail as deep into Peconic Bay as I could. Max had taken me there once before and it was a trip I had liked, wide open and swift, so I turned the boat out into the bay, tightened her up, and aimed her west. I'd never liked going through the path of the ferries with the sails up. I'd always wanted the power of the outboard just in case things got a little too close. But Max had always laughed at my caution, so this day I tightened my grip on the tiller and told myself, piece of toast, no problem. But I couldn't take my eyes off the white two-dimensional shapes of the ferries sliding soundlessly over the water. I watched them put distance between each other, and then one after another on opposite shores I watched them slide into their piling berths.

I urged the *Nemaste* on—Go where I am going. *Va! Va! Va!*—wanting her to make it through while they were unloading and loading their passengers. I tightened the sails, willing to heel her over some more, but the *Nemaste* skimmed the water gently, and if I could have walked on water, I could have walked faster than she was sailing. My palms began to sweat. One ferry eased away from the shore and gathered up speed. She seemed to look only straight ahead and plow forward without any concern for what may have been coming into her path. Then the other ferry eased out as well, and from my seat at the tiller, I imagined that we were all three set on a perfect collision course and we would meet and sink in the middle of the Sound.

I held on to the tiller with both hands and watched the ferries like a cat would watch a strand of wool drawn across a thick carpet. My back legs nearly rocked with anticipation. Max would have laughed at me. "You're nowhere near them," he might have said. And this is what I told myself and wanted to believe. They were moving faster than I had estimated and I— I was moving slower. One passed before me with plenty of room. It was only for the second ferry that I had to change my course and I pleased myself by knowing exactly what to do. I turned with plenty of water between us and we passed each other on our port sides, and then when I was well past her I turned into her heavy ferry wake. I rocked gently and noticed a couple standing at the back of the ferry who were watching me. I remembered how I had stood at that same point at the beginning of the summer watching a lone sailor move in behind the ferry exactly as I was doing. I suddenly knew how I would look to them, and I wondered if they imagined a man in my cabin who was calling up to me that very moment, or if they knew I was solitary and singular. To show them I was alone but not lonely I raised my hand in salute and the man waved back. I imagined the woman wishing she were me, and I smiled.

I had never seen the bay as beautiful as it was that day. The sun was strong and right over me, and although some light rain had been predicted for later that evening the clouds were high and wispy, and if I watched them carefully I could detect them moving across the sky with the speed of a minute hand on an old watch. And the water was alive with tide life and currents and I laughed out loud as I steered through the riptides between

Jessup Neck and Cedar Beach. All around me it sounded like breakers on an unseen shore, surely frightening to me had I not been through them once before with Max. He had told me how once he'd been motoring with someone up from Shinnecock Canal at night, in the dark of a new moon, and when they had hit the riptides everyone had panicked, thinking they were going to hit the shore. They had even turned back in confusion. But I piloted through, like the keeper of some great secret.

The wind picked up after a while and I could have sailed the *Nemaste* real tight, had her sailing on her ear, but I was cautious and kept her at a tilt that didn't steal my breath away nor weary my legs by keeping them jammed into the opposite bench. Her centerboard hummed beneath me and the wind brushed the sun from my body and kept me cool.

I hadn't known I would feel this way, that the previous sailing experiences I had had would jell so strongly and that I would feel like I'd been doing this all my life with no great time lapses of being marooned on land. I almost felt as though there had probably been other lives I had spent on boats, so close was the motion of the water to the beat of my own heart.

I attempted great things that day. I sailed in every possible direction, like I might have made love with Max in every possible position. I came about and I jibed. I jibed on purpose and I jibed by mistake. I swung the boat around buoys like I'd seen them do in races on TV, and with the wind at my back I played with the jib sheets and the main until I got the sails wing on wing, one sail on each side, opened like the wings of a great bird, and I let her soar to her heart's content. She forgave me my inexperience and my ungraceful touch as an experienced lover would forgive a young virgin her awkwardness.

Only when I grew hungry did I finally stop. I drew her up close to the shore and turned her into the wind. Her sails flapped wildly, and with my heart in my throat, I abandoned the tiller and ran forward to uncoil the main halyard and pull the sails down in great powerful handfuls. Then, trembling with the effort, I lifted the Danforth anchor out of its rusty holder and dropped it with a splash into the water. I let the *Nemaste* drift back in the wind and felt her dig in. Done.

With the kind of confidence I think ten-year-old boys must feel when they master a skateboard, I ate a can of stew cold out of the can with a fork, sopping up gravy with a hot dog roll. And then I drank a diet cola while I ate potato chips out of the bag. Pleased with myself, smiling, I laid down on the bench and looked up into the late summer sky. The sun had passed to the west and the heavy clouds that had been promised were building. I would use the head and then I would sail for a cove Max and I had once found and anchor there for the night.

I underestimated the time it would take me to get to the cove Max had marked on my charts, but the sunset was so spectacular I remember thinking that it would surely be on the eleven o'clock news. I realized it was getting late and turned the *Nemaste* into the wind to put her in irons and let her stand motionless in the water while I quickly ran below to snap on the mast lights and running lights and to grab the large flashlight and a sweatshirt. I was struck with the incredible beauty and electric lavender aura that filled the cabin, stirring my memories of some past sunset, but the wind rattled the sails and I ran up top to keep sailing.

Traveling slowly east, needing to tack against the wind, I swear I would have put the motor in if it hadn't been for my ancient need to please my father. Like a bird coming to a place where there'd once been a birdfeeder years before, I perched on the bench and tried to do the right thing. It was growing darker and the shore was becoming difficult to see. The horizon was fading into darkness and electric lights of unseen buildings came into sight against the deepening purple sky.

And somewhere deep inside I was beginning to tremble— not my hands or a fluttering in my throat, but my bones, my deepest parts shuddering with something that was coming back to me, something I wanted to hold back, but something that was coming with the power and immutability of high tide. The thought of sailing in the dark was beginning to fill me with terror, and the thought of sailing alone ... *like a crack of lightning, an image of my father on the floor beneath me flickers through my mind*—I bolted up and got to my feet. I tilted the tiller up. I would sail standing.

I no longer knew where I was. The purple of the sky deepened, and the only stars that shone were revealed erratically behind torn rags of churning clouds. A heavy moon appeared unsteadily off to the east. And nothing else, nothing else looked familiar. The land became a stranger. I tried to see the ferries, but I no longer knew if I was even sailing toward them. It was as though someone had spun me around and set me down in some shadowy kaleidoscope world. I shone the flashlight on the compass, but in my panic I could no longer remember which direction I was supposed to be sailing. I needed to stop the boat, to get her still, and to anchor somewhere for the night.

Looking for land off to starboard I turned the *Nemaste* that way, shining the light over the waters, like I had done for my father so many years before when we'd gone night fishing. I would play with the light, throwing it across the glinting surface to see how far it would go, like shining a flashlight up into the stars, and then I would point the light straight down to the water beneath me and illuminate the green glass and all its life. This night the bay was like churning black oil all around me. With one hand on the light, one on the tiller, I steered her slowly in. I would stop and anchor, and sleep. And then, I told myself, this terrible trembling would leave me. Silently I slid along the swelling water, trying to judge how close I could get, how close to the land without scraping bottom. Then there in the dappled drifting moonlight my flashlight caught a lone mooring, a red and white ball with its stiff antennalike rod sitting in the water. I sailed past and watched it. A mooring would be better than an anchor, would hold me faster, and wouldn't slip as I lay sleeping. I wondered whose it was, wondered if they'd be back that night. I turned and passed it once more and decided to tie up to it. If anyone came back, they could chase me away.

So I turned and sailed out into the water to an open space where I could take the sails down and then motor her up to the mooring. But suddenly I was seized with an awful feeling that if I motored in, if I dared to drop the motor into the slick blackness, something bad might happen, that I *had* to sail up to it, and there was just no other way. I got the *Nemaste* out away from the land and the mooring and got her in irons. Quickly I pulled down her jib, leaving only the mainsail up. Then I loosened its halyard, trailing its line back to where I could reach it at the tiller. And then, once I was at the tiller again, I turned her away from the wind and headed toward the mooring. With the dim beam of the flashlight, I could faintly see the whiteness of its ball. I knew I would have to come up on it right into the wind, timing my approach and my turn into the wind so I would stop exactly beside it.

I glanced at the telltales in the dark, forcing myself to think everything out clearly and separately. I would approach the mooring this way, with the wind filling my loose mainsail and then turn just this way—I tried it. It felt too fast, so I cut too soon, and running forward, pulling down the mainsail in handfuls, I reached the bow just as the antenna was passing me on the port side about two oar lengths away and the boat turned away from it. From somewhere inside me I wished that Casey were with me to hold the tiller steady into the wind again so that I could run forward to the bow. And then before the wish was even complete I remembered that it was me who had sat at the tiller all those times, and my father who would walk forward. Casey'd never been on a sailboat at all.

At some point, I didn't even know when, I had scraped my fingers on something and now they pounded with pain. Ignoring it, I raised the mainsail. I would try again. Out away from the mooring I sailed, turned, and headed back. This time I would go slower, cut in tighter. My spine was like a ramrod. I held the tiller so tight my fingers ached, even though I could remember my father's heavy hands on the tiller, so relaxed and gentle. I went further this time, cut back to the mooring and drifted up to it. The sail blocked my view, but I caught glimpses of the mooring, barely there, bobbing out front, coming closer. The sails were luffing and I abandoned the wavering tiller and ran forward, again pulling down the sail. The halyard tangled and I had to yank at it and pull and by the time I made my way to the bow the antenna was right there. I gripped it, but the *Nemaste* was drifting forward too fast, carried by the wind and the vacant grip of a floundering tiller. I got the metal end of the antenna in my hand and felt it slipping away. I scrambled along the gunwale, fiercely gripping the antenna as it and the boat drifted away from each other. I hung on to the rails of the boat with my other hand and my feet, my shoulder pressed into the guardrail, and my arm extended out over the edge, my hand clutching the mooring that was dragging me off the boat. I carried the whole weight of my boat in my left hand. All that kept the mooring and the boat connected was the soft tissue in my shoulder between the bones. Weakening, I felt the antenna tear from my hand and felt the slice of metal through the flesh of my fingers.

The boom then bounced around and the *Nemaste* was staggering. Frustrated and in tears, I yanked the anchor from its rusty holder with my cut hands and flung it into the water. Kneeling by the bow, I couldn't tell by a delicate tug on the line if it had caught in the bottom or not. All that I could see and hear was a deep darkness of swellings and lappings. I couldn't tell if I was fastened safely to the earth, or if I was finally drifting for good, lost and detached on dark phantom waters.

*O*nly one light worked in the cabin of the *Nemaste* and that one was dim. I tried smacking the other fixtures, and when they didn't light I remembered Max telling me to charge the battery once in a while, but I hadn't thought of it till that night. Holding the chart close to the dim glow, I tried to figure out where I was, but I could barely make out the creeks from the points. I turned the light off to preserve whatever was left in the battery for the running lights so that no one would plow into me in the darkness. Then, feeling around with my hands in the forward berth, I pulled Max's sleeping bag out and drew it around my shoulders. I was freezing. I sat on the bench opposite the table and tucked my feet up under me. I was as tender with myself as though I were tucking Casey in while she tossed in some unseen nightmare. I felt the tenderness in my hands and with one hand I reached up and touched my head. I stared at the table across from me but could barely see its outline. And then, I don't know why I did it—probably for the same reason some movie heroine stumbles in the dark to check a disturbing noise downstairs—but I got up, trembling and dragging the sleeping bag with me, and I sat on the bench at the table.

I sat where I'd sat that night, across from where my father had sat. There was such a deep darkness. I closed my eyes and remained motionless, listening to the water lapping beneath me. And I was lulled by moving water as I am always lulled by water, and I went somewhere I'd never been even in my dreams, except for once, and that time it was not a dream.

My father's breathing is heavy and raspy, each breath sounding like a stroke of sandpaper across an old oak table. He stares at the playing cards in his left hand, and then thoughtfully he presses his other fist against his lips and puffs out his cheeks. His breathing stops for a moment, until he pulls two cards out of his hand and tosses them facedown on the table.

Then he looks up at me and grins. "Run for your life, sweet patootie." A long brown bottle of bourbon sits next to the cribbage board.

It's a cool night, and over my bathing suit I have put on one of my father's large sweatshirts, one with a hood. Even in the cabin I leave the hood up and I am gripping my cards with fingers that I try to cover with the cuffs. I stare at my cards and make my decisions. I toss down my two cards over his. And I don't look as he tips the bottle up to his face.

"Aren't we going to fish, Daddy?" I say into the cards. I glance up at his eyes when the bottle is down. He keeps his hand on it.

"Nah."

"How come? I thought you were coming out to go night fishing."

"I don't feel much like it now. Your mother ruined it for me. Your mother's the kiss of death to anything I might enjoy."

"But *I* want to fish. Can't I put the flashlight in the water?"

He shakes his head and puts an eight down. "Eight."

I pout and put down another eight. "Sixteen, pair for two." I peg my two points.

He drops another eight on his pile. "Twenty-four for six." Now he is grinning at me. A stupid, heavy grin.

"So take your six points," I say crankily. But he doesn't. He just sits there looking at me and grinning.

"Stop," I whine.

"Stop what?"

"Stop looking at me like that."

"Like what? The cat can look at the queen."

Our eyes lock, both of us defiant, his with a touch of malice that I know comes from the brown bottle.

I peg his six points and drop a seven on the pile. "Thirty-one for two."

"Did I ever tell you, Elizabeth, that your eyes are the color of the North Sea before a storm?"

I don't answer him, but he won't stop looking at me.

"I'll bet the boys love to look at you, Elizabeth."

I scowl at him and he laughs. "But not when you have that puss on." He lays his cards down. "Come here," he says.

I peg my two points and stay in my seat.

"Elizabeth," he says. That is all. Just my name, with that

certain tone, and I must slide off the bench and go around to stand before him.

"What?"

He pushes my hood off the back of my head and runs his hands over my hair. I pull my hands up into my sleeves. "Come here," he says again and obediently I crawl up into his lap as his heavy arms go around me.

"Why can't we go fishing, though, Daddy?" I say up close to his face.

"Not tonight, patoot," he answers and the odor of his breath is terrible, like a dreadful smoky medicine that will steal my own breath away. I turn my face away from him and press the side of my head into his shoulder. Face to face with the brown bottle, I close my eyes and listen to his breath blowing past me and his lungs rattling inside him. While part of me wants to settle into his warm, fatherly embrace, there is an edge to me that stands guard, an edge that scrapes along the side of the brown bottle. I try to draw away from him but he holds me fast.

"Be still," he whispers, and, tense and alert, I am still. I hear the bay lapping against the bottom of our forest green sailboat and he holds me. He holds me.

"Your crib," I finally remind him. He hasn't counted out his crib yet.

"I forfeit," he says. "I'm done with the cards for the night."

"You mean I win?" I slip out of his arms when he reaches for the bottle, and this time I watch in fascination as his heavy lips encircle the bottle's end and bubbles glug inside. My father drains the bottle. It's empty now and I stand before him.

"I win?" I ask again.

His eyelids and eyebrows seem thick and heavy, and his lips pull into a sloppy smile. "You win."

I start to clean up the cards. "Let's fish then," I press.

"Enough!" he shouts and the cards explode from my hands. I cover my ears. I watch as he rubs his face roughly with his hands, over his stubbly cheeks, over his puffy eyes, then over his head as though he's smoothing a cap on. Then he says quietly, "Get ready for bed, Elizabeth. Take off your clothes and get into your sleeping bag."

"I'm not tired," I dare to whisper.

But he just nods gently. "Yes, you are, Elizabeth. Now."

I am glad Peter is not here. I actually think that. I feel protective and strong and think how it's a good thing there's only me. I pull out the sleeping bag and unfold it on the narrower bench. I smooth it flat and turn and wait for my father to leave.

"Well?" he says.

"I have to get undressed." For the last year or two a veil of understanding has slipped between us, the unspoken acknowledgment that he doesn't come in the bathroom when I'm in the tub, that he looks the other way, that he leaves the cabin while I undress. But now the cat is watching the queen.

He holds out his hand to me. "Give me the sweatshirt," my father whispers.

I stood up so abruptly that I cracked my head on the flat roof of the cabin. I cried out with the same sound a mother might make as she helplessly watches her baby roll off the edge of the bed. I clutched Max's sleeping bag around my pounding heart. There were too many ghosts in the dark cabin that night, so I went out to sleep under the stars.

But there were no stars. I looked up into the chaos above me, the soft squall clouds scudding rapidly across the face of a full moon, and I could almost feel the moon drawing the ocean up toward itself in a full and swollen tide. The horizon that met the sky was a band of haze, coming clearer only when I looked away. And the faintly illuminated clouds above me looked like the innermost folds of a womb.

Oh, how I had longed to make constellations that night. To pin them all to the sky. My mother and father stretching across the northern sky, bound to each other where they belonged for as long as the stars stayed put, and over there, to the west, I could've hung Charlie with his hand on the head of his faithful but fearful dog, Duke, and Max—Max making a spoon disappear into his ear, his elbow a star, his eye another. I would have placed my grandmother on the deck of a cruise ship, here the smokestack and there her iron grip on the railing. And I would have pinned Casey to the night sky, too, sitting her at the helm of a sailboat, Casey, proud and whole, stars marking the rudder beneath the water, and brighter stars marking her flashing smile, and a lost husband at the bow, or would it be my father? Maybe it is me at the tiller . . . I kept forgetting that Casey never sailed, that I needed to put her standing on a corner somewhere and the bright star would be the ember of her cigarette. And when that jangled a nerve deep inside my jaw I thought of the southern hemisphere and how there I would pin up all the characters from *You Again,* and some of those stars would be on the edge of the northern stars, a great overlapping and weaving of constellations for astronomers and astrologers to decipher.

I thought how some memories were like constellations. Sometimes they are hidden in other hemispheres, sometimes they're covered with clouds or dimmed by daylight, but they are always there, always waiting to tell their stories.

But this night there were no stars. I slipped my bare feet into the zippered cocoon of the sleeping bag and stretched out on the bench. I looked up into the clouds and felt the boat rocking aimlessly beneath me. Soon the rain splattered my face.

I heard it patter loudly on my sleeping bag, but I wouldn't go in the cabin. Instead I dug down into the thick bag and zippered it up over my head.

"I'll do it, I'll do it," I answer him. On the shelf are my summer pajamas, a shirt and shorts of a soft thin cotton. I pull them onto the bench and pull my arms inside the sweatshirt as though I am a great turtle and I'm going inside to change. My father doesn't stop watching me and shame hums its tune—a tune that will become a theme throughout my entire life.

But for now it is enough that I slip out of my bathing suit beneath my father's sweatshirt. I am not far from him, and before I can slip my pajamas over my feet he reaches and clasps the strings from the sweatshirt hood and draws me to him. "Daddy, stop," I say, and I am startled at how much I sound like my mother up to her elbows in the kitchen sink when he comes up behind her. "Cut it out."

But he doesn't say a word and his face is transformed. He is smiling, a soft, crooked smile, and he's watching my bare legs as he reels me in like a dull catfish.

Suddenly I bolted upright in the rain and thrust my head out of the sleeping bag, out into the air where I could breathe. And though my eyes were opened to the night world about me, and though my hands pressed over my ears, I could not stop the panic and the images that were coming back to me.

My father pulls at the shirt slowly and forcefully tries to raise it up, but I've secured my fists on the hem inside and I am as tenacious as a puppy locked to a shoelace. He lifts me onto his lap, still tugging at me. Then he sighs, and in the cabin stands and tries to sit me on the table, but I am limp and resistant. "I said I'll do it," I whine, folding and flapping around in his embrace. He releases me for a moment to sit on the table, just stroking my shoulders and my arms that are rigid inside the shirt.

He is deliberate and slow and the crooked, swollen smile never leaves his face. Still he is silent, although all his energy and urge is focused on my shirt and what I hide beneath it. I show no one what is beneath it, not even my mother, not even a friend, because of my secret—the faint swelling that has been circling my tiny nipples.

No soldier has ever protected a border with more intensity than I protect the sight of my young body this night. I grapple and struggle against my father, and then soften when he suddenly presses his forehead against mine and closes his eyes. My guard lowers and I wait, feeling his breath on my face.

"Daddy—" I plead.

Then laughing cruelly, he rips the shirt from my hands, but as he grips it to rip it off me, he tips forward swiftly with a jerk and I hear his forehead crack like a gunshot against the part of the cabin roof that extends like a shelf over me. I scream and pull the shirt down over my body again. I stare at his face, for his brow has opened like a kangaroo's pouch, and I see the bone beneath. He is staggering blindly, blood running into his eyes. I don't see what is happening. I don't know. I am suddenly out in the cockpit, crying.

"Elizabeth." I hear him call to me softly, and turning I see him silhouetted in the door to the cabin. He is coming after me. "Wait, patootie," he whispers, and he reaches out. But I am standing on the bench. "No!" then the gunwale, "No, Daddy, no!" and as he steps out into the cockpit, one hand on his head and the other reaching, brushing against my thigh, I step off the side of the boat and plunge into the bay.

Suddenly I was very still and calm. I saw a little girl floating there in the water, crying and calling out to her drunken father. The memory had been there all my life, but I had never turned toward it before, never took it in, or opened myself fully to its terrible gusts. Abruptly it was all remembered; it was all laid out before me like a new chart with every place I'd ever been, marked and noted. I watched as the little girl fought against the heavy, sodden sweatshirt that covered her small gleaming secrets and pulled her down, and I watched as, struggling for the breath and her life, she took all that had just happened and rolled it up and tucked it away in some empty corked bottle as though she would never have to see it again, thinking if only he would come for her, if only his strong body would lean over the side and lift her up out of the water.

Now it was whole. I laid back down in the rain and felt myself surrender to a deep and absolute mourning, not just for the dead man the Coast Guard had found in the early dawn, but for the little girl I had lost that night. Rain mixed with tears and I felt a congratulatory gentleness in the air that opened the way for me. Inside my sleeping bag I cupped my hands over my breasts. They had grown to fill a big man's hands, and had once nourished a small baby who herself would die before her own breasts were fully grown.

I cried for it all, anchored there in the bay. The rain kept on, and soon I felt its cold drops seeping through the sleeping bag and running down between my thighs and around my neck. But I did not get up. I passed the night out there in the cockpit, under the invisible constellations, and once I was empty of all I'd been holding and I was finally certain there was no dead man lying on the floor beside me, I slept.

I've come to believe lately that if *Charlie's old Duke had had the opportunity to experience a lightning storm firsthand, if he had run through a field under lightning bolts and rumbling thunder, he might have been better later on in other storms—once he had proven to himself that he could survive the worst. For imagining the worst can leave deeper scars than experiencing the worst. And now, unlike Duke, I knew I had run through rain fields pursued by a tempest and I had survived. When I stood on deck the next morning, it was as though I had been rinsed clean of fear and shaken out. I saw where I was. A sparkling sun had dried the outer skin of the sleeping bag, the anchor had held through the night, and off to the east I saw the clean silhouette of a ferry.*

Deliberately and without fear, without Max, I hooked up the ladder and jumped off the side. I would like to say that I swam around the boat four times and dove for oysters, but fact is, I plunged in for only a moment, right near the ladder, to feel my body sink, but mostly to feel my body rise up again on its own.

And then, once I was dressed and before heading back, I put up my mainsail halfway and ambled over to the mooring. I cut into the wind at just the right heartbeat and the Nemaste *stopped dead in the water for me to pick up the mooring antenna. I didn't tie up to it; I just held it for a minute, wishing someone had been there to see me do it. Maybe you. You could have taken my picture.*

I renamed the boat soon after I sailed her alone; she is no longer the Nemaste. *I scrubbed and sanded the letters off once she was on dry land for the winter, and put on new ones, beautiful black letters with white outlines on her red stern:* Pumpkin Moon. *A couple of old salts told me it's bad luck to rename a boat, but they have nothing to teach me about bad luck. I make my own luck, and I have a hunch my karma drawer is emptied, vacuumed, and new-born clean.*

And I take her out by myself all the time now. Charlie predictably softened on his promise of only one year at his dock. So the Pumpkin Moon's *a regular sight in the waters of the Peconic Bay, the first boat on the water in the spring and the last one out in the fall, even into late November, when it is cold but wonderfully windy. Nowadays when I turn her bow at a slant to the wind and I see her sails swell and feel her tilt way over, I feel a swell of such indescribable joy, the balance of wind and water and power at my fingertips. I feel myself surge forward. I think maybe next summer I will sail out past Gardiners Island, through Block Island Sound and maybe even to the sea. I want you to know how happy I am.*

I should tell you that Max is gone from my life, and while I've never seen him again I sometimes find myself looking for him when I pass trucks and diners on Long Beach Road. But if we were to meet again, how would I begin? Would I say "I'm sorry, Max," or "Where've ya been?" Knowing Max, maybe I could just say "Knock, knock." I would have to tell him that I had known all along how to sail—that there truly was a jib etched on my palm— and that everything he had tried to teach me had been solid and seaworthy. I would also like to tell him about my new book, and how I finally got the rest of my advance. And I'd have to tell him how I used that story about his father, and also how I wrote a good portion of the book on board the boat, tucked away in that little cove we'd found together. Alone, with my little college typewriter before me on the fold-up table, I was like an industrious spider, tossing a strand of words here, a longer sentence there to that distant mooring, always stretching truth and illusion, to see if it would hold me. And it did. It held Charlie, and I bet it would hold you and Max too, if either of you were ever to stop in a bookstore and notice it there beside You Again.

I regret that for so long I had wanted to forget the truth of things, but the truth had pressed heavy on me for too long. It was hard to tell anyone what it had been like to see my own daughter arrested and thrown in the back of a police car in front of the house. And I let the memory of it slip into the deep abyss where the memories of my own father had drifted. And watching Casey kicking and spitting and then seeing metal handcuffs snapped round her grimy little wrists was somehow inextricably bound to having my father tighten my sweatshirt around my own struggling arms. It all lent itself so well to forgetfulness, to lies, to storytelling.

I had even wanted to lie to you when Casey died, wanting to hurt you as hard and as deeply as I could. I used to think of looking into your eyes and telling you that the police finally found Casey's broken body in Hempstead, in a crack house, or I had thought of telling you that some commuters noticed three pieces of her on the railroad tracks at the station. For this I am so sorry, for the truth the police told you was bad enough. That I found her myself that night, and that I saw with my own eyes and with my own shining flashlight, our daughter lying in a still heap on the floor of our garage.

It was not long after she died that I was out walking alone on a beautiful autumn morning under a canopy of blazing orange and yellow trees when I noticed a huge morning moon hanging weightless in the sky, and then I saw the pumpkin, big and thick and orange, smashed against the curb.

Casey was all I could think of. Casey, and you. And me, and how everything seemed smashed and lost, beyond any reckoning or reason. That was when I began the lie about the hit-and-run. But now there is only room for truth. I can tell you gently that the hypodermic needle was still in her dirty arm, the tender part of her arm where you used to press your lips and blow to make her giggle when she was small. And now as I say this, I am empty of malice. I ache to lay my hand on the back of your neck where your hair always touched your collar.

Time heals if it is tempered with truth, and I've come to see that there are new autumns, and hills upon hills of pumpkin patches bearing new pumpkins every year.

I know this because, each year, when I finally put the Pumpkin Moon on land for the winter, and drive back along the North Fork, I see them piled like full moons at the roadside. So I end my story here for you, full circle. Come close to me for just an instant if you can. I have a hope for you: I hope you, too, are free.